By the Gate

River View Series, Book Two

Jeanette Taylor Ford

Cover by Dave Slaney

Best Wishes,

Jeanette

x

LONGSHIP
Publishing

My sincere thanks must go to my editor Angela, whose work was really cut out with this one!
Also my friend Lee West and to Adam Rigby for their help and advice regarding matters of the law and procedures of court and to Anthony Davis who advised me about records of cars pre-dating the DVLC

Thanks to all my author friends for their support and encouragement, especially those at Longship.

Once again, thank you to my awesome cover designer, Dave Slaney

By The Gate

Now that spring is in the air
I wonder if you will be there
If I go along the river, and wait
At our place, by the Gate?

Now that summer is in the air,
Will we walk without a care?
And as the warmth touches my face
Will you hold me in your embrace?

Now that autumn is in the air,
Will we still feel the love we share?
I'll take your hand and look into your eyes
For real love we cannot disguise.

And so, as we remember the past,
When we vowed that our love would always last
In my winter, will you still wait
And look out for me, by our gate?

J.T.F.

By the Gate
Chapter 1

"Oh, my back!"

Elwyn Price stopped digging and straightened up with a groan. *I'm definitely not as young as I used to be,* he reflected. *I should have got the lads to do this.* He moved his head slowly round, feeling it crack, attempting to bring relief to his neck and shoulders.

The holes were for a new fence, since the old one had been destroyed in a gale and shortly he would have to move his herd outside. At present they were overwintering in his cattle sheds. The fence was to make sure his cattle were not tempted into Mrs Baxter's garden. That young woman had been very gracious over his daughter Glynis' cruel stupidity and had never let it get in the way of her neighbourliness. When his Mary had been ill a while back, Lucy Baxter had been really kind, making bread, pies and all sorts 'to keep you men going' as she said cheerfully.

Lucy was a chef and a baker and ran a business called 'Aunt Bea's Pantry' that specialised in all kinds of jams and pickles. She also owned the land on which his herd grazed and several fields around her house, the remains of River View Farm. Much of it had been sold off years ago and had expanded the tiny hamlet of Sutton-on-Wye, now exalted to village status. Lucy had fallen in love with Kenny, who owned the garden centre and nursery, built on some of the land that had belonged to River View Farm. And that had been the trouble with his Glynis, he reflected. Before Lucy had come along, Glynis had been infatuated with Kenny and became jealous when Kenny started looking Lucy's way.

Glynis had never been an easy child; he remembered how she always had to 'get back at' her brothers and had often been quite vicious. He wasn't at all surprised to hear what she'd been up to in order to frighten poor Lucy, egged on by the lies and empty promises of Lucy's ex-fiancé. He was sorry and embarrassed. At one time he feared that Lucy might decide to take the field from him. But Lucy was not like that – she wouldn't punish him for his daughter's misdeeds and in fact she made a special effort to befriend them.

Elwyn resumed his digging, and,thinking about Lucy, he really understood why Kenny Baxter loved her. The farmer was a taciturn man, didn't get on all that well with people, but he understood love. When he first clapped eyes on his Mary, he thought she was the prettiest girl he'd ever seen. There had never been anyone else after that. Mary seemed to understand him and could always get him to do things that others couldn't. It had hit him badly when she was ill. She'd caught pneumonia and had to spend time in hospital and took longer to convalesce but Lucy had done her very best to help. Oh yes, Elwyn knew why Kenny loved Lucy; she was a girl in a million.

When his spade hit something hard, it brought the man's thoughts to an abrupt end.

"Hello, what's this?"

Upon closer inspection, his heart plopped in his chest. Sliced in half by his spade was a bone and near it, sticking out of the side of the hole, was what he was sure was a skull, a human skull.

For a few mad moments, Elwyn was tempted to ignore it, fill the hole in and dig somewhere else without letting on to anyone. However, his conscience nagged at him that this was probably a person who had gone mysteriously missing, and someone, somewhere, might need closure. Although a pleasant spot, it was definitely not somewhere a body should have been buried, with nothing to mark the spot - suspicious, of course.

Cursing under his breath, for he knew his fencing would be seriously delayed, he put his spade over his shoulder and stomped his way out of the field.

Chapter 2

Lucy Baxter hummed to herself as she went about her housework. Her little boy, John, was having a nap and she was trying to achieve as much as possible while she had the chance. John was just toddling and he kept her constantly on her toes, entertaining and keeping him out of trouble.

She had just switched on the washing machine when there was an urgent knocking on her kitchen door.

"Mr. Price!" she said, surprised to see the farmer looking agitated. "What's the matter? Has something happened to Mary? Come on in."

He stepped inside and took off his woolly hat.

"Thank you, I won't come in any further because of me boots."

Lucy glanced down at his mud-covered wellingtons and nodded.

"I hardly know how to tell you, Miss Lucy, but I was in your field digging 'oles to put up a new fence – you know, the gales flattened the old one – and bless me in there weren't a body in one o' them!"

"A body? Do you mean to say you've found a corpse in my field?"

Lucy was wide-eyed at the thought.

"We-ell, not exactly a corpse, more a skeleton, but it's an 'uman skeleton, I'm sure. It shouldn't be there, Miss Lucy, that field has never been a graveyard, to my knowledge. For generations it's been farmland."

"My goodness, we must inform the police. Can you put a cover over it or something? I'll call them."

"Yes, I'll do that now. I'll leave you t' call 'em then, shall I?"

"Absolutely. I'm sure you will hear from them shortly. I'll do it now before John wakes up."

Elwyn pulled his beanie back on his head and stepped outside. Lucy watched him stride away before going indoors to fetch her phone.

*****

Kenny Baxter was also busy working. He owned the garden centre and nurseries that were near to River View Farmhouse grounds, but not that close, there being a couple of fields between them. When his phone rang, he stuck his spade in the ground and pulled it out of his pocket.

"Hello, Lucy, my love, what's up?"

When he heard what his wife had to say, he called to a man working near him.

"Joe, mate, tell my mother that something's come up and I have to pop home? I'll be back shortly."

"Okay, gov. I'll do that." Joe downed his fork and set off for the shop where Sheila, Kenny's mother manned the till.

Ken hurried along the river path in the direction of his home and in a few minutes he came to the field where Elwyn had been digging. He made his way over to where the hole was, now covered by a piece of wood. He lifted the plank and peered inside. Elwyn was right; he could indeed see a skeleton there, or part of one. The rest was still hidden. He replaced the wood and hurried to the farmhouse.

*****

They had to wait a while for the police; it was at least a twenty-minute drive from the city and a skeleton was not exactly an emergency. However, when Ken took them to the spot, they took a look and put the plank back.

"And who found this, sir?" The constable who seemed to be the senior of the two asked Kenny.

"Farmer Elwyn Price. The field belongs to our property but he rents it for his herd of Herefords. He was digging holes to erect a new fence. His farm is across the river; there's a bridge a bit further past my nursery. It's called West Bank Farm. I expect you'll want to speak with him?"

"Yes sir. But you say this is your property?"

"My wife's actually. She inherited it a couple of years ago from her aunt."

"So, Mrs Baxter hasn't been here for very long? About three years?"

"That's right."

"And how long did her aunt own the property?"

"Around forty years, I think, but she only lived there full time for the last few years of her life. Until then, she was caring for my wife Lucy in Lucy's father's home in Hereford."

"I see."

He snapped his notebook shut.

"We'll go and speak to Mr Price. We may well want to see your wife at some point, sir."

"Of course. Can I see you to your car and then I can give you directions to West Bank Farm?"

"Thank you, that would be helpful."

The two policemen walked with Kenny back to River View Farmhouse and, after they had their directions, drove away.

"So, what are they going to do?" asked Lucy as Kenny dropped in to see her.

"They are off to see Elwyn. I expect they will be back."

"Will they dig up the body?"

"No doubt they will and then it'll have to be sent for forensic examination."

"It's very odd, isn't it?"

"It is. It must be quite old; that field has been a cow field for as long as I can remember. It's not been used for crops during my lifetime, I'm sure of it."

"Been there for a long time then. Poor soul, whoever it was. Do you think we will ever know who she or he was?"

"Well, they can do so much these days, what with DNA testing and all. We'll have to wait and see."

*****

When Kenny returned to work, he had to sort a problem for a customer and, as a consequence of that, the incident slipped his mind until the end of the day.

It was his usual practise to call in at the Nursery house to say hello and have a cup of tea with his mum, her husband Tom, who happened to be his Lucy's father and his granddad, Joseph, who lived with them. His mum, Sheila, always left work earlier in order to get home to get the meal on or to spend time with her husband.

"So, son, what was all that about then? Why did you have to go home? Is Lucy alright?"

Sheila asked as she poured his tea.

"Yes, she's fine."

"Oh good…Well?"

"Well what?"

"Stop being obtuse, dear! What was the problem?"

Kenny pondered for a moment; the police had said they wanted no one to know about the skeleton until it was dug up and safely away. But, family was family and surely he could trust them to keep it to themselves?

"Well, I'm not really supposed to say, but, the thing is, when Elwyn Price was digging in the meadow to put the new fence up, he found a skeleton."

A stunned silence followed his statement, then –

"A skeleton?" Tom was the first to recover.

"What sort of skeleton?" asked Sheila.

"A human one, Mum, or there wouldn't be any point in calling the police, would there?"

"How did it get there?"

"Well, I have no idea, I'm sure! It must have been there a long time; it's always been a meadow far as I know."

"That's right," said Joseph. "It was a meadow when I was a lad and I'm pretty sure it was afore that."

"Hmm, strange," said Sheila. "What did the police say?"

"They are going to send a team over in the morning to dig it up properly. We will have to wait and see what happens after that."

Chapter 3

Detective Inspector Dan Cooke, West Mercia Police, entered the station at Hereford the next morning after a couple of days off.

"Morning, sir," said Sergeant Johnson at the desk.

"Morning, Bert, you okay?"

"Yes sir, just fine."

"Will you have coffee brought to my office, please, Bert?"

"Of course, sir. Did you have a late night?"

"Oh, we have my wife's sister staying with us and her baby kept crying in the night. Not used to it, you know. Glad to come in for some peace, tell you the truth! Can you find me some paracetamol or something? Got one heck of a headache."

"I think I have some, sir. Mind you, coffee won't do that any good. It's water you need."

"In that case, I'll have water in my coffee. Don't be long, there's a good chap."

Bert grinned behind his boss, then spied a young constable.

"Hey, Rob! Get DI Cooke a coffee, will you please, lad? And take him these." He chucked a silvery blister-pack to the constable, who caught it deftly.

"Right away, Sarg."

Not long later, Dan, sitting with his head in his hands, looked up as the door to his office opened and PC Rob Atkins came in with a tray bearing a mug of coffee, a bottle of water, a couple of biscuits on a plate and the tablets.

"Oh, thanks, Rob. I see the sergeant insists that I have water!"

"Yes sir. Did you hear what happened yesterday, sir?"

"No, I'm not with it yet. Enlighten me."

"A skeleton has been found, sir."

"Oh yes?" Dan was only mildly interested. "Where was that, then?"

"Sutton on Wye, sir."

"Sutton on Wye?" repeated Dan "Whereabouts in Sutton on Wye?"

"In a meadow, sir, belonging to a Mrs Baxter, sir."

Dan's head shot up and he winced.

"Really? What's happening about it?"

"A team is going out there today to dig it up and bring it back, sir."

The detective hurriedly popped a couple of pills into his mouth, downed the coffee, which fortunately wasn't as hot as it should have been and grabbed his coat from the peg on the wall.

"Find Grant and tell him to bring the car right away. I'm going out to Sutton to see what's going on."

The constable exited the room immediately. Dan followed at a more leisurely pace after tucking the water bottle into his pocket. Bert was right about drinking water for his headache but he hadn't time to wait.

"Why didn't you tell me about the body out at Sutton on Wye, Bert?"

"You were in a bit of a state, sir, I thought I'd let the tablets kick in first."

"Oh well, I forgive you then. I'm going out there as soon as Grant comes with the car."

"I thought you would sir, after what happened out there a couple of years ago. Seems the body has been found right in that lady's property, sir. She seems fated, doesn't she?"

"Looks like it. Ah, here's Grant. See you later, Bert."

With that, he exited through the double doors and the sergeant returned to his computer.

*****

Twenty minutes later, they pulled up outside River View Farmhouse. The kitchen door opened and Lucy appeared, looking impossibly young with her hair tied back in a pony-tail. On her hip was a small boy. A small white dog, which closely resembled a hairy hearth rug, danced around the Dan's feet and he bent to make a fuss of her.

"Hello Clarry, I think you remember me."

"Detective Inspector Cooke! How nice to see you again – and Detective Sergeant Grant. Come on in. Would you like something? A freshly baked scone?"

Stepping into Lucy's kitchen was a gorgeous, aromatic experience. The smell of freshly-baked bread, mingled with that of new scones just out of the oven immediately made his mouth water. Regretfully, he shook his head.

"Sadly, no, much as I'd like to take you up on your offer, for I know your scones are wonderful. We should get out to the field and see what's going on. I knew nothing about this until this morning, I've had a few days off, being visited by my sister-in-law and family. Glad to get back to work, I have to say!"

Lucy laughed; it was a delightful sound. Lucy was like a breath of fresh air. Thankfully, he felt his headache lifting; obviously the tablets were doing their work – or was it this young woman chasing away his cobwebs?

'Now, now,' he chastised himself. Lucy was such a nice girl, who could help but like her?

"Can you be able to show us where we should go? The team isn't here yet, I take it?"

"No, I don't think they are. Hang on, let me get my boots and coat on and wrap this young man up and I'll be right with you."

The two men watched as she stuffed her son into a padded all-in-one suit.

"What's his name?"

"John, after his granddad," she said in answer, smiling. She pushed little boots onto the child's feet and set him on the floor, where he stood, eyeing his feet. The boots were green and looked like frogs; obviously the child was fascinated by them as he turned first one foot and then the other. A few moments later Lucy was zipped up in her jacket, her own wellies on and ready to go. Dan looked ruefully at his shoes.

"I have some spare boots if you two would like to borrow them? Kenny has several pairs."

"Thanks, much appreciated."

Once the two men were appropriately shod, the little party set out for the field. They went via the river path to the wide gate to the meadow. Although the gate itself still stood, there was a large gap beside it where the hedging had been blown down; the roots torn and broken and even large branches lay on the ground where the gale had whipped them from the trees. There had been a couple of gale-force winds that winter. Elwyn had obviously decided to erect the new fence slightly behind where the hedging had been and angle it to meet the gate.

The meadow was rather muddy and the two policemen were glad of their borrowed Wellington boots. They soon reached the place where the farmer had come across the bones and Grant moved the boards so they could peer into the hole. Just as they did so, they heard a shout and saw men coming towards them. They had come to dig up the skeleton.

"I'll leave you to it then," said Lucy. "It's quite cold out here and I don't want John out for long. I'll be at home if you need me."

"Right you are, miss," replied one of the men who had just arrived.

Dan watched her go, her son perched in his usual place on her hip, then turned his attention back to the job in hand.

The men erected a small tent over the hole so they could work in the dry.

"Don't go at it like a bull at a gate!" he ordered. "Be careful with your tools, try to work around the bones as I'd like to get it out with as little damage as possible."

It was indeed a chilly day and Dan paced around trying to keep warm as he waited for the men to do their work. A table had been set up inside the tent and, as each bone came from the hole, it was laid out upon it.

Time ticked slowly by. It was a tricky task to lift the skeleton without further damage and Dan wished he had a team of archaeologists instead of these clods who were not nearly as careful as archaeologists would have been.

An hour later, Lucy appeared, mini hearth rug by her side, carrying a bag. It transpired she had brought flasks of hot chocolate for him and his team and they gratefully partook of the warming liquid.

"Where's the boy?" he asked.

"Oh, he's down for a sleep so I thought I'd bring these to you now. I mustn't stay in case he wakes up, although he usually sleeps for a good hour or so. If you have time when you're done, come back to the farmhouse and you can have that scone," she twinkled. "I'll come back for the flasks later."

"We'll bring them back for you, ma'am," said Grant.

"That'd be great. Thank you."

It was another hour before they were sure all the bones were up. They found something else too. It was dirty and tarnished but still recognisably a small silver cross on a chain.

Chapter 4
February 14th

With music playing softly, there was an expectant air in the room. Samuel rose stiffly from his chair at the edge of the dance area and held out his hand.

"May I have this dance?"

She looked up at him, smiled and took his proffered hand. She was surprisingly light on her feet as they glided as one across the dance area, they made little sound on the wall-to-wall carpeting. They moved as one to the slow waltz, born of many years of practise; they had been champions.

Soon, they were joined by other couples, hesitant at first, then with growing confidence, while others sat and enjoyed watching.

Against his will, his traitorous mind floated back more years than he usually cared to remember – another place, a lifetime ago, at his first dance. He could still remember the hint of perfume rising from her shining brown hair, her shy smile as he nervously put his hand on her slim waist. He wasn't such a good dancer then, but, as he gazed down into those warm, deep blue eyes, he realised it didn't matter, just as he knew he would remember that time for the rest of his life. It was the moment he first fell in love...

The music changed from one tune to another without a break and they followed, their feet on automatic pilot. Some of the other couples stopped and sat down but Samuel and his Emily danced on, ever the showmen.

When the music faded away, everyone clapped, and, smilingly, Samuel took his wife of over sixty years back to her armchair and sank down next to her.

"My, that felt good," he grinned, patting her hand. "Can't keep it up like we used to though."

Emily smiled and was about to reply when a cheerful voice was heard, along with the rattling of a trolley.

"Tea time, everyone!"

Cessy was manning the trolley, aided by Glynis. The sound of rattling teacups and cheerful voices followed as the little round tables, especially brought out for occasions such as this, were laden with drinks, dainty sandwiches and cakes. This was Sutton Court Nursing and Care Home's version of a Valentine Tea-dance and everyone happily tucked into the delicacies on offer.

As Samuel quietly sat, sipping his tea and recovering from his exertions, he allowed his mind to wander back to when he was a young man, reliving the times he spent with his first girlfriend. They had grown up together as neighbours, she'd lived at the newly-opened nursery and he at River View Farm. He was a little older than her, and although they attended the same schools, he was in the year above her but they played together, doing all the things kids do in the country, fishing in the ponds on his farm, climbing trees, generally getting into mischief as children will. Gradually, of course, they grew and their activities changed. He spent more time working on the farm or playing football with his friends if he had the chance, she with her friends, doing whatever girls do when they get together. Almost without him noticing, she blossomed into a beauty, by far the most attractive girl in the village and it seemed she had been waiting for him, because when he asked her to dance, she slid into his arms and fitted naturally as if she belonged there. Even after all those years and the loving marriage he'd had with his Emily, sometimes he felt a longing for his first love which made him feel guilty. There were times when his arms seemed empty, unfulfilled...

"Would you like a cake, Sam?"

At the sound of Glynis' cheerful voice, Samuel was abruptly brought back to the present.

"You were miles away then," she laughed as she held out a plate to him. He smiled at her and took a small cake in the shape of a heart with rather garish red icing swirled on the top. He gave a half grimace, half grin, waving it at her. She laughed again.

"Sylvie's been experimenting."

"Ah! Well, I'll just bite it and not look," he said, "I've no doubt it will taste lovely if Sylvie made it."

It did indeed and he finished the cake with relish. Having been brought back to the present, he sought more food and was soon happily eating his little sandwiches and another violent red fairy bun.

*****

Sam and Emily were not residents of Sutton Court. They lived in the village in a neat little bungalow on the new estate the opposite end to the Care home. They went two afternoons a week to the day centre to socialise and get out of the house for a while. It was good to see their friends who were already resident here. Sam reflected that growing old was not much fun but he and Emily had fared better than others – until now.

At eighty-nine, soon to be ninety, Sam still cut a fine figure. His early years had been spent farming. It was in his blood; his dad had been a farmer as had his father before him and like as not, many generations going back. However, eventually, the farm had been sold and Sam found another career; he went to university and became a teacher and retired a headmaster. He'd met Emily at university, who also became a teacher but it was the discovery that they loved ballroom dancing that brought them together. They had married after gaining their qualifications. Emily was a year behind him.

He'd had a good life with Emily; their mutual love of dancing had kept them fit and had also taken them all over the country taking part in dance competitions They knew a lot of people, had made many friends, but always came back to Sutton-on-Wye in beautiful Herefordshire. To them, there was no better place to live.

Now, his Emily was not so fit; she had cancer and this was the reason they went to the day centre at the Home. Emily sometimes went on her own to give Sam some respite from caring, after all, he was not so young himself. He liked to go walking and his favourite walk was the path along the river, at the back of River View Farmhouse, where he had grown up.

After the Sutton Court mini bus dropped them home, the pair settled down to watch the television for a while. Sam was thankful there was no tea to get ready, they'd had sufficient to eat at the dance. Soon, it would be time to help Emily to bed. Often she went even earlier, her energy reserves were low now. Today, it had been good; almost like old times as she had glided, still in tune with him, to the slow waltz. He knew she'd overdone it but it had been important to her. It was their own little celebration, for they had first danced together on Valentine's Day, all those years ago. It would be their last, for he could tell that it was coming upon her fast; he could see a change in her every day. It wouldn't be long but he intended to make sure he was with her every minute he could from then on.

Chapter 5

Detective Inspector Cooke looked at the bones laid out on the pathologist's table. They had been arranged so that his inexpert eye could see that the whole skeleton was there, the two pieces of the leg bone broken by Elwin's spade aligned.

"Female, around sixteen or seventeen, I'd say," the pathologist informed him. "Complete, and in surprisingly good condition, given that she must have been there a long time."

"How long?"

"Oh, sixty – seventy years; nearer seventy, I'd say. We need to do further tests; carbon dating, DNA and so on, which of course will take some time. But in the preliminary stage, that's my best guess. Given the state of the neck vertebrae, I'd say she was strangled; there's evidence of unnatural breakage there."

Dan looked up.

"So, Stan, it looks like we have a seventy-year old murder on our hands."

Dr. Stan Wilson nodded.

"It does indeed."

*****

Lucy was not really that surprised when D.I. Cooke and P.C. Grant turned up at the farmhouse a couple of days after the skeleton had been taken away.

"Hello there," she said, as she opened the door. "I thought you might be back. You are just in time to help me."

"Oh yes?" The DI smiled charmingly at her, eyebrows raised quizzically.

"Yes. I've just made a new cake that I want to try out on someone. Sit down at the table and I'll cut you a slice each. I'd be glad of your opinion."

"Happy to oblige, ma'am." D.S. Grant couldn't look happier at the prospect of sampling a cake. DI Cooke smiled and sat at the table ready for his portion.

Once her guests had a piece of cake and a cup of tea in front of them, Lucy sat down, awaiting their verdict. She watched the DI take a bite of his cake, idly reflecting that he was a handsome man, although he must be around forty. Still, that's not really old, she thought to herself. Out loud, she said,

"Well, what do you think?"

"Delicious," pronounced Cooke, taking another bite and his sergeant nodded vigorously in agreement. "Although of course, we are really here on business, about the skeleton, you know."

"Of course; I knew you would come when you had something to tell me."

"Erm, yes, well, we don't know too much yet. It seems it has been there for some years, around seventy, our pathologist reckons. It's a young woman of around sixteen or seventeen and it appears she was strangled."

"Oh, poor girl! What a dreadful thing – and to think she's been lying in my field all those years! I bet her parents, whoever they were, had a terrible time when she went missing. I can't think of anything worse than losing a child, even one as old as that. I couldn't bear it if anything happened to John."

"No. Quite."

"I don't see how I can help you, Detective Inspector. As you know, I've only been here three years."

"Of course. But you know the people in the village. Can you tell me of any who have lived here a long time?"

"We-ell, there's Mr. Price's dad, he's pretty old. And there's my husband's grandfather, Joseph Baxter. He's not as old as Mr Price senior, but he's getting on. He may well have heard if anyone had gone missing from hereabouts years ago. It's possible that she may not be from round here, of course."

Dan nodded. "Yes, we've thought of that. We are trying to trace the missing persons records from seventy years or so back but not having computers in those days, it's going to be a long task but we have people on it. It would be very helpful if any locals could shed light on the matter though, save us a lot of time."

"I can see that. Why not try Mr. Price and Joseph? I'm sure that they would know whatever went on in this village for about the last hundred years or more!" Lucy laughed.

The policemen stood up, having finished their cake and tea.

"We should go and see Mr. Price anyway as he found the body to tell him our findings so far. Hopefully we can talk to his father as well."

As Lucy waved the two detectives off in their car, she heard her son's cry from upstairs. She shut the door quickly and hurried to fetch John from his cot.

*****

"You say it's a young woman? How strange," mused Elwyn. "I've been hiring that field for many years, ever since Lucy's aunt bought the farmhouse. I've never known it dug or ploughed in all my years living here."

"The pathologist reckons she's been buried nigh on seventy years, sir."

"Oh well, that's afore my time. My father might know something though."

"We were hoping we could talk with him."

"Oh? I'm sure he wasn't involved in anything."

"We don't think he was, sir, it's simply that he's been here a long time. He might have heard tell of a young woman going missing if she's from around here."

"That makes sense. I'll get the wife to ask him if he'll talk with you. He's rather frail now and keeps to his room a lot. Mary!"

A woman appeared at the kitchen door in answer to his call. Her rosy cheeks and ready smile were attractive in a mature way.

"What's the matter, my love?"

"Mary, my dear, would you mind asking Dad if he would talk with the detectives please? They want to pick his memory."

"Oh yes, won't be a tick."

Mary hurried off up the stairs, and, moments later, they heard her voice calling,

"You can come up. Father will see you in his room."

"If you've finished with me, I have work to get on with," Elwyn said to Dan.

"Of course, sir. We just wanted to tell you what we know about your skeleton. Thought you'd be interested."

"Indeed I am. I hope it won't be too long until I can get on and finish the fencing in the field?"

"When we are sure there's no more evidence there, we will contact you. Shouldn't be long now."

Elwyn nodded and went out the back door. The detectives followed Mary upstairs. They were shown into a large bedroom which had been made into a sort of bedsit, with the bed and bedroom things in one half of the room and the other half was a sitting-room with a couple of armchairs with a small table between and a television in one corner. Obviously, Mary had gone to a lot of trouble to make this room a pleasant and convenient place for her elderly father-in-law to spend his time.

"Dad, this is Detective-Inspector Cooke and Detective Sergeant Grant. They want to ask you about something."

"Oh yes? What's that then?" Sid's voice was surprisingly strong for an old and frail man. Dan went forward to shake the old man's hand, casting his appraising eye over the figure in the automatic recliner chair. His upper body was quite bulky; Dan suspected this was a once-muscular man now in decline through immobility. But the face was alert, the eyes watchful.

"Sit down, sir," offered Mary as she indicated the chair that faced the invalid.

"Thank you," Dan sat in the chair. Mary drew over a kitchen-type chair from beside the bed for the sergeant to sit on and he nodded his thanks.

"I'll leave you to it then. When you've finished, just come on down."

"Okay. Thank you. Good of you to see us, Mr Price. You have a very nice room here."

"I do but you didn't come here to talk about my living conditions. What did you want to talk about?"

Dan cleared his throat.

"Can you tell me how long you have lived here, Mr Price?"

"Always been here, man and boy. Never lived anywhere else. I took over from my father and now my son works the farm, helped by his sons. That's the way of farming families. I'm useless now, as you can see. Had an accident about ten year ago."

"I'm sorry to hear that, sir. But it's good that you've been here so long, it's because you have that we wanted to talk with you."

"Oh? How's that then?"

"Did your son tell you that he found a body?"

Sid looked up, startled.

"A body? Where? Who is it?"

"Well, we don't know. He found it when he was digging in Mrs Baxter's meadow, you know, the one where your son keeps his herd. Bones of a young woman. Been there about seventy years, we reckon. We wondered if you can recall hearing anything about a young woman going missing, round about 1945/46? We thought, as you've lived so long in the village, you might have heard something. After all, the village was much smaller in those days, wasn't it?"

"Yes, it were. But I never heard tell about a missing woman. Who is she?"

"Well, we don't know, that's what we are trying to find out."

"I'm sorry I can't help you. Goodbye."

Dan paused for a moment, looking at the old man. He had slumped down and appeared to be taking no more interest.

"Come on, Grant, we aren't going to get anything more. Sorry to have bothered you, Mr Price."

The old man barely moved and showed no interest at all as they left his room.

Once they had gone though, he lifted his head and stared at the door for a long time.

Mary was cleaning the living room when they went down. She showed them to the door.

"He couldn't tell us much. We won't bother him anymore, it's obvious he doesn't remember anything."

"His mind wanders rather these days," she said in an apologetic manner.

"He might want you to go up to him. We'll be off now. Thank you very much. Goodbye, Mrs Price."

"Goodbye, sir."

Once they were in the car, Dan said,

"What did you make of the old man, Grant?"

"I'm not sure, sir. He seemed very alert, in spite of his disability and yet, when we mentioned the girl, he seemed to change."

"You are right. It's my opinion that Mr Sidney Price knows something about this and he's using his infirmity to hide it."

Chapter 6

The police detectives' next port of call was Baxter's Nursery. They went into the garden centre, knowing that Sheila or Kenny would be there and they found Sheila at the main checkout.

"Hello there, Mr Cooke," said Sheila pleasantly.

"Good to see you again, Mrs Dixon. How are you?"

"Oh, just fine, thank you. What can I do for you?"

"I was rather hoping to have a chat with Mr Baxter senior. Is he at home, can we go and see him?"

"I'm really sorry but my father-in-law has gone to stay with my daughter for a few days in Ross-on-Wye. I expect you could see him there, if you like. May I ask what it's about?"

"We're just looking for older residents of the village who might possibly remember a young girl going missing around seventy years ago. I know Mr. Baxter would have been a child then but he might have heard something."

Sheila nodded. "It's possible. The village was a hamlet then, a very small community. I'm sure everyone knew everyone else's business. That's what it was like in those days. Come to think about it, it's pretty much the same now really, although there are more people living here. What do you know about the body that was found, if I may ask?"

"It's no secret. We know it is of a young woman of about sixteen or seventeen and she has lain there for around seventy years."

"I see," said Sheila thoughtfully. "I'm sure Joseph would help you if he can. I could give you my daughter's address."

"It can wait. Do you know when he will be back?"

"Next weekend. He never stays long because my daughter's always so busy. And the children can get too much, although he adores them. Small doses, you know."

"Yes, I can imagine. Can you tell me about any other people who would have been here at that time?"

"Well, I'd say the best person would be Samuel Williams. He moved away but he grew up here and lives in the village again now. In fact, his family owned River View Farm and he would have been around eighteen at the time. He certainly would know if anyone had gone missing and of course, the body was buried on his land."

"Hmm, interesting. Yes, we must certainly talk with Mr. Williams. Can you tell me where to find him?"

"Dorothy Avenue, number 16. There are three roads of fairly new-built houses and bungalows at the end of the village. They were named after the builder's wife and two daughters – Dorothy, Charlotte and Victoria."

"Must have been a builder with connections," grunted Dan.

"I'd say so," grinned Sheila. "I hope you get the information you are looking for and don't hesitate to come back if we can help you more. I'll think about others who might have been living in the area, perhaps in Long Sutton or Sutton Rise."

"Thank you. If you do think of anything, just call and leave a message for me."

She took the card that Dan handed to her and smiled. "Of course."

Sheila watched the two men as they walked out and back to their dark, unmarked car, seen clearly through the large plate-glass windows. She thought about the young woman lying buried in the meadow and then of her parents, whoever they were. 'Poor, poor things,' she muttered to herself, 'what a terrible thing to have a beloved daughter just disappear without trace.'
*****

Dorothy Avenue was a street with a mixture of houses and bungalows that were pleasing to the eye and didn't look too out of place in the country surroundings.

Number 16, a bungalow of sand-coloured bricks with large picture windows and a glass porch had a small front lawn, neat as a new pin with daffodils bobbing their golden heads in the narrow beds that surrounded it. In the corner by the next-door neighbour's fence, a tidy rockery glowed with fresh alpine greenery that would flower later on. Here and there small bunches of heather threw splashes of colour, white, pink and pinky-purple and miniature daffodils danced as valiantly as their larger relations.

'Very nice,' thought Dan as he knocked on the front door, having opened the porch door. There was no answer; he knocked again.

"There's no one in!" a voice called and Dan turned to look at the young woman just coming out of the house next door. She had a toddler in a push-chair with her.

"So it seems. Do you have any idea where Mr. Williams might be?" Dan flashed his ID card and she came over to look at it.

"Oh, you're police?" She frowned.

"Plain clothes."

"Ah. Well, Mrs Williams – Emily – is very ill, you know, and she's been taken to St. Michael's Hospice. Went yesterday, poor soul. I expect Sam – Mr. Williams – will stay there with her until – well, until she, you know – dies. Won't be long now. Sam has done his best to care for her at home but they know how to make the passing easier at St. Michael's."

"Of course. They do a wonderful job there," agreed Dan, solemnly. "I don't think we'll bother Mr Williams just now. We only wanted to speak with him because he's an older resident of the village. It's to do with something that happened around seventy years ago; we are looking for people who might remember it."

"Oh, I see. Is it to do with the body that was found in the field?"

"Yes. We are trying to find out if anyone went missing at that time."

"Why don't you try Sutton Court? I'll bet there'll be someone there who would have been around at that time. In fact, come to think of it, there's Flo, Florence Hind. She's my great-aunt and she used to live in one of the farm cottages that are now part of Nursery House. Her memory is sharp as a razor, too – I wouldn't mind betting she could tell you if anything happened."

Dan smiled at her. "That sounds hopeful. We will go there, eh, Sergeant?"

"Yes, sir, sounds good."

"Thank you very much for your help, Miss – er, Mrs...?"

"Sue. Sue Smith; I used to be Sue Marsh. Just tell Aunt Flo that you met me."

"Thank you, Mrs Smith, much appreciated."

The two men walked back to their car and waved to Sue as she walked past them.

"Just when I was beginning to lose hope, Grant, what with Joseph Baxter being away and now Sam Williams not at home," said Dan, "it seems all is not lost after all. Sutton Court it is then. Let's go!"

Chapter 7

The sweet, sickly smell of vanilla, mingled with a faint aroma of urine met the noses of the two policemen as they were given entrance into Sutton Court, although it wasn't overpowering and they soon became immune to it as they waited for the matron, Cecelia Milton. The young woman who had admitted them informed them that she was administering medical aid to a resident but would be along shortly. She indicated the chairs for waiting visitors but they remained standing.

As he waited, Dan took in his surroundings. It house had clearly once belonged to gentry; it retained its elegance and was decorated in warm colours, giving it a welcoming feel. The walls were a soft cream but the chairs were padded in a light green with gilt edgings. The curving staircase with shallow stairs had a balustrade and handrail that was gold, as were the light switches. There were even a couple of alabaster busts in niches in the walls. A gilt table held a gorgeous display of spring flowers in a glass bowl. In a way, it was hard to tell they were in a nursing home. Obviously, the present owners wanted to retain the illusion of grandeur by keeping this entrance hall and staircase, even though the stairs probably were not used much.

As if to put a lie to this thought, a woman appeared, descending the stairs. She came rapidly towards them, smiling in welcome, although her eyes were apprehensive. Smoothing down her blue nurse's dress, she held out her hand.

"Good afternoon. I'm Cecelia Milton, owner and matron of Sutton Court. How may I help you?"

"Pleased to meet you, Mrs Milton, my name is Detective Inspector Dan Cooke and this is Detective Sergeant Grant. I was wondering if we could ask for your help?"

"Certainly, if I can. Would you like to come into my office? It's just through here." Cessy led the way through a door off the main hall, near the front entrance.

This was a room with a definite function. The desk of light wood was modern, a computer sat to one side of it. Along one wall, shelves held blue ring-binder files, each clearly marked and in alphabetical order. On the opposite side to the shelves were several small metal drawers and beside them a cupboard with glass doors. Dan could see that various bottles of pills and other medications were clearly visible within the cabinet.

"Do sit down," Cecelia went to sit behind the desk; the officers sat on chairs the other side. Dan idly reflected that it was not often he was the one sitting in front of a desk instead of being the person behind.

"How may I help you?"

"Well, you may have heard that a couple of weeks ago, a body was found in a field here in the village?"

"Yes, in Lucy's meadow, wasn't it?"

"You know Lucy – erm, Mrs Baxter?"

"Of course. We are great friends, Lucy's a lovely girl – or I should say, young woman. But that doesn't explain what you want of me, Mr Cooke."

"How long have you lived in the village, Mrs Mason?"

"Twenty four years. My husband was left Sutton Court in his uncle's will. We had to do a lot of work on the house, it was in quite a dilapidated state but we finally moved in twenty four years ago, in the May of nineteen ninety one."

"I see. Anyway, today we met a young woman who said her aunt, or her great aunt, lived in the village seventy years ago and is a resident here at Sutton Court. We are looking for people who were around here at that time. Her name is – erm – Florence Hind?"

"Oh, you mean Flo! Yes, she's lived in Sutton all her life, I believe."

"Would it be possible to see her, please?"

"Of course. I'm sure she will be delighted to talk with you. She's bright as a button and loves having visitors. I'm sure she would indeed be a good person for you to talk with. If you wouldn't mind waiting here for a moment, I'll go and see where she is."

"Thank you, that would be most helpful."

"Nice lady," remarked Dan after Cecelia had left the room.

"Indeed, sir," Constable Grant nodded. "Quite a place, don't you think?"

"It is. They've done a good job with it."

Five minutes later, Cecelia reappeared.

"Flo said she would be happy to see you. She was sitting in a room with other residents so we have put her in a small room so you can talk with her privately. If you would like to follow me, I'll take you to her."

They went into the large hallway towards the staircase. They walked down a smaller hallway to the left, which had a few double doors leading off. Through glass panels, the men could see into a spacious lounge and then an equally large dining room. The matron opened a door to their right and they went into a pleasant small room, comfortably furnished with a couple of armchairs and a small two-seater sofa. An old-fashioned fireplace with a marble mantelpiece held a clock and a few ornaments of figurines. The large window looked out onto an ornamental garden with a fountain playing in the middle of a round pond.

'Very pleasant', thought Dan.

The door opened again as a wheelchair was pushed into the room. Sitting in the chair, a rug over her knees, was a small woman with a cloud of white hair surrounding a surprisingly unlined face.

"Here we are," said Cecelia as she brought the chair to a halt, positioned so that the men could sit in the chairs and talk easily. "Flo, this is Detective Inspector Cooke and Detective Sergeant Grant. They would like to pick your memory."

"Hello, Mrs Hind, it's good of you to see us." Dan held out his hand.

"Oh, call me Flo, young man! Mrs Hind makes me feel really old."

Her voice was clear as a young woman's and Dan and Grant grinned at each other. Dan had a good feeling about this woman.

"Flo, then, thank you. We met a young woman called Sue Smith, used to be Marsh, she said we should come and talk with you."

"Ah yes. My Sue. Good girl, comes to see me often. Well, how can I help you, Inspector?"

"If I can call you Flo, then you must call me Dan."

"Thank you. Dan it is. What do you want to ask me?"

"You've lived here all your life, I understand?"

"That's right, yes. I grew up in one of the farm cottages that were knocked together to make one house that belongs to the Baxters."

"So Sue said. I wonder if you can cast your mind back to around nineteen forty five or six. Can you remember if a young girl went missing about that time?"

"Hmm, let me see. The only thing I can think of is that young Rosemary. She went off with a man. He was a stranger and appeared in the village about a month before she went missing. Oh, he was a show-off! He had a car and liked to drive around in it for everyone to see. The local girls went mad for him with his slick-backed hair and expensive tweeds. He thought he was the real bees-knees.

"Anyway, one night she sneaked out of her house with a suitcase, leaving a note saying she was going away with him and was going to be married. She said she would get in touch with them when they settled somewhere, but there was never any word from her again, y'know. Her poor mother nearly went mad with grief but she insisted that she would hear from Rosemary. Month in, month out she waited. A year went by and then two. Poor Agnes, although she had another child, she just gradually went downhill and died about five years after Rosemary disappeared. Everyone reckoned she died of grief. Her poor husband didn't know what to do, he got old before his time but he still had his son to look after when his wife died. He kept working but he lost loads of weight. He'd lost his precious daughter who had been the apple of his eye and then he lost his beloved wife. I don't think he ever recovered, you know. And then there was that poor lad who was only about eight when his sister went missing and he was more or less left to bring himself up the best way he could without much from his parents, or at least, not much from his mother."

Dan and Grant looked at each other – jackpot!

"Did you know the family well, Flo?"

"Of course I did – we lived next door to them."

"I see, well of course you would know them well in that case."

"Everyone knew everyone's business in them days, Dan. That was the way of things. Not like nowadays when folks don't even know their next-door neighbours."

Dan nodded gravely.

"You are so right. We're very grateful to you, you have a wonderful memory."

"Oh, my head is fine, young man. It's these stupid legs of mine that don't work anymore. There doesn't seem much choice in old age, you know, it's either the mind that goes or the body. I'm glad I still have my mind really but I'm not much keen on the body going the way it is!"

"I'm sure. I bet you are good at being friends to the others though."

"Oh yes, I try to help them keep their minds going. I am lucky too because I have family and friends who come to see me. Some of the poor folks in here have no one to visit them. Oh yes, I'm lucky. And it's lovely here, they look after us very well."

Flo put her hand out to Cecelia, who smiled and took it in hers.

Dan stood up.

"Well, we have enjoyed meeting you, Flo and you have helped us tremendously. Oh, this Rosemary, can you tell us her other name? Does any of her family still live in the village?"

"Oh, dearie me! Didn't I say? Silly me! It's Baxter, Rosemary was Joseph Baxter's big sister."

Chapter 8

Once back in their car on the car park at Sutton Court, Dan sat back and gave a low whistle.

"Joseph Baxter's sister, my word! I never expected that. I wonder why Sheila never said anything?"

"Perhaps she doesn't know about it, sir."

"Yes, you could be right. She doesn't strike me as someone who would deliberately withhold information."

"I agree, sir. Straight as a die, I'd say."

"Unfortunately choice of word there, Grant, but you're right."

"What do we do now, sir?"

"I think we'll just pop back to the nursery and get the daughter's address and then we'll call it a day. We'll go and see Joseph in Ross on Wye tomorrow."

"Oh, Mr Cooke! I was about to call you," Sheila greeted Dan and Grant when she'd opened the door of the Nursery House in answer to their knock. "Do come in."

They stepped inside the house.

"You were going to call me, Mrs Dixon?"

"Yes, I've just had a phone call from my daughter. Joseph is not well and he wants to come home. Kenny is going over this evening to fetch him."

"That's very fortuitous, Mrs. Dixon, because we came back to get your daughter's address so we could see Mr. Baxter tomorrow. We've had a very interesting discussion with a resident of Sutton Court, a lady called Florence Hind."

"Oh yes, I know Flo! She used to live here, I believe, before the cottages were knocked into one."

"She said that, yes. She also said that Mr Baxter's sister went missing seventy years ago."

Her hands on either side of her face, Sheila gasped.

"My goodness! I never even thought of her! But she ran off with some man."

"That's what Mrs Hind said. But she also said that the family never heard from the girl again. In my book, that means she went missing."

"You're right, Mr Cooke. My father-in-law never talks of her, I only know from what others have said in the past. His mother had already died before I knew them, in fact, I think Joseph was not that old when his mother died. His father never spoke of Rosemary at all and of course he was very old when I met my first husband, Kenny's father."

Dan nodded in understanding.

"According to Mrs Hind, he never got over losing his daughter and then his wife."

"He certainly wasn't a very happy man. Don't get me wrong, he wasn't nasty, he just had a sad air about him. I hadn't been married very long when he died; it was a happy release for him I think. Poor man. I really didn't know him that well."

"Well, we won't keep you any longer. I will call tomorrow to find out how Mr Baxter is. If he's not up to talking, it can wait. After all, that body has lain in the ground for a long time. A few more days or weeks before we can identify her won't hurt."

"Thank you, that's very considerate of you. Joseph often isn't well but that's not surprising at his age. I do my best to make sure he's looked after properly and Kenny and Tom, my husband, are both very good and do their best to help."

"He's not a candidate for Sutton Court then?"

"Oh no! There's no need for that. Joseph would hate to leave his home and we can manage."

"That's excellent. He's a lucky man to have you."

"He's been a wonderful father-in-law, it's the least I can do for him."

"Quite. Well, we must be away. As I said, I'll give you a call in the morning. Good evening to you, Mrs Dixon."

"Goodbye, Mr Cooke, Sergeant Grant."

"Ma'am," replied Grant and followed his boss out of the house.

When they had gone, Sheila went to find Tom, she needed his calmness because, for some reason, she was feeling somewhat ruffled.

On their way back to Hereford, the two policemen talked about their discoveries.

"What will you do if Mr Baxter is not well enough to talk with us, sir?"

"No matter. I want to see if there are any reports of any other missing persons – and to find out if Rosemary Baxter was ever reported missing. At some point we need to get a DNA sample from Joseph Baxter to see if she can be identified that way."

"Of course, sir."

"Technology has come on in leaps and bounds the past few years. Identifying a skeleton would have been almost impossible not so long ago. Makes detective work a bit easier but it's still mostly legwork and searching for answers that eventually solves the questions, along with a large dose of intuition."

"Indeed."

"Don't you love being able to drive out into the country on these investigations, Grant? Herefordshire is so attractive. It makes a nice change, when most of our work involves the seedier side of life in the city."

"Yes sir," Grant agreed but seemed somewhat doubtful about the joys of the countryside. Before long, they were driving in the city towards the police station.

"It's quite late, Grant, go home now and enjoy your evening. I've a feeling we might have some tedious work ahead of us tomorrow."

"Hello, Mrs Dixon? This is Dan Cooke. How is Mr Baxter today?"

"Hello, Mr Cooke. I'm afraid my father-in-law is rather poorly. He seems to have taken a chill. Could you wait a couple of days before you come to see him? His doctor is coming later so we'll know more after that. At the moment, he is still sleeping and he won't be getting up today because he is running a temperature."

"I'm sorry to hear that. I will call again on Friday. In the meantime, if he improves and is able to talk with us, would you let me know, please?"

"I will indeed."

"Thank you. Goodbye for now."

When Sheila put the phone down, she turned to Tom, who was sitting at the kitchen table eating toast. Butch sat patiently beside him, watching the toast going up and down.

"I'm worried, Tom. If this body turns out to be Joseph's sister, what will that do to him? I'm bothered that he might not be strong enough to cope with it."

Tom reached out and took her hand.

"He is stronger than he seems, my dear. Let's take it one step at a time, Let him get better first, then we will know if he can deal with it. If it is his sister, he deserves to know. He also deserves to know what actually happened to her. Although it seems impossible to find out what occurred so long ago, things have a habit of coming out somehow. I have a feeling in my bones that this mystery is going to be solved."

Sheila looked at her husband, to whom she had been married for only a couple of years and her heart turned over with love for him. He was always so calm that he made her feel peaceful just by being with him. He was right, one step at a time. With that thought, she kissed Tom and set off upstairs to check on Joseph.

He was awake but looked far from well. He smiled weakly at her.

"I'm sorry to be a nuisance, my dear."

She bent down to kiss his hot cheek.

"You are never a nuisance. You know how much we all love you. We're going to get you better. I phoned the surgery. The doctor's coming to see you later."

"No need for that," he protested.

"I'll be the judge of that. Now, I'm going to get some water and a flannel and cool you down."

A few minutes later, she returned with a bowl and proceeded to gently dab his face with the lukewarm flannel. He closed his eyes appreciatively. She took the duvet off, replaced it with a sheet and a blanket and opened his pyjama top and sponged his chest.

"There now, does that feel better?"

He nodded.

"Thank you, my dear."

"Do you fancy anything to eat?"

He shook his head slightly.

She poured some water into a glass from a jug she had brought up earlier and popped a straw into it.

"Here, you must try to drink a little."

He managed to take about half the glass, which was good, then he laid back again with a sigh. She smoothed his hair back from his forehead, kissed him again and left him to sleep.

It turned out that Joseph had a chest infection and the doctor gave him antibiotics. With Sheila's careful ministrations, he gradually improved. However, he was not well enough to talk with Dan Cooke until after the weekend. None of the family mentioned that the police suspected the body might be Rosemary and Sheila hoped that the elderly man would cope when he did eventually find out.

Chapter 9

Samuel sat by his wife's bed; he knew her time was near. His fingers gently touched the white hair that framed a face so pale he could barely see where the hair stopped and her skin began. He remembered when her hair had been blonde, like spun silk against her soft cheeks. When it turned white, she hadn't looked any different.

Her eyes had first attracted him to her – they danced with life and laughter. They were so blue and they drew you in. When she looked at him, he felt he could drown in those pools that seemed so deep and yet sparkled as sunlight on water.

He recalled how she was with him, their families, and the children she taught at school. She treated everyone as if they were important to her and they loved her for it. Their one sadness was that they couldn't have children. They discussed adoption but somehow it hadn't seemed right. In the end they decided not to and put all their energies into their respective jobs and their dancing.

As he held her hand, so small and still, he thought about how Emily glided lightly in his arms and easily picked up new steps and moves; she was a delight to dance with. It seemed that every time he danced with her it felt like their first. It didn't matter how long they had been together or how many dances or competitions they entered, it always seemed a fresh, exciting experience. She was his whole life, his heart, his everything. He was a lucky man. They'd had a wonderful life together and now she was slipping away from him.

A nurse came in to check on Emily. She looked at Sam with compassion. He had sat there for four days, refusing to leave his wife, only to go to the bathroom. He ate slept here, on a bed next to Emily, He slept only for short periods, terrified to sleep long in case she slipped away without him watching over her, comforting her and waiting for her hand to go from his into her guardian angel's hand on the other side of the veil. The nurse did what she had to do, then touched Sam on the shoulder and went out.

Emily's eyes flickered open. Sam applied a little more pressure on her hand so she would know he was there.

"Sam?"

Her whisper was barely a breath in the still room.

"I'm here, my darling."

"I love you."

"I love you, my dearest."

He kissed her softly on her brow.

Her eyes closed again, her breathing shallow. Not long later, her arms stretched out and eyes still closed, she lifted her head from the pillow with a smile on her face, as if greeting someone. She sank back down and just as Samuel took her hand again, he heard a rattle in her throat and then silence.

Samuel sat still, holding her hand. He made no sound, but a tear from each eye trickled slowly down his cheeks. He sat for a few moments and then reached for the bell.

****

Dan and his team had been busy. They had searched, without success, for any reports about Rosemary Baxter going missing. It seemed that her disappearance had not been raised with the police, nor had the newspapers been aware of it. She had simply slipped unnoticed into oblivion. What had her parents been thinking of? Hadn't they cared? According to Florence Hinds, the mother never recovered from the shock of losing her daughter. So why didn't she report the girl missing? She was so young, under the age of consent, which in those days was twenty one.

They found reports of other girls who had gone missing and found dead, one in Devon, another in North Wales, and again in Yorkshire. All had been raped and strangled over the period of around eighteen months. All were young women and they had all been in quiet country locations. However, none of them had been buried as their girl was; all had been left where the dirty deeds had been done for someone, anyone, to find. The papers were full of the murders and it was obvious to all that there had been a serial killer about.

Dan ended up frustrated and, for the time being, defeated. His eyes hurt and so did his head as he tried to think what could have happened to Rosemary, if it was her.

"Go home, Grant, go home everyone. We can't do anything else right now. Enjoy your weekend and let's hope Joseph Baxter is well enough to talk with us soon."

****

Dan had a difficult weekend, trying to think around the newspaper reports and puzzling over why the Baxters hadn't reported their daughter missing. Monday morning brought him into work, tired from lack of sleep, his brain having refused to let him rest.

Shortly after he arrived at the office, he had a phone call.

"Detective Inspector Cooke."

"Hello, Mr Cooke, this is Sheila Dixon. I called to let you know that Joseph is much better now and says he will see you if you care to come over."

"I'm glad to hear that, Mrs Dixon, we'll be over within the hour. Thank you for calling."

He pressed a button on his desk phone.

"Bert, is Grant in yet? Oh good. Would you ask him to get the car please? We are going out to Sutton-on-Wye."

"Very good sir."

"Oh, and bring me a coffee, would you? I need one before I go."

Young Johnson appeared with his coffee, and no sooner had the door shut behind him, the phone rang again.

"Detective Inspector Cooke."

"Hello, this is Susan Smith, you remember I met you last week outside my house?"

"Yes of course. What can I do for you?"

"I thought you should know that my neighbour, Sam Williams is home again if you still want to see him. He's still very delicate though, after his wife dying."

"Thank you, Mrs Smith. We may want to see him. We will be careful with him, don't worry."

****

Sheila's smiling face greeted them as she opened the door. At her invitation they stepped inside.

"Joseph is in the living room waiting for you. Please be gentle with him because, although he's much better, he is still not completely well."

"Don't worry, we will."

"Would you like tea or coffee?"

"Not for me, I've just had a drink."

Walking into the living room, he saw Joseph sitting in a recliner chair, a blanket around his knees. He looked a little pale but his smile was bright and welcoming. Dan went over to shake his hand.

"Hello there, Mr Cooke, it's good to see you again. I understand you want to talk with me about something. I'm mystified but I'll help if I can."

"Thank you. It's good of you to see us."

"Sit down, sit down."

They sat down, Dan on an armchair opposite Joseph and Grant on an upright chair beside his boss. Dan cleared his throat.

"You are aware that a skeleton has been found buried in River View meadow?"

"Yes, what of it? Do you have any idea who it might be?"

Dan hesitated; was the man strong enough to hear the answer?

He looked at the old man, who gazed back at him steadily.

"I'm sorry to say this because it's going to be a shock to you but we are beginning to believe it might be your sister, Rosemary."

"No!" The shock was evident. Dan got up and put his hand on the man's shoulder. Joseph made a valiant effort to gather himself.

"What makes you think that?"

"Well, I admit we only have some scanty evidence at the moment. We know the skeleton is that of a young woman of around seventeen. Our forensic experts say the body has been there about seventy years and we know that your sister disappeared at around that time."

"It's true, she did. She went off with a man."

"I know you were young at the time but can you tell me why your parents never reported her missing?"

"I didn't know that they hadn't. But I do know that she took a case full of clothes and left a note for my parents. I remember my mother crying when she read it."

"Do you know what the note said?"

"I never saw it but Mother told me Rosemary had said she was going to be married and was going to live in London and would contact them again once she had settled down. I heard my parents talking about it."

"Hmm, I wonder what happened to the suitcase."

"No idea. I presumed she took it with her. If you didn't find it with her, then the body might not be her, might it?"

Dan nodded gravely.

"I suppose that is true. It would be helpful if we could have a sample of DNA from you, if you wouldn't mind. That would tell us once and for all if the body is that of your sister."

"Of course. No problem."

"Grant will do that, won't you, Grant?"

"Yes sir. I have the stuff in the car."

"Good man. Go and get it, would you?"

When Grant had gone out, Sheila came in to see if Joseph was alright. She took his hand.

"Don't worry, my dear. Although I am shocked that it might be our Rosemary buried in the field, I'm in control. It's just that it brings back so many bad memories, you know."

"Yes, I do know. I'm sorry I didn't tell you but I didn't want to bother you when you were ill."

"Of course not. I understand, my dear. But I can't believe it is Rosemary – we were all so sure she had gone off with that man."

"Would you tell us about your sister?" asked Dan. "What was she like?"

"Well, as you know, there was a big gap between us because she was nine years older than me. I was only eight when she left home. But I remember her being kind and caring. She was like a second mother to me because I was often left in her care when Mother had to see to things on the farm. She had long, light brown hair like mine was and blue eyes, also like mine. She was very pretty and always looked good whatever she wore and whatever she did. She could look good in the old dress she wore around the house or in the dungarees she wore when doing farmwork. It was Father who was employed at River View Farm but everyone used to help at busy times, such as harvest time. I remember that she actually went out with one of the sons at the farm, and he was crazy for her. They went out for quite a long time until she met this other man."

"Can you tell me who the new man was?"

"I don't remember anything about him really only that I didn't like him and he had a car. I remember the car particularly because you didn't see many in those days."

"Can you remember his name?"

"Yes, it was Gilbert Trent. I remember because I have searched the records for their marriage, I even went down to Catherine House in London where the records were but I found nothing. The records are in Somerset House now. And with all the family history sites and records available online now, I've searched them too but have never found anything at all."

"Hmm. Thank you for that. Oh, was the name of the lad from River View Farm Samuel Williams?"

"Yes, that's right. He lives in the village now, in one of the new places down the road."

Dan nodded.

"That is so. For a matter of interest, do you know how he took it when Rosemary finished with him so she could be with this – Gilbert Trent?"

"He took it very badly. He was very much in love with my sister, I think. I never saw him much but I was friends with his younger brother, James and James used to say that Sam was like a bear with a sore head after Rosemary dumped him."

"Interesting. Thank you very much for that. You've been very helpful, Mr. Baxter. If you'll just let Grant take your samples, we will leave you in peace."

Joseph opened his mouth obediently as Grant took the saliva samples and popped them in a sterile bag.

"Thank you. We'll be in touch again once we have the results."

Once in the car, Grant said,

"So, could this Samuel Williams have killed the girl in a fit of jealousy?"

"Always possible, Grant. Next stop, Dorothy Avenue."

Chapter 10

Samuel showed them into the lounge of the bungalow. He insisted on brewing tea and so they sat on the settee and waited while he made the brew. He brought a tray with three mugs and biscuits on a matching plate. He set it down on a small table, handed out the mugs and offered the biscuits. Grant and Dan both took one and Samuel then eased himself into a chair with his own. Dan admired the fine china mugs which had a dainty violets design.

"My wife would only use fine bone china. She said things tasted much better from it. She was a real lady." Samuel sighed.

"We are sorry about your wife, Mr Williams. Emily, wasn't it?"

"Yes, my Emily. We would have been married sixty years in November."

"That's a long time. Many people never get that far. Were you young when you married?"

"Twenty eight. We met at university, we were both mature students doing a teaching degree."

"I see. How come you were at university so late?"

"Well, as I lived on a farm, I fully expected to become a farmer after my father. But he was killed in the war and my mother, my younger brother and I struggled on trying to run the farm afterwards. After Dad died my mother's heart was less and less into farming and so eventually we decided to sell the farm because my brother and I wanted to do other things. So, we sold up in nineteen fifty one and the money paid for a cottage for Mum and university for me and James became a carpenter. I'm sure we've all been happier for doing that.

"I know that Mum was much better in her little cottage, not having to worry about the farm and how to keep going, although I was doing most of it by then. In fact I had been since during the war. I left school and worked on the farm full-time because it was a full-time job. We only had two elderly workers to help us."

"It must have been hard. The reason we wanted to talk with you is because you lived here in the village seventy-odd years ago. You heard about the skeleton that has been found? Now we know that the meadow where it was buried belonged to your family."

Samuel nodded his head.

"Yes, I heard – and yes, the field was ours. How odd, I never noticed anything untoward. During the war, the field was ploughed and planted to grow crops. When the war was over, we decided to let it become a meadow again. It had originally been a meadow, you see, but the Ministry of Agriculture insisted that we plant it as food was scarce during the war. It was still scarce afterwards for a while but the heart went out of us when Dad died and so I left it to become a meadow again; I couldn't deal with everything on the farm and one field less to work made a difference. Once it was back to grass, I started keeping more sheep. Fortunately, the Ministry was okay with that and we gradually became more of a sheep farm, although we did grow some crops, mostly to feed the sheep during the winter."

"I see. If you had kept ploughing the field, she might have been found."

Samuel nodded.

"Highly likely, I'd say, although it depends on where it was buried – you say it was a 'she'?

"Yes, forensics have concluded it was a young woman of around sixteen or seventeen. Do you remember hearing of anyone of that age going missing from around here?"

Samuel frowned.

"No…no, I don't think so. Do they think she was from around here?"

"It seems likely. Murderers don't usually take bodies far unless they had transport, and not many people had transport in those days."

"Yes, that's true."

Samuel got up and put his cup on the tray and sat down again.

"I don't really see how I can help you, Mr Cooke."

"Well, we suspect that the body may be that of Rosemary Baxter, who disappeared around that time."

Dan watched Samuel's face carefully as he mentioned Rosemary's name. The man looked up.

"Rosemary?" he whispered. "No!"

"You knew her, I understand."

"Oh yes, I knew her." The bitterness in Samuel's voice was evident. "That Gilbert Trent knew I loved her but he went all out to get her. There were other attractive women in the village but no, he had to have her."

"You loved her? Would you like to tell us about her?"

"Not really, there's not much to tell. She was my first girlfriend and my first love. She was beautiful and I thought she loved me. But her head was turned by the attentions of an older man, more mature than me, a man of the world and he had a car. I tried to warn her about him but she wouldn't listen. I was beside myself as I sensed that he was no good. Why would someone like him be in our village? She knew nothing about him, where he came from or anything but she didn't care. He completely turned her head and in the end she went off with him and we never saw her again."

Samuel glanced at Dan. The distress was gone and his look became a hard stare.

"She went off with him. There is no way that body could be Rosemary."

At that, Dan stood up.

"Well, thank you for being so frank with us, Mr Williams and for the tea. We will bid you good day for now. You won't be going away at all in the near future? We might need to see you again."

"Oh no, I'm not going anywhere. I have to see my Emily buried and I have no plans for going anywhere afterwards."

"Of course. Our condolences once again, Mr Williams, and thank you for your help."

Samuel saw the detectives out and waited on the doorstep until they had driven away. Then he shut the door and made his way to the lounge with the intention of taking the tray through. Instead, he sat down abruptly on the settee. Rosemary! It was such a shock being asked about her. Now, the loss of his Emily hit him harder than ever before; the only two women he had ever loved, apart from his mother, were both gone from him. He had no-one to turn for comfort. Overwhelmed, he put his head in his hands and wept in great, heavy sobs.

Chapter 11

Kenny always tried to pop home at lunch time; he hated to miss any opportunity to spend time with his wife and little boy.

Lucy greeted him as usual with a kiss, then hurried over to prevent John from putting his bowl of food on his head. Kenny ruffled his boy's hair and sat down to eat his dinner. Clarry sat at his feet, wiping the floor with her little tail.

"I saw Aunt Bea this morning," began Lucy.

"Oh yes? What does she want you to do now?"

This was a normal conversation for them, for anyone else it would have been bizarre. Lucy's Aunt Bea had been dead for about four years. However, sometimes she either appeared or 'spoke' to Lucy when there was something that needed doing, or someone was in trouble.

"She wants me to visit Sam Williams. She says he needs someone to care for him because he's alone in his grief. Not something I relish the thought of but I understand that someone should do something, poor man."

Kenny nodded.

"Yes, you're right. When will you go?"

"This afternoon if I can. Do you think your mum would babysit this young man for a while?"

"I'm sure she would, you know that she and your dad and my granddad love having him."

"I'll give her a call while you're here to watch John."

Lucy hurried from the room, phone in hand. Not many moments later, she was back.

"All settled."

She removed the now mostly empty dish from the high chair and deftly wiped John's face with a damp facecloth.

"Shall we go and see Gran and Granddad, little one?"

John smiled up at her, excitedly slapping his hands on the tray of the highchair. She lifted him out and handed him to Kenny to play with him for a few minutes.

"I'll go and get our things while he's with you, my love," she said and left the room. She returned to find John in fits of gurgling laughter at the faces his dad was pulling. Lucy laughed along with him because her baby's delighted sounds were so funny. Eventually, Kenny kissed his boy and his wife and handed the baby over to Lucy.

"I must get back to work. I'll see you later, my love."

"I'm worried that I won't know what to say to Sam."

"You will, it will come to you, don't worry." Kenny kissed her on the nose. "You always manage to do the right thing somehow and I'm sure your aunt will help if you get stuck."

She nodded and looked at him lovingly; he always knew how to make her feel better.

"You're right. I love you."

"I love you, my sweet. Now I must fly."

When Samuel opened the door, Lucy could see immediately that he was upset. His usual upright form drooped as he attempted to shield his face from her.

"Hello Sam, I felt you might need some company, so here I am."

"I'm alright, I'm fine on my own."

"No, you're not. I can see you're not. Come on, let me spend some time with you." Lucy reached up and kissed the man, putting her arms around him. It was his undoing, and the dam burst again. Lucy gently ushered him into his house, pushing the door shut behind her with her foot and sat beside him on the settee, her arm around his shuddering shoulders. She gave him her hanky, thankful that she always used man-sized ones.

"There now, there now," she crooned to him as if he was a child.

"I-I'm sorry," he managed.

"No, don't be sorry, it's natural, don't worry." She continued to hold him and gradually the sobs subsided. She had her arms around him and her head on his shoulder and he tilted his head towards hers. The comforting embrace lasted a while; Lucy realised she hadn't needed to be concerned about what to say but she was glad she had come. The poor man needed to be held and comforted so he could mourn.

After a while, Lucy said,

"Shall I make you some tea? Or something to eat?"

"I'm not hungry but I would like a brew."

"I'll get it."

"No, I'll get it." He rose unsteadily from the sofa and Lucy followed him into the kitchen, which was neat as a pin, except for a tray with three used mugs and a solitary biscuit on a plate. He saw her eyeing it.

"I had the police round this morning."

"The police?" she said, startled. "What on earth for?"

"They've been talking with people who have lived here a long time – because of that skeleton that's been found, you know."

"Oh yes. Were you able to tell them anything?"

He didn't answer but concentrated on pouring the now boiling water into the teapot. He took the dirty mugs off the tray and put them by the sink and took two clean ones from the cupboard.

"I loved that Emily always had nice china," remarked Lucy. "I prefer it too. We used to talk about it when I visited and she used to tell me when she had found some that she liked."

"Oh yes indeed. My Emily was a real lady in many ways. She wouldn't have cheap rubbish and she always said that tea tasted better in fine bone china rather than chunky mugs."

Lucy noticed that Sam's hands were rather shaky so she picked up both the mugs and carried them through, setting them on the small table. Sam followed her through.

"How are you coping?" she asked once they had sat down.

"I thought I was doing well," replied Sam, "although of course I miss her dreadfully. I've had a lot to do, arranging the funeral and informing people and so on. But the house feels so empty without her, even though she spent the last weeks mostly in bed."

"I can understand that."

There was a silence while they sipped their tea.

"It seems the police think the body in the field might be Rosemary Baxter," volunteered Sam.

Lucy looked up in surprise.

"Rosemary Baxter? Is she any relation to…?"

"Joseph Baxter. Yes. She was his sister."

"Gosh! I never even knew he had a sister, he never speaks of her."

"She was nine or ten years older than him and he was only about eight when she disappeared."

"I see – oh my goodness."

"We all thought she'd gone off with this bloke, a smart guy with a car."

Lucy noticed the bitterness creeping into Samuel's voice.

"You sound like you didn't like him."

"No, I didn't. These days he would be called a creep. But she liked him."

"And you weren't happy that she liked him?"

"No, I hated it. I was in love with her."

"Would you like to tell me about it?" Lucy asked, gently. He looked at her for what seemed like a long moment, then nodded.

"Do you have time?"

"Of course. I didn't come here to rush off again straight away. I felt in my bones you needed someone."

"Maybe the Good Lord knows I needed someone to talk to."

"I'm sure He does."

He closed his eyes for a moment and seemed to shudder. Then, he drew in a breath, opened his eyes and began to speak.

"It was nineteen forty five and I was seventeen, about to turn eighteen. My father had gone to fight in the war and my mother and brother and I were struggling to keep the farm going, with the help of two elderly farm hands."

As Sam began to speak, he was transported back through the years. He felt the coldness of a damp February day, the sort of chill that gradually seeped right through and into the bones. He heard again the lowing of the cows in the cowshed, smelled the unmistakable aroma of a farm…

Chapter 12
Sam's Story

1945, February 14th

"You going to the village hop tonight, mate?" Sidney Price asked.

Samuel stopped pitching hay in the barn, wiped his brow with his sleeve and looked at his mate.

"Oh, I dunno. I'm not much of a one for dancin'."

"There'll be loads of girls there," said Sidney, slyly. "Come and try your luck."

"Luck for what?"

"Come on man, use your imagination! You live on a farm, for goodness' sake."

"Not for that!" Sam was indignant."

"You never know." Sidney winked. Then he laughed. "Just kiddin'! Go on, be a sport, it'll be a laugh."

"Okay then. But we've got to get this done first and I have to feed the chickens because Jim is staying late at school today."

"Of course, but it's ok, I'm here to help. You're going to work with me tomorrow."

The two young men set back to their work with vigour. They had a system. Because they both worked on their families' farms and there was a shortage of workers, they helped each other, finding many jobs were better and quicker done with two. They were hard workers, so it worked well and their mothers were happy with the arrangement as it suited both places.

Later, Samuel tramped to the farmhouse, weary after his hard day. His mother, Maggie, had a delicious-smelling hotpot ready for him and hot water for his wash.

"Hello Ma," he kissed her cheek after he'd shed his boots at the door.

"All right son?"

"Yeah. I think Cindy will calf soon. Bit early, but I'm pretty sure."

She nodded. "You would know, son. You're good with the animals. Now, get your wash. Jim will be in shortly."

"I'm going to the village hop tonight with Sid."

"Are you indeed? Well, that's not like you, son. But I daresay you deserve a bit of fun. It's usually a good do, so I hear."

"Why don't you come too?"

"Oh no, I'm far too tired. Dances are for the young. Me armchair's calling me."

"You're not old, Ma!"

"I feel it. Anyway, I should be in with our Jim."

Sam turned back to the sink and, stripped to the waist, had a thorough wash. Just as he was towelling himself dry, his younger brother, Jim came in, along with a blast of cold air.

"Cor, shut that door, kid!" Sam shivered. "I dunno, I think we might yet have some snow, you know? It's cold enough."

"It is that, son," his ma agreed. "Now, get your clean things on and come to the table."

It wasn't long before the three of them were sitting and eating, the hot food warming their bellies and Sam felt the tiredness beginning to leave him.

"Ee, I bet you're going to look at all the girls!" Jim teased his brother and ducked his head quickly as Sam took a friendly swipe at him. Sam never intended to hit him anyway, he just flapped his hand, making some of Jim's hair waft in the draught.

"Shut up, you!"

Jim laughed and Sam looked indignantly at his mother, caught the twinkle in her eye and joined in the merriment.

At length, the meal was finished and the dishes taken to the sink. Usually, the boys did the washing up in the evenings.

"I'll do it and Jim'll help me. Go on up and get ready or you'll keep Sid waiting when he comes for you."

Sam needed no second bidding and went off up to his room.

When he descended the stairs merely fifteen minutes later, dressed in his best, he saw his mother's hand raise to her chest as she smiled at him tremulously. He knew she saw his father in him and that she missed her husband and longed for the day when he would be home. As they all did. Indeed, he couldn't wait for the time when his dad would be back in charge of the farm again.

The minute Sid knocked on the door, Sam was ready to go. He kissed his ma on the cheek again, ruffled Jim's hair ('Gerrof' said Jim) and went out.

Being February, it was already dark and because of the blackout there were no street lamps. In any case, there weren't any in River View Lane. However, the two young men were used to walking in the dark and were soon in the village, nearing the village hall. They could hear the music already, although the only light was when the door to the hall opened and closed as people went in. The windows had blackout curtains. Sam thought he would be glad when they had light again; it seemed the war had bought blackness in more ways than one.

Inside, the village hall was decorated with crepe paper streamers across the ceiling and a trio of musicians, a fiddle player, an accordion and a drummer were playing a tune that immediately made Sam want to dance, although he didn't really know how. Quite a number of people were already dancing. As the lads made their way in, Sam looked around. Visions of young women, all dressed beautifully, hair and makeup making them look their best, quite took his breath away. Their partners, mostly young men all looked neat and tidy in their Sunday best.

They helped themselves to a drink from the long trestle table at one end of the room and stood watching the dancing for a while. Then, leaving their drinks, they each picked a girl sitting at the side, obviously waiting hopefully to be asked to dance. Sam's first partner, a girl he only knew by sight from the next village, Long Sutton, was there with her friend who lived in Sutton-on-Wye. She introduced herself as Cynthia, a nice enough girl, fairly pretty, he thought. When the music stopped he took her to her chair and Sid delivered her friend Julie and then they looked around to see who else they could ask. In that moment, Sam saw a beautiful girl, her hair long and flowing over her shoulders and wearing a blue dress that seemed to accentuate the colour of her eyes. He went over to her, heart thumping.

"Rosemary?"

"Sam."

"Is that really you?"

"Well, I'm not anyone else, that's for sure!" As she laughed, her whole face lit up and he was enchanted. He could see his little friend in her; her smile and laugh were exactly the same but she was a new creature to him. Surprised to find he felt somewhat shy, he stood in front of her for a moment, not knowing quite what he should do; he just wanted to stand and look at her, drinking in her beauty. She smiled and took his arm.

"Shall we dance?"

As if in a dream, he put his arm hesitantly round her waist, aware of her shapeliness, her womanly lines. As she drew close, the hint of perfume rose from her hair. He wanted to bury his face in that soft brownness, barely aware of the music and no longer conscious of the people around them. Rosemary looked up into his eyes and he knew that he was in love.

Even when the music stopped, they stayed locked in each other's arms until someone shook his arm.

"Hey mate! Hello Rosemary, how are you? My, you've turned into quite a beauty, no wonder Sam can't take his eyes off you!"

"Hello Sid. You okay?" Rosemary smiled at Sidney and Sam knew the first twisting of jealousy. However, it was short lived because Sid had a girl with him, a pretty red-haired girl, Amelia, Rosemary's friend.

"Shall we sit together?"

"What?" Sam gathered his thoughts together with difficulty. "Oh. Yeah, sure. I'll get us some more drinks, shall I?"

"That would be good, mate." Sid slapped him on the shoulder and turned to organise chairs around a small square table. Sam went off to get them some drinks and soon came back with them on a small tray.

As they sat around the table, supping their drinks, Sam could hardly bear to take his eyes away from Rosemary. How womanly she had become without him realising! He watched her laughing at something her friend said and was completely bewitched. He jumped when Sidney clapped him on the shoulder again.

"Come on mate, bring your bird and let's dance."

Sam obeyed, holding his hand out to Rosemary and she slid into his arms once again.

The evening passed in a dream, and all too soon it was time to leave.

"Can I walk you home, Rosemary?"

"I'd like that."

Sidney and Amelia were nowhere to be seen, so Sam helped Rosemary on with her coat and, slipping on his, they went out. It had turned colder and she pulled her scarf closer about her. Sam took her hand in his and put them both in his pocket. They walked like that along the village street then up the lane to her home. Rosemary lived with her family in one of the cottages on his farm; her dad was a farmhand. They stopped at her door and she turned to face him.

"Thanks for seeing me home, Sammy," she said.

"My pleasure. May I see you again?"

"Oh yes."

"Tomorrow? I only see to the animals on Sundays. I could be free about two."

"I'll wait for you at the meadow gate. Goodnight, Sammy."

"Goodnight, Rosy."

They looked at each other for a moment. Sam didn't dare do what he wanted but she stood on tiptoe and kissed him lightly on the lips. Moments later, he took her in his arms and kissed her tenderly.

"Goodnight, then. See you tomorrow."

"Goodnight."

He watched while she let herself in and then walked to the river path as it was a shortcut to the farmhouse. Unable to stop smiling and giving a little skip or two, he made his way home, heedless of the cold and the dark, the river lapping and gurgling beside him.

Chapter 13

That spring and summer were the most wonderful time of Samuel's life. Rosemary's love gave him a spring in his step and renewed energy for his work on the farm. At every opportunity they walked hand in hand along the river and when the warmth of summer came, they lay together in the grass, kissing and talking of their dreams for the future. Because they were too young to get engaged, he gave her a little silver cross on a chain.

"A promise to be going on with, a reminder of how much I love you," Sam said as he put it around her neck.

Their meeting place was the gate to the meadow, or what had been a meadow, opposite the stone bridge that crossed the river. Nothing made his heart leap more than the sight of her sitting atop the gate as he walked the river path towards her. Or he would wait for her there, leaning casually against the gatepost as he watched for her arrival.

The field nearest to River View Farmhouse and had always been a meadow until the Ministry of Agriculture made them plough and plant it to help with the food shortage so at this time it was the same as the other fields with crops growing there. But it was still always referred to as 'the meadow'. Once the war was over, Sam was determined it would be a meadow once again, as soon as possible.

It was in September when the telegram came. 'Regret. Stop. Private Williams killed in the field. Stop. More information to follow. Stop.'

The war was officially over, so the family couldn't believe it – how could he have died when the war was over? It turned out he'd been killed by an unexploded land mine. It was a big blow to the little family that was eagerly awaiting the return of husband and father. They had kept the farm running for him, now he wasn't coming home.

Sam wept bitter tears in Rosemary's loving arms. She kissed his wet eyes and smoothed his brow. He hugged her fiercely and she held him until the dam dried out. At first his mother, was too proud to show her grief but the girl's caring attitude also helped her to cry the cleansing tears needed in order to carry on. Even the young Jim was soothed by Rosie's presence; she was a light in their darkness.

Somehow, life went on, with Sam continuing to bear the brunt of the running of the farm. His mother's heart had gone out of it but they couldn't see what else they could do but to carry on. Food was still needed after the war and their farm produced well.

His friend Sid's dad did come back and commended both lads highly for all they had done while he had been away. He was a great blessing because now Sam had someone to turn to for help and advice and helped him to find workers for the farm. Men were returning home from the war and needed work so there were plenty to choose from. Sam and Sydney continued to work hard doing their share of work on the two farms.

All was going well and Rosemary and Sam planned to marry the following Autumn after the harvest, 1946.

However, a stranger arrived in the village and stayed at the local pub, the Pig and Bottle. With his slick-backed hair and expensive suit, he was soon noticed by the local girls, who hung around the pub in the hope of catching his eye. He had a car, too, and that was an attraction; there weren't many about; only the owner of Sutton Court had one. His name, he said, was Gilbert Trent and he was in the area looking around for a property to buy as he had a fancy to live in the country. But he wanted to find out first if he liked the area.

Sam and Rosemary were out strolling by the river one day as they often did when Gilbert Trent approached them. He doffed his hat and stopped to talk. He seemed very friendly but Sam was suddenly aware of the way Gilbert looked at Rosemary, flirting with her and undressing her with his eyes. He felt his hackles rise and started to walk away. Rosemary followed and caught up with him.

"I'm not sure I liked him, Sammy. The way he looked at me made me feel uncomfortable."

"I didn't like the way he looked at you either, Rosie. Promise me you will stay away from him."

She shivered and tucked her arm through his.

"I promise," she said.

After that meeting, things started to go wrong. Sam didn't notice at first. It began with Rosemary being unable to see him sometimes. She was working in a shop and they had to stock-take, she said. She'd had to do that before so he didn't take any notice. But this time it seemed to go on longer than usual.

Sidney called round one evening, and said,

"What's this with Rosie and that bloke Gilbert?"

Sam caught in his breath. "What do you mean? She's at the shop, stock-taking,"

"She's not, mate. I've just seen her with him in his car, driving down the main street."

His heart felt like it had risen to his mouth; he felt he could hardly breathe. He looked hard at Sidney.

"You're not kidding me, are you? She told me she would stay away from him."

"No, honestly. Would I lie to you? I saw them, honest."

Sam shot out of the house and ran with everything he had to Rosemary's house. At his knock, little Joseph answered.

"Where's Rosemary, Joseph?" asked Sam, panting for breath.

"I dunno. She went out in a car with that bloke."

"Did she say when she would be back?"

"No."

Sam walked away despondently. In the days that followed, Rosemary avoided him. When he did catch her in, for he kept calling round, she opened the door but a crack. When he pleaded with her to talk with him, she said,

"Go away, Sam. We're over. I'm seeing Gilbert now," and shut the door.

For a moment he stood there, shocked, then he hammered on the door again. She opened it and he stuck his foot in it.

"What happened, Rosie? I thought you loved me! We were going to be married."

"I was too young to know, Sam, and Gilbert is a man of the world. He is older and mature. He knows what life is all about. And he makes me feel like a woman."

Sam drew in his breath sharply.

"You haven't! I mean..."

"No, we haven't. Not that it's any of your business now. We'll wait until we're married, Gilbert says."

"Married! But you were going to marry me! You changed so quickly, how could you?"

"I think it was because I didn't know any better."

"Rosie, don't do this! I'm sure he's up to no good, there's something about him."

"Take your foot out, Sam, and don't come here again."

Miserably, he realised he was getting nowhere so he removed his foot. The door shut behind him. He made his way slowly back to the farmhouse. He hardly knew what he was doing, could barely put one foot in front of the other. Sidney was no longer there when he got home. His mother looked up when he came in and frowned, concerned.

"Where have you been, son? Are you alright?"

He said nothing, just walked past her and went to his room, shutting the door behind him.

The next few days he acted like a robot, doing what he had to do, barely talking, never mind laughing. His mother looked at him through worried eyes and even Sidney was concerned; he had never seen his friend like this.

"Plenty more fish in the sea, mate," he would say.

"Not for me," was the reply. Sid could think of nothing more to say after that.

About a week later, he heard that Rosemary had left her home with a suitcase, leaving a note for her parents to say she was going with Gilbert and getting married.

She was never seen again.

Back in the Present

When Samuel came to the end of his story, the two sat in silence for a few minutes. Lucy mulled over what she had been told. Poor Samuel, to lose his first love in such a way. Although it was rare for the first love to be 'the one' but it must have hurt the young man very much and it seemed shadows of that pain lingered, even now he was an old man.

How tragic that a girl's young life had been snuffed out before she had a real chance at life. What can have happened?

"You must think me silly to still feel upset about Rosemary all these years later," remarked Sam, "especially when I've had such a happy life with my Emily and I should be thinking about her at this time. I *am* thinking about her, I miss her dreadfully, but the knowledge that they think this body might be Rosemary has brought it all back and the pain with it. How could she have ended up dead? Although I wasn't happy, she was. She was looking forward to being married."

"It's all very strange and tragic. Do you think Gilbert Trent killed her?"

Samuel sat with his head down and his hands trembled in his lap. She reached out to touch them and he clutched her hand.

"He must have," he said eventually, in a low voice. "I can't think of any other explanation."

****

"It was so sad," Lucy later reported to Kenny. "Poor Sam, he is suffering so much over the loss of his Emily but now the police think that our body in the field is Granddad's sister, Rosemary, Sam's first love."

"So, he's had a double whammy, with Emily dying and now finding out his first girlfriend has been dead all this time."

Lucy looked at Kenny fondly and nuzzled his cheek. He put his arms around her and pulled her to him. She was his first love and he remembered well how he'd felt when he thought he would never have her. He constantly thanked his lucky stars how things had worked out for him. He adored her and had never wanted to be with anyone else. He felt for Samuel, whom he had known for most of his life. It was sad that he and Emily had never had any children but Emily had always found children to mother around her and Kenny had often spent time at their house, along with other village kids.

Knowing his Lucy, she had done a good job in helping to sooth Sam, but he resolved to visit the elderly man himself very soon.

"You're such a good girl. Do you know how much I love you? You were my first love, you know."

Lucy kissed him.

"I do know how much you love me. I didn't know I was your first love though, I hope I'll be your last."

"There is no doubt about that. I don't think I could ever find anyone to match up to you."

"Flatterer!" She teased him. "It's you who is perfect, not me. There was a time when I thought you were too perfect – you did so much for all sorts of people that I thought you were too good to be true!"

"Moi?" Kenny was wide-eyed. "You mean you haven't noticed that I leave my socks on the bedroom floor and the top off the toothpaste? And when you make cakes I nick them?"

"Of course I know you're not perfect now!" Lucy laughed. "It's amazing how you come down to earth once you're married!"

Kenny looked hurt.

"I haven't come down to earth. I still run home to you whenever I can to assure myself that you are here and you're mine. I don't think I will ever come down."

"Silly! You know that I think I'm the luckiest woman in the world so don't push it!"

He tickled her then and she giggled and squirmed. Their pretend fight ended in them sinking into the sofa and doing some serious kissing until Clarry decided they'd had enough and pushed her nose between them and they broke apart, laughing, and made a fuss of her.

****

Joseph hardly knew what to think or how to feel. The revelation that it might be his sister buried in the field had completely thrown him. He could not get his head around the fact that his sister had been dead all those years when his parents had waited to hear from her, confident at first that they would.

He had to be honest with himself. It had been his growing fear over the years as he had hunted in vain for records of a marriage or the birth of a child, or any life experience that might leave a record. It made sense that she was dead. He had never been able to convince himself that she had died straight after leaving here; she had been so happy and optimistic about going with her lover, so sure she was getting married and going to a new life. How tragic that it seemed to have stopped as soon as she left.

A tear trickled down his cheek. Rosemary had been so full of life, always happy and helpful to their mum looking after the young Joseph like a second mother to him, there being an eight year gap between them.

She had taught him so many things, especially gardening, working a plot together. He loved going out about with her and she taught him about trees and chased him. They'd made a kite which they'd flown together. She'd even showed him how to fish in the river but never allowed him to go alone. He recalled how she would sit on his bed and tell him stories she made up. He'd often thought about them, that they should have been written down and published.

He'd waited and hoped she would come back or they could go and visit her wherever she lived and he would ask her about writing down the stories but of course it had never happened.

Joseph concluded that he really shouldn't have been surprised at the Inspector's suggestion; the more he thought about it, the more he became convinced that it was indeed his sister.

Chapter 15

The day of Emily's funeral dawned dull and overcast.

'*That's how I feel,*' thought Samuel as he got up and pulled back the curtains. He looked at the bed, crinkled on one side, immaculate on the other. He couldn't seem to stop sleeping on one side, even though it had been some time since Emily had actually been there with him. Would ever get used to sleeping on his own, indeed, to living alone? He sighed and for a moment was tempted to get back into bed and pull the covers over his head and let the day carry on without him.

'*Go you on, Sam! I'm waiting for you, don't forget.*'

Samuel could almost hear Emily speaking in his mind. In spite of his mood, he smiled at the phrase 'Go you on', a Norfolk saying, she'd told him, picked up from her Norfolk-born mother. It meant, 'stop messing around'. He knew he couldn't go back to bed anyway; he'd never been able to go back to sleep once he was up.

As it was only half past seven, he had loads of time before the funeral at eleven o'clock. The funeral car would come for him at ten forty-five so he would have a shower and get dressed later. What he needed was a cup of tea.

In his pyjamas he padded into the kitchen to put the kettle on. The room filled with the sound of classical music from the radio, making him feel worse so he turned it off. He felt restless. Once the kettle boiled he made his tea and stirred it until it reached the right colour. He fished the teabag out and threw it in the bin, then took his mug and went into the living room. He put the television on and watched the news but it was so bad it made him feel awful so it switched it onto another channel, found an old episode of 'Morse' and settled down to watch it, to take his mind off the coming funeral.

The programme lasted a couple of hours. During the adverts were on, he made some toast and ate while he watched.

When it finished, he took his plate and mug to the kitchen and slowly made his way up the stairs to shower and shave, ready for sending off his Emily.

Kenny and Lucy arrived at at ten-thirty. They were to ride in the car with him to give him moral support. Lucy squeezed his arm and he managed a smile for her.

The limousine and hearse arrived promptly and they wound their way slowly through the village and stopped outside the church. The vicar was waiting by the door and they followed the coffin, decorated with a single arrangement, into the church and up the aisle.

Unable to sing the hymns, Samuel sat and listened to the service. It had an unreal quality about it, like it had nothing to do with him and Emily. He couldn't look at the coffin at the front of the church, couldn't imagine his Em inside it.

When it was time to go, he allowed Lucy to take his arm and, as he stumbled, Kenny put his arm out to steady him. He could feel the eyes of everyone in the church on him and amazed at how many there were, but then everyone in the village knew and loved Emily.

After the dim interior of the church, the sun was blinding. How the weather had changed from dull and dreary to so bright. It was a little chilly, it was still only April after all, but the sun made it bearable. They followed the coffin over to the plot that Sam bought many years ago, where he and his wife would lie together in their final rest. At that time, neither of them could imagine a time when one of them might be gone. But always efficient, Samuel had wanted to make sure they had a place in the village churchyard and not to be buried in a cemetery further away because they both loved the village.

Now though, he had a fleeting wish that they had decided to be cremated; he hated internments. He did his best to hold it together and did so until he had to throw a handful of earth onto the coffin, when thoughts of Rosemary came unbidden into his mind. He thought of her having lain all those years in the earth with no one who loved her aware she was dead. Looking down on the coffin of his beloved wife, Samuel realised that now both of his loves had been claimed by the earth, out of his reach. That truly dreadful thought weakened his knees and he collapsed to the earth at the edge of the deep hole.

****

"Sam, Sam!"

Lucy's voice filtered through to his fogged-up brain. The brightness of the sun made his eyes hurt behind his closed eyelids. He put out a hand tentatively along the ground towards the voice. His hand was gripped by a smooth feminine one. He squinted one eye open.

"Lucy? What happened?"

"It's alright, Sam. You fainted. Probably the stress of the day. Trouble is, as you fell, I think you may have broken your leg so we've called for the paramedics. They are on their way."

He became aware of pain in his right leg.

"I-I need to get to the village hall. All those people…"

"Shush now, don't you worry about them. You must keep still – you don't want to cause further damage. You have seen the funeral through and the rest you don't need to be concerned about. It's time to care for you now."

The old man allowed himself to relax on the grass, his head pillowed on someone's jumper and covered by someone else's coat and a blanket someone had brought over from their house opposite the church.

He had no idea how long it was before the sounds of the siren filtered through to his mind. When the paramedics examined him, he groaned so they gave him a welcome shot of morphine, for which he was grateful, and soon the ambulance was speeding towards Hereford hospital.

Chapter 16

"Kenny, I'm worried about Samuel."

Lucy turned to her husband with a worried frown. They were sitting together in their lounge at River View, relaxing after the eventful day of Emily's funeral. John was in bed and the two were alone.

"As if burying his wife wasn't bad enough, he had to fall and land himself in hospital."

"Well, in some ways, it might be good. He won't be on his own for a while. I must say it was unexpected though, he's never struck me as the fainting type."

"He is old though, he must be nearly ninety. Anything can happen at that age."

"I suppose you're right. We must make sure he has visitors, we can't let him feel we don't care."

"Well, I'm sure my mum won't let him go without visitors. I bet she already has a rota drawn up – you know what she's like!"

Lucy giggled; she did indeed so, she wasn't surprised when her mother-in-law called the next day to ask when she could visit Sam!

"Of course, dear, we don't know how long he will be in hospital, especially as he doesn't have anyone at home to help him when he comes out."

"If you can have John this afternoon, I'll go and see him today and find out what the situation is. I must say he looked pretty poorly when I left him yesterday; I fear there may be other things going on besides injuring his leg."

"Poor man – and such a shame he doesn't have children or any other family to watch over him."

"I think he and Emily have always looked upon us and others in the village as their family. It is a shame they had no children, for they would have been wonderful parents."

"They would indeed. Well, I'll be off now, love. See you when you bring John round later."

****

Lucy was even more concerned when she returned to the hospital. Samuel lay still in the bed, his face had an unhealthy pallor, barely conscious. She sat on a chair next to him and took hold of his hand. At her touch, his eyes flickered open.

"Oh, hello Lucy, my dear."

Concerned at his whispered voice, Lucy held his hand to her cheek.

"Hello Sam. Aren't you feeling so good?"

He shook his head very slowly and his eyes closed again. Lucy looked around and saw a nurse walk by on her way to another patient.

"Excuse me."

"Yes? Can I help?"

"Can you tell me who I can ask about Mr. Williams' condition? I thought he only broke his leg but he seems to be really poorly."

"Are you his next of kin?"

"I'm his granddaughter." Lucy felt bad about lying but knew they wouldn't tell her anything otherwise. "He has no one else." That, at least, was the truth.

"Mr Williams shattered his knee when he fell and he is having strong doses of morphine to keep the pain under control. It's likely he will need a new knee. We are keeping him semi-sedated until the doctor decides what needs to be done. We are concerned about some other issues, so are running some tests."

"What other issues?" Lucy felt alarmed.

"I am not at liberty to say. You will have to talk with the doctor. Can we put your name in the records as being his next of kin?"

"Of course."

"Come to the desk when you are ready to leave and we will fill in the necessary details."

"Right. Thank you."

Lucy turned to Sam; she couldn't explain why but she was now very worried about him.

****

When Lucy went back to fetch John from the Nursery House, Sheila sat her down and gave her a cup of tea.

"What is it, my dear? Is Sam alright?"

"Well, I don't think he is really. They said that he was semi-sedated because of the pain. His knee is shattered apparently. But I had a feeling…oh, I don't know, perhaps I imagined it. I think the heart has gone out of him now that he's lost Emily."

"I know how he feels, poor love. I felt like that when my poor John died. And Dad did too, when Mam died, didn't you, Dad?"

"Oh yes, indeed I did," agreed Joseph. "I didn't want to live without her. But life goes on and you learn to cope somehow. Although she's never far from me, I often feel as if she's right there beside me."

"I'm sure she is, Dad. Ah, there's our little man, he's been out on the nursery with his daddy."

Lucy caught the little one as he tottered and swung him into her arms.

"Hello darling. How's my boy? Have you been out with Daddy?"

He nodded at her and Lucy smiled at Kenny who had come in with him. He kissed her briefly and tousled little John's hair.

"Must get back to work. I'll see you in a bit."

"Alright my love. Say goodbye to Daddy, John."

The little one waved at Kenny, who waved back at him and then was gone. Lucy set John on his feet and he trotted over to Joseph, who picked him up and jiggled John on his knee until the little one was laughing merrily.

"Those two get on so well," remarked Sheila fondly. "Now, back to Sam. Do you have any idea how long he will be in hospital?"

"Not really. Certainly for a while because they are going to operate on his knee and are doing other tests. I'm afraid I pretended to be his granddaughter and next of kin, otherwise they wouldn't have told me anything at all."

"Well, you might as well be because he doesn't have anyone else as far as we know."

"I'm sure there's no one."

"We'll take it day by day and work out how to look after him when he comes out. We'll cross that bridge when we come to it."

"Yes. Right, come on then, my little man, we need to get home so I can put dinner on for Daddy. Thank you for having John, Sheila."

"Oh, no trouble at all, we love having him, don't we Dad?"

"We do indeed, although I soon won't be able to jiggle him on my knee if he keeps growing at the rate he is!"

*****

Later that night, Lucy lay awake in bed next to Kenny as he slept peacefully. Her thoughts of Sam were keeping her from sleep. Through a crack in the curtains and she could just see one tiny star. When she reflected on that star and how far away it was, it made her feel insignificant. Her mind kept going around and around, reminding her of Samuel's grey face on his pillow and the weak whisper of his voice. She recalled his story of his love for Rosemary and how distraught he'd been at finding she was running away with another man.

A nagging doubt crept into Lucy's mind. Could Sam have been responsible for Rosemary's death? The question kept surfacing and yet she just couldn't believe it of him. He was so gentle and loving, could he really have killed the girl he'd loved?

In the dim, starlit room, Lucy senses her Aunt Bea's presence.

"What is the answer, Aunt Bea?" she whispered but all she heard in reply was the faint sigh of a breeze rustling the leaves on the tree outside the window.

Chapter 17

Over two weeks later when D.I. Cooke and D.S. Grant turned up at Nursery House. Kenny and Sheila were at work in the garden centre but when she saw the two police officers Sheila called Joe to take over the till so she could be around for Joseph. This visit could only mean one thing…

"Mr Baxter," said Dan when they were seated in the lounge, "we've had the results of the DNA tests and it has confirmed that the body was that of your sister, Rosemary."

Joseph nodded slowly.

"I had already come to the belief that it would be, Inspector. The circumstances of my sister leaving and the fact that we never heard of her again, seemed to speak for itself. How tragic that her life was cut short, just as she thought it was getting exciting for her."

"It is indeed tragic, sir, and may I offer my condolences? I don't know if we stand much chance of finding out who killed her but we'll give it our best shot. We also can't find any trace of Gilbert Trent; where he came from or where he went. We did find some cases of young women being raped and murdered over a period of months before your sister disappeared; we are trying to find out if there was a connection. They seemed to stop after your sister's disappearance."

"Are you saying that you think this Gilbert Trent might have been a serial rapist and killer?"

"It's beginning to look that way sir, although why stop after your sister? There are some inconsistencies between your sister and the others, in that the others were all left in barns or under bushes where someone would eventually find them."

"And my sister was buried," mused Joseph, thoughtfully. "Not consistent at all really. Why bury Rosemary if he dumped the others? Doesn't add up, does it?"

"No sir, it doesn't. I'd say the serial killer didn't hang around long after he had achieved his aims so perhaps Miss Baxter's killer was someone different after all."

Joseph nodded slowly, thoughts whirling around in his head.

"Oh, I nearly forgot sir, I meant to show you this last time we came. Have you seen this before?"

Dan held up the cross on a chain that had been found with the skeleton. It had been cleaned and shone as if new.

Joseph stared at it hard.

"I'm not sure, but I think Rosemary did have a cross like that. She always wore it under her blouse, so I never really saw it properly."

"Ah, I see. The thing is, it wasn't around her neck. It was loose in the grave. It might have been placed on her but as the body decomposed, it fell further down."

"Maybe whoever killed her broke it and threw it in after her when he buried her? He wouldn't keep it in case someone found it and it became evidence, maybe? I don't have the mind of a killer, so I don't really know. It's a suggestion, I suppose."

"It is indeed a suggestion. The only thing is, it's not broken."

"In that case, I'm flummoxed! Perhaps you will find out, Inspector."

Detective Inspector Cooke nodded gravely.

"We'll certainly do our best, sir."

"I was wondering… would we be able to bury her again with a proper funeral?"

"Oh yes, sir. We'll let you know when we release the body. Forensics are still doing tests on it, although I don't know what else they can find out now. Oh, I don't suppose you have any photographs of her?"

"I do, but you will need to give me time to find them."

"No problem, in your own time, sir. Let me know and I'll send someone up for them."

Sheila had said nothing to this point but now she spoke.

"We have people going into Hereford every day to visit Samuel Williams so we can easily deliver them to the police station, save someone coming out here again."

"That would be helpful, Mrs Dixon, thank you. How is Mr Williams?"

"He hasn't been at all well but he's beginning to recover. I think they'll soon discharge him but he will be sent somewhere to convalesce because he has no one to look after him."

"I'm glad to hear he's doing well. We've been waiting to talk with him again but we didn't want to while he was still poorly."

"Thank you for being so understanding, Inspector," Sheila said, warmly. "Are you ready to leave now?"

"Yes, we're all done here. Thank you for your help, Mr Baxter and I'm sorry to be bearers of bad tidings. I did hope to come here and tell you that it wasn't your sister."

"Don't worry, Inspector. Although I am sad my sister has been dead all these years, at least it has cleared up the mystery of why she never got in touch. Unfortunately, it has opened up all sorts of other questions."

"Indeed it has, Mr Baxter, and we'll do our very best to find the answers to those questions. Good day to you, sir and Mrs Dixon. Please extend my best wishes to your husband, son and daughter-in-law."

"I will indeed. Goodbye for now, Inspector, Sergeant."

Sheila sighed as she shut the door behind the policemen. She went over to her father-in-law and put her hand over his.

"I'm so sorry about Rosemary, Dad."

"So am I, my dear, so am I! She had everything to live for. How could someone snuff the life out of a beautiful young woman like that?"

****

Later in the day, Joseph found his photograph album and picked out several of Rosemary. There weren't that many of her as a young girl but as she grew older there were more. There was one of her holding a him as a baby. There was another one of the four of them when he was about four, Rosemary fourteen, all looking very stiff and starchy as professional photos often were in those days. Hmm, come to think of it, they might have been younger because his father had gone to war in 1940, so there were no more formal family photos, although there was one with her posing with their dad in his soldier's uniform and a beautiful one of her sitting on a gate, laughing at whoever was the photographer. She looked so happy, her eyes shining with love. It looked like the gate to the very meadow where she had been buried all those years. Yes, there was another, with her sitting on the gate and a young Samuel beside her, his arm around her. He felt a pang inside; how happy they looked! Not long after that everything changed...

The last one he found she was holding a bucket, a scarf tied round her head as she often had when working, and in the background was a car. He recognised that car, it was Gilbert's. Certainly the police should have that photo; it might help.

Tom scanned each photo on his computer and reproduced them on photo paper.

"So you don't have to send the originals; you don't want to lose them."

"You're right, Tom, thank you. I'll put these back in the album."

"She was very pretty, wasn't she? Even in these small photos you can tell."

"Yes, she was a lovely girl and always very kind to me. What a pity she met that Gilbert Trent, for she'd probably have married Samuel and lived here in the village, maybe even at River View; it might still be a farm."

"That's true. But then Lucy and Ken wouldn't be living there."

"Also true and I'd hate to think that they would never have found each other. Things are as they are."

"I tell you what, Joseph, I could make those photos larger for you; perhaps you'd like to have one in a frame?"

"Oh, that would be lovely. I'd like the one of her sitting on the gate. Oh, and it might be helpful to the police if you enlarge this one with Gilbert's car in the background."

"Hmm, yes indeed. I'll do that."

Tom went off and soon came back with the two photographs. Joseph looked carefully at them, especially the one with the car. He could actually see part of the number plate; oh yes, that might indeed be helpful to the police.

Tom had brought an envelope big enough to take the photos. Joseph put them in and wrote 'For the attention of Detective Inspector Cooke' on the front. Tom took the other photo, saying he would be back shortly. Later, he returned with a frame from the garden centre, the enlarged photo of Rosemary encased within and presented it to Joseph. Joseph smiled in delight and held out his hand to his daughter-in-law's husband. They gripped hands in understanding and the old man set the photo on the sideboard where he could see it.

*****

Later that night, as he was relaxing in bed, Joseph had a sudden thought. He sat up in bed, feeling the need to go downstairs and putting on slippers and dressing gown, he slipped as quietly as he could along the landing and down the stairs.

Blinking in the sudden light as he switched it on, he picked up the envelope with the photographs in and took the one off the sideboard. Holding the two enlarged photos side by side, he examined them carefully.

"Thought so." He breathed the words softly to himself, then, replacing the photos back into the envelope and the framed one back on the sideboard, he quietly made his way back to bed.

He lay mulling over his discovery and it was quite some time before he eventually fell into a troubled sleep.

Chapter 18

"Oh hello, Joseph, this is a surprise. What can I do for you?"

"Good morning Mary. Sorry to disturb you. I was wondering if I might visit Sid for a while? There's something I'd like to talk with him about."

"Of course you can. He's in his room, watching television. Come on in."

Joseph stepped carefully over the threshold and followed Mary up the stairs to the bedsitting room that was Sid's.

She opened the door to the room.

"Dad, Joseph is here to see you."

"That's nice. Come on in, Joe, my boy."

As Joseph went into the room and greeted the old man in the recliner chair, Mary shut the door and went away giggling at the thought of Sid calling Joseph 'my boy'. Joseph was well on the way towards eighty!

Joseph went towards the seated man and they gripped hands.

"It's so good to see you, Joe, thank you for coming."

"How are you, man?"

"Oh, not bad, considering, you know? Sit down, do. Make yourself comfortable. I've no doubt Mary will be bringing in some tea now you're here. She's a good girl, spoils me rotten. Lucky to have her, me and Elwyn."

Joseph sat down and they chatted for a while about this and that.

Sid was right; Mary did appear carrying a tray with a teapot, two mugs, a milk jug and sugar bowl and a plate of home-made cookies. Joseph looked at them with pleasure.

"I was just saying to Joe that you spoil me. Thank you very much."

Mary poured out the tea and gave each man a plate with a cookie on and their mugs of tea and then left them to get on with it.

"So, how's all your family? I haven't seen your Lucy for a few days, I miss her cheerful face."

"She's been pretty busy; she's taken on the responsibility for Samuel Williams while he's been in hospital because he has no relatives."

"She's a good lass. Poor Sam, it's a pity he and Emily never had any children. They are such a comfort in older age. But I don't think Emily could have them, you know. Something wrong with her tubes."

"That's sad. Poor Emily, she would have been such a good mother."

"She would indeed."

"Actually, I came to ask you about Samuel. Did you know the DNA has revealed that the body found in the meadow is that of my sister, Rosemary?"

"No, I didn't know it had been established. I'm very sorry, Joe. So sad, she was a beautiful young woman."

"Yes, she was. But at least I now understand why she never got in touch. When I think of all the years my parents waited and hoped to hear something from her, it makes me sad. It answers questions but it also poses more. Sid, do you remember if Sam gave Rosemary a necklace? A little silver cross on a chain."

Sid frowned as he pondered.

" I remember her wearing one but I don't know where it came from," he said at last.

"So you don't know if she gave it back to Sam when she broke with him?"

"No. Sorry."

Joseph leaned in closer.

"You were his closest friend, Sid. Do you think Samuel could have murdered Rosemary?"

Sid gasped.

"Why on earth would you think that?"

"Well, I know he was very upset when she broke it off with him. I remember him meeting her one day in the farmyard and he was trying hard to persuade her against going with Gilbert. She became very cross and shouted at him to go away. Do you think he killed her because he was jealous of Gilbert?"

"No, I don't. What I do know is that Sam would have done anything to protect Rosemary. He never, never would have killed the girl he loved."

"It's alright, Sid, don't get agitated. I was just thinking aloud, that's all."

"Well don't. Sam is innocent. I was his friend. We were always together, especially after they broke up. He didn't kill her, I know it in here."

Sid pointed to his chest. Joseph nodded in agreement.

"I don't think he did either. I would never believe it of him. But I had to ask, Sid, you know that don't you?"

The older man nodded slowly.

"Yes, I suppose you did. It looks bad for Sam, doesn't it?"

"I certainly think the police might well think it was him, yes."

****

"A young woman brought this in for you, sir. She said to make sure you got it."

Dan looked up at the constable who was holding out a large brown envelope.

"Thank you, constable."

Dan opened the envelope and out spilled the photographs. He examined them carefully.

'Hmm, pretty girl. How sad.'

When he came to the enlarged one with the car, he read the small piece of paper attached to it by a paper clip:

This is the car that belonged to Gilbert Trent.

Now that really was a clue; he could see part of the number plate. There weren't many cars around in those days so he should be able to find out who the owner was. He was pretty sure that Gilbert Trent wasn't the fellow's proper name.

What they needed to do next was see how much information they could glean regarding the other murders, try to find out if a strange man with a car had turned up in the area. There were bound to be elderly folk around in those areas who might remember. After all, murders don't happen every day, especially in quiet country places.

****

It was Cecilia's turn to visit Sam. The hospital was negotiating a place at the convalescent place in Redhill. However, she had other ideas.

"Why don't you come to us at Sutton Court, Sam? You know everyone there and you know we'll look after you. We have a spare room; in any case, we'd always find somewhere for you. What do you think?"

"That would be very nice, Cessy, thank you. It would be good to be among my friends again. I've missed everyone and I'm really fed up with being in hospital."

"I'll see Staff on the way out. We have often had people for convalescence at Sutton Court. Leave it with me."

Cessy was as good as her word. Two days later, Sam arrived at Sutton Court by ambulance. His bed was ready in one of the lovely downstairs rooms in the new wing.

It didn't take long to settle in. Every member of staff already knew him and a succession of friendly faces came by to greet him.

The next day, in came Glynis, who gave him a kiss on his cheek and said,

"I'm so glad you've come here, Uncle Sam, welcome home to the village."

Chapter 19

She was sitting on the gate, smiling and waving. He was walking towards her, his heart drawn to her, his arms aching to hold her. Even as he walked, she appeared to get further away. Faster and faster he walked until he was running, running along that river path, trying to reach her. However fast he ran, she and the gate receded further at the same speed until she was the size of a doll in the distance. He opened his mouth to call out to her but no sound came out. He tried and tried again to no avail. His limbs felt heavy; he moved slower and slower and eventually stopped and looked at her. He could see her somehow, although she was far away, see she looked sad, her eyes pleading with him. Again, he opened his mouth and his arms. No sound…

"Sam, Sam!" He opened his eyes, his heart pounding. He saw Peter looking at him with concern.

"You were having a bad dream, Sam."

Peter took a towel and gently wiped the sweat off his brow.

"There now. Would you like a drink of water?"

"I'd love a cup of tea, lad."

"I'll get you one."

Sam lay, waiting for Peter to return with his tea. He remembered his dream; ever since Rosemary had been found she had haunted him, occupied his thoughts during the day, his dreams at night. She was always out of his reach; as hard as he tried to get to her, she moved away, just as she had in real life. He'd thought she was his but in the end she chose another and put herself out of his reach for ever.

Now, at the time when he should be morning his Emily, Rosemary dominated his mind, making him feel utter despair.

Peter returned and helped Sam to sit up in bed, propping him up with pillows and the old man gratefully sipped his drink. Its warmth comforted him.

"Would you like a sleeping tablet, Sam? They usually knock you out and you have dreamless sleep."

"That would be good."

"Mind you, they make you feel like sh** in the morning," warned the night nurse.

"I don't care. If they help me sleep without dreaming, that would be good. If they give me a hangover, it'll be worth it. I've been having bad dreams ever since my Emily died."

"No problem; I'll go and get it now so you can take it with the rest of your tea. Won't be a tick."

He was as good as his word; he was soon back and Sam popped the pills with his drink.

"Will you stay with me for a few minutes please, Peter?"

"Of course." The nurse brought a chair closer to the bed and took the old man's hand.

"I am sure you must miss Emily. She was a lovely woman, Sam. In fact, we all miss her."

"She was indeed. I loved her very much. She was my whole world..."

Peter watched Sam as the sleeping tablets did their work, then he lowered the slumbering man by gently removing the excess pillows and settling him more comfortably in his bed.

****

Elsie Rowe sat with the newspaper on her lap. Although it was a few days old, she had hung onto it. It wasn't the front page news that had caught her eye; but one on the second page:

'Skeleton found Buried in Village Meadow' the report of a body found in a field in Herefordshire, thought to be that of a young woman of about seventeen and had been there about seventy years.

Over the many years of her life, Elsie had read about disappearances and quite a few bodies being found and each time it brought back memories of her sister, Agnes. However, Agnes had not been buried but had been killed after first being brutally raped and left dumped under a hedge in a field on their own farm. For some reason, maybe it was the age of the girl, this story reminded her even more of her sister. The news report said that the body identified using DNA and was one Rosemary Baxter, sister of Joseph Baxter who still lived in the village. *Poor man*, thought Elsie, *what a shock it must have been to discover that his sister had lain dead in a field close by when it was thought she had run off with a man.*

The old lady let her mind drift back over the years to when she and her sister had been teenagers. In 1945, Agnes was almost seventeen, Elsie only fourteen. In spite of the age gap, the sisters had been close. Both girls were healthy with rosy cheeks and strong bodies. As with many children growing up in farming families, they were used to hard work around the farm in Devon. They had two older brothers, Eric and Raymond and a young one called David. Their father and Raymond had gone off to fight in the war and Ray had not come back. Agnes had grown into a beauty with her raven hair and perfect complexion. David and Raymond also had the dark hair and dark complexion, taking after their mother while Eric and Elsie had drawn the short straw and had the red hair that the combination of dark and blonde parents produced. Elsie had hated her 'carrot hair', as she called it and envied her sister's dark beauty but they were still the best of friends.

Until that man came to the area in his flashy car. Elsie was sure it was the car that turned her sister's head; Agnes set herself up to attract him, doing her makeup carefully and wearing her best dress whenever she thought he would be around. She was successful too; it didn't take long for him to look her way. Soon after, Agnes could be seen proudly riding around with him while he, wearing his dark glasses and casually smoking his pipe, took it all in his stride. She no longer had time to spend with her younger sister; all her thoughts were with her man and she spent as much time as she could with him.

Their father did not approve; after all, Agnes was still only sixteen and, according to their parents, decent sixteen year olds didn't hang around with men 'like that'.

Else recalled the row when their father announced at the table one evening that he'd warned the bloke off and paid him a bribe to go away.

"You can't do that! He wouldn't go without me, he loves me!"

"I think you'll find he has gone already; he took my money pretty quick. He is much too old for you, sweetheart, he must be at least thirty. Be sensible, girl, and wait for a young man more your own age. In any case, you are far too young yet; you're nowhere near twenty one."

The man had indeed gone; Agnes had run to the pub where he'd been staying and was told he had checked out several hours before. The landlord and those in the pub were the last people to see her alive. She'd never arrived home and, in the early hours of the morning one of the new farmhands found her under a hedge. She had been a virgin but she'd been brutally deflowered and strangled with her own stocking.

The family were already in morning over the loss of Ray during the conflict; now they had to face the terrible reality of their beautiful daughter's murder.

Chapter 20

"Elwyn, I'm concerned about your dad."

Elwyn looked across the table at his wife as he was eating his dinner.

"Oh yes? How's that then?"

"Not sure. I think something is worrying him."

"What could be bothering him?"

"I dunno, but something is, I'm sure of it. He's not sleeping well either; I hear him moving around in the night. That bed of his creaks something awful."

"I don't hear anything."

"Of course you don't. You sleep like the dead. But it keeps me awake. Sometimes I go in to him but he gets cross and tells me to go away. He won't tell me anything. Would you try to talk with him, please, love?"

Elwyn nodded. '"Okay." He resumed eating and silence reined again, not an uneasy silence, for Elwyn was a man of few words and Mary was used to it. She had no doubt that Elwyn would talk with his father because he always did whatever she asked. It had given him a terrible fright when she was ill a couple of years ago. Her husband could be taciturn and people found him difficult but she understood him and loved him all the same and knew he loved her. He was a hard worker and had always strived to give her and their children all they needed.

When they finished their meal, she gathered the plates to wash up and Elwyn made his way upstairs to visit his father as usual. He saw his dad every evening anyway but tonight he had a mission.

They had eaten alone tonight because Glynis was working and young Alice had gone to do homework with her friend in the village; her dinner would keep warm under a saucepan lid. Mary always had Elwyn's dinner on the table as soon as he came in after his hard day's work on the farm, although he wouldn't have complained if she hadn't. Their two daughters were more flexible; when Glynis was working she ate at Sutton Court with the residents and Alice would be home soon. Mary made a cup of tea and took it through to the lounge. She switched on the television and sat down to relax and await her husband.

Before he came down, Alice arrived in a whirl.

"Hello Mum." The girl bent to kiss her mother.

"Hello love. Homework go alright?"

"Yes, Ben helped me sort it, I'll be able to do it now. Honestly, he's better than the teacher in explaining things."

"He's a clever lad, you're lucky to have him for a friend."

"I am. Gosh, I'm hungry!"

"Your dinner's under the saucepan lid. It won't need long in the microwave."

"Thanks, Mum!" Alice left the room and shortly after Mary heard the microwave bleeping. The lass would take it up to her room where she would eat it glued to her computer while listening to thumping music through her earphones. Mary often warned her she'd end up with hearing loss but of course she was ignored – young people always knew better after all...

Mary watched the news and then the One Show. Just as it was ending, Elwyn appeared in the room and sat down next to her. She looked at him expectantly.

"Well, you were right lass, something is bothering him but he wouldn't tell me what it is. He wants to visit his friend Sam, insists he has to see him, so I'll take him over to Sutton Court tomorrow."

****

"Sid, how good to see you!"

"Hello there, mate!"

"Hey Sid! Hev ya come to see how the other 'alf lives?"

In spite of his anxieties, Sid loved the greetings that came his way when he entered the large lounge at Sutton Court. He searched for his friend and eventually saw him sitting near one of the bay windows and was shocked at the sight of him, he looked so frail.

However, when Sam spotted Sidney, he levered himself out of the chair and came over to his friend, walking a little unsteadily with the help of a zimmer frame.

"Sid, my friend, how good to see you."

"Sam, how are you? I should have come before."

"Don't worry, I know it's difficult. As you can see, I'm still alive." Sam's grinned and Sidney was glad to spot a glimmer of humour, a glimpse of the old Sam, there in his eyes.

"I had to see you. We need to talk."

Sam nodded solemnly.

"We do indeed."

Turning to the carer who was wheeling Sid, Sam said,

"Could we go to my room, please Kay?"

"Of course. About turn!"

Kay deftly did a turnaround with the wheelchair and headed off in the direction of the nursing wing with Sam following slowly behind with his walker. Fortunately, it wasn't far and they were soon in the pleasant room that had been allocated to Sam.

Once Kay had got them settled, Sam in his armchair and Sid nearby but at an angle so they could see each other easily, she hurried off to fetch them a drink and biscuits.

"Nice room you have here, mate," said Sid once Kay had gone. "Lovely view of the garden."

"It really is. I enjoy watching the birds and the squirrels. The fountain is wonderful too; I find it quite mesmerising.

"They keep the grounds well, don't they?"

"They do but it's a lot for three gardeners; Kenny and his nurserymen contribute quite a bit, I am led to believe."

"He's a good lad."

Sam nodded. "Yes, and that wife of his is simply lovely, such a kind lass."

"She is that. She's never let our Mary or Elwyn feel bad about what our Glynis did to her."

"No, she wouldn't. Mind you, Glynis is doing well here, she's a very good carer."

"Found herself, I think."

The two men nodded in agreement and fell silent for a few moments, each lost in their own thoughts. It was broken by Kay coming back with two mugs of tea and a plate of small cakes and another of dainty sandwiches.

"Seeing as you're visiting at tea time, you may as well have your tea together here," she said cheerfully.

"I'm sorry to visit at a mealtime, I had to wait until our Elwyn had time to bring me over," said Sid.

"It doesn't matter, visitors are welcome any time – except in the night of course!" Kay giggled. "Enjoy your food. I've included a selection of fillings, so you can take your pick and eat as many cakes as you like."

She handed each elderly man a plate and made sure the trolley was positioned so both could reach the food easily.

"I'll leave you in peace now. Just ring if you need anything."

The two elderly men helped themselves to what they fancied, not talking much but enjoying the company and watching the birds' antics outside. It was pleasant sitting there together; the two friends hadn't been together for a long time. As they enjoyed their food, they were both well aware that they were delaying the conversation which they knew they must have before Sid left.

When Elwyn came back for his father, he was glad to see him looking much happier. Sidney bade his friend goodbye and happily agreed to come again, whenever Elwyn could bring him. The other residents waved cheerfully as he wheeled him past and Kay and other members of staff also called cheery goodbyes and 'come again'.

Mary was also relieved to see her father-in-law looking relaxed and no longer worried as she helped him settle for the evening. She listened to him as he happily chattered away and reflected that she hadn't heard him so talkative for a long time.

Chapter 21

Dan frowned as he stood looking at the photos of Rosemary pinned on the incident room board.

"You know, Grant, there's something about these photos that bothers me and I can't think what it is."

Sergeant Grant came to stand beside his boss and also examined the pictures.

"She was a very pretty girl," he observed.

"She was that," agreed Dan. "A terrible thing, Grant. It's always the pretty ones."

"So it seems sir. Mind you, if I was a killer I'd probably go for the most attractive one I could find."

"Yes. The male species usually aims for beauty."

"In my experience, the beautiful ones give the most trouble, one way or another," grunted Grant.

Dan clapped him on the shoulder and laughed.

"You're probably right, man! Although I'm sure they are not all trouble. Look at that young Mrs Baxter, for instance, she seems very kind."

It was Grant's turn to snigger.

"You rather like our Lucy Baxter, don't you sir? Better hope your missus never gets wind of it – she'll kill you!"

Dan laughed heartily.

"Don't worry, she won't. But you have to admit that Lucy is like 'Mr Kipling' – she makes exceedingly good cakes! In any case, my Linda wouldn't hurt me, she knows I adore her."

"You're a lucky man, sir."

"I am."

His eyes narrowed.

"It's that necklace that worries me, the cross they found buried with her. She's wearing it in these pictures – see? It's clear in the one Mr Dixon enlarged for us. In the other one, she's not wearing it. We know it's a later photo because that's Gilbert Trent's car in the background; it was probably him who took the picture. It bothers me, Grant. It bothers me why a necklace that she wasn't wearing any more was found buried with her."

"Are you sure it's the same one, sir?"

"Well, of course, one can never be exactly sure but it certainly looks like it in these pictures."

Mr Baxter said he remembered that she always wore it but she's not wearing it in the younger pictures so she must have had it later. She is wearing it in the photo with Samuel Williams. What does that say to you, Grant?"

"That she had it when she was older."

"Quite. And who gives necklaces to girls?"

"Parents? Boyfriends?"

"Quite. Obviously, Joseph Baxter doesn't remember when or where it came from but there's someone else who might know."

"Samuel Williams?"

"Well, yes, Sam Williams but I don't think he's going to tell us. I was thinking of our friend Flo."

****

Dan and Grant pulled up at Sutton Court in their plain car. Dan had taken the precaution of calling ahead and Cessy opened the door to greet them.

"Flo is waiting for you, gentlemen, in the conservatory. Glynis will stay with you, if you don't mind, to be a chaperone."

Glynis! Dan cringed inwardly; that was the young woman who'd tried to frighten Lucy. He hoped she would feel okay about being there while they talked with Flo.

They followed Cessy to the Conservatory and found Flo, sitting in a comfortable chair and Glynis standing beside her.

Dan nodded to her,

"Miss Price."

"Inspector."

"Hello there, Inspector, what can I help you with now?" Flo's voice cut across his thoughts. Now, Dan walked towards the old lady and took her hand.

"Thank you for seeing us again. Do you remember Detective Sergeant Grant?"

"Of course I do! I'm not senile you know! Hello, Sergeant."

"Mam."

"Now, what can I do for you two lovely gentlemen this time?"

Dan held out the cross and chain out to Flo.

"Do you by any chance remember seeing Rosemary Baxter wearing this?"

"Can I take a closer look? My eyesight's not so good."

She took the necklace and peered at it.

"Why yes, it looks like Rosemary's alright. She showed it to me when he gave it to her. She said it was a promise because they were too young to get engaged."

"He? Who gave it to her, Flo?"

"Why, young Samuel of course! He wanted to marry her, I told you that before. I fine remember the day he gave it to her. It was not long after he heard about his dad being killed in the war. Rosemary was so excited; he was a lovely lad and she couldn't have done better. He was set to inherit that farm and they could have had a good life together. But she had her head turned by that – that – fancy bloke with his flash car and poor Sam lost heart for the farming after that. Not many years later, they sold the farm."

"We have seen a photograph of Rosemary when Gilbert was seeing her. She wasn't wearing the cross."

"No. She gave it back to him. She told him she was seeing Gilbert and gave the cross back to Sam."

****

"Dad! Mum!" Glynis rushed into the house after her shift. Realising they were up in her granddad's room, she burst in.

"Whatever's up with you, our Glynis?" Mary was alarmed.

The young woman looked around at her family. Three pairs of eyes looked at her enquiringly.

"The police came to Sutton Court today – they think Uncle Sam committed a murder!"

Chapter 22

"What are you talking about, our Glynis?" The alarm on Mary's face was mirrored on everyone else's.

"That detective bloke, Cooke, came to Sutton Court to talk with Flo Hind."

"Pah! That woman!" spat out Sid.

"Dad, shh! What happened, girl?" Elwyn put a hand on his dad's shoulder.

"They showed her a necklace, a silver cross on a chain. Flo told them that Sam had given it to Rosemary when he was courting her – she said that Rosemary had gone round to show it to her – she lived next door to them, didn't she? Then she told them that when she broke off the engagement, she gave the necklace back to Sam. Then they went straight to his room and I thought they were going to arrest him for murder!"

"That woman!" Sid was contemptuous. "She always was a gossip; it's time she learned to mind her own business!"

"Hush now, Dad. So, what's happened to Sam? Did they take him away?"

"No, he's still at Sutton Court. They haven't arrested him yet but it's obvious they think he did it. They questioned him a long time and when they left they suggested that he gets a solicitor. Cessy was really cross and really told them off because she said that Sam wasn't well enough to be treated like that."

"Bless her! Poor Samuel."

Sid snorted again.

"Poor Samuel indeed! That copper is barking up the wrong tree! Obviously can't see further than his nose. I nee – oh!"

"Dad!" Mary rushed forward as Sidney clutched his chest and slumped forward.

"I think he's having a heart attack!" shouted Glynis. "I'll call an ambulance!"

She hastily opened her mobile and quickly gave them instructions.

The paramedics arrived in about fifteen minutes. By that time, Sid was barely conscious but was still breathing, if shallowly. They were very thorough in their checks and while they were doing so, the ambulance arrived. They soon carried him in, with Elwyn by his side and were speeding back to Hereford, blue lights flashing.

****

Samuel was feeling shell-shocked. As he lay in bed, he thought back to a few hours earlier when Detective Inspector Cooke and Sergeant Grant had come to his room. Cessy had been with them, her eyes watchful. She'd stood beside him while they questioned him.

"Mr Williams, have you seen this before?"

Sam took the chain offered to him with shaking hands. He knew it alright. When he had heard about the body being found, this necklace had been constantly on his mind. Until now, he hadn't known if it had been discovered and hoped against hope that it had not, for he knew questions would be asked. Glynis had warned him just before the policemen came to him that *Flo had told them about the chain, that he'd given it to Rosemary and that she'd given it back to him.*

"It looks like the necklace I gave to Rosemary Baxter when I was going out with her."

"Do you think it's the same one?"

"It could be. I can't be sure. It's a long time since I saw it."

"And did she give it back to you when she broke up with you?"

"Yes."

"What happened to it after that?"

"I don't know. I lost it."

"Mr Williams, I believe this is the same necklace you gave to Rosemary. I believe you were so jealous of her relationship with this other man that you killed her."

"No!"

"You couldn't bear the idea that she was planning to go away with him and you thought you'd stop her going. Perhaps you tried to talk her into leaving him?"

"I certainly tried to talk her out of it, yes."

"Perhaps you tried and she wouldn't listen and you got mad with her. Perhaps you lost your temper and things went too far?"

"No! No, I would never hurt Rosemary! I loved her! I could never hurt her!"

"How come this necklace was buried with her?"

"I don't know."

"I think you do."

"I don't."

"I think you got mad, killed Rosemary and then buried her and put the necklace in with her."

"No, I didn't. I told you, I did not kill her, I loved her. I loved her," Sam's voice faded into a sob.

Cessy went over to him.

"It's alright Sam, it's alright." She turned to the policemen. "I think you should go; can't you see how upset he is?"

Dan sighed and squared his shoulders.

"Mr Williams, we will be investigating this further. In the meantime, I suggest that you get a solicitor. Good day to you, and to you, Mrs Milton. We will, no doubt, be in touch again."

Dan turned and walked out of the room and Grant followed.

"Glynis, would you see these gentlemen out please?" Cessy called to the young woman, who was hovering nearby.

"Of course."

Cessy watched them for a moment, then hastened to his side.

"I didn't do it, Cessy." Sam looked up at the woman, his eyes full of tears. It almost broke Cessy's heart to see it. She smoothed his hair.

"No, Sam, I don't believe you did."

"I'm glad someone believes me," he mumbled.

"I think you'll find that most people will believe you."

"But apparently not the police. I could spend what's left of my life in prison."

"Well Sam, I'm a great believer in right prevailing. Things have a way of working out and I'm sure this will work out for you. Right now, I'm going to get you something to eat because you've missed your tea. Tonight I will give you a mild sedative to help you sleep. You are not to worry because worry can stop you getting better. How does that sound?"

"You're too kind, my dear. Thank you."

"Right. I'll go and see what I can find for you to eat. Shall I turn the television on for you?"

"Yes please."

Cessy turned the television on and gave the remote to the elderly man.

She returned a short time later with a bowl of soup and a roll. Sam watched as she set it down on the small table near his chair.

"Thank you. It smells lovely. Would you mind doing me a big favour and get hold of Paul Gamble and ask him if he can come and see me please? I don't know any other solicitor."

"Of course. I don't know if he deals with this kind of thing but he'll be able to advise you. I'll do that now while I'm thinking about it. I'll leave you to eat your soup. Do you fancy some sponge pudding and custard?"

"Thank you."

The evening had passed slowly. Sam had not been able to concentrate on the television. He was glad when it was time for bed.

Cessy came in with a warm drink and the tablets. He enjoyed his drink and was thankful that soon he would sink into a comforting sleep that would block out all thoughts of the terrible turn his life had taken.

*****

It was a long night for the Price family. Sid hovered on the edge of death for several hours. The hospital staff suggested that they go home but Mary would not leave his side so Elwyn stayed too. After all, it was his father.

"You need to get your rest, love," he told Glynis. "Can you call the lads and let them know what's happened? "

"I will, and I'll get leave from Sutton Court so I can help with watching over granddad. Do you think we should let Uncle Sam know?"

"Let Cessy decide. I would think he can't take any more shocks for now. We are hoping Granddad will recover and it would be silly for Sam to worry about his friend, he has enough to worry about."

"Do you think he killed that girl?" Glynis lowered her voice to a whisper. "I know Granddad doesn't think so."

"I can't believe it of him, he's such a gentle man. He's incapable of killing anyone. Your granddad knows him better than any of us and if he said Sam didn't do it, then I believe him."

Glynis nodded. "I don't believe it either. I wish that detective would get his act together and see that Uncle Sam is innocent."

"I hope so too because otherwise Sam will spend the rest of his life in prison."

Glynis and Alice kissed their mum and dad and drove home.

Chapter 23

Amazingly, Sid rallied and in the morning Elwyn and Mary were told that the danger had passed and they should go home to rest. Glynis came back with the car and her parents drove home in it, promising to return later.

"Glynis."

The young woman hardly heard the man in the bed say her name; it was barely a breath on his lips.

"I'm here, Granddad."

She took his hand.

"Th-that police bloke. I need to see him."

"Who?"

"That detective – whatsisname – Cooke."

"When you're better, Granddad."

"No. I have to see him now."

He tried to raise himself in his agitation but Glynis gently pushed him back into his pillows.

"I'll call him. Don't get upset. I'll go and call him now."

"A preacher, I need to see a preacher."

That didn't sound good. Her granddad hadn't been to church in many years. Although he kept a Bible by his bed she had never seen him reading it. A preacher and the detective – it sounded like her granddad had something to confess. Surely he hadn't killed that girl?

As Glynis was asking the Sister in charge how she could get hold of a chaplain, who should come into the ward but Tony Trevithick, the vicar of Sutton-on-Wye.

"Oh, Reverend Trevithick! I'm so glad to see you!"

"What is it, Glynis? I've come to see your grandfather. Your mother called me this morning about his heart attack and I thought I should see how he is."

"He's been asking for a minister. I was just trying to find out how I could get hold of a hospital chaplain."

"Ah well, I've saved you a job then. Where is he?"

"You need to get gowned up, Reverend," said the Sister. "Everyone has to do that in Intensive Care."

"Of course."

Glynis went out into the corridor to call Detective Inspector Cooke.

Luckily, she got through to him straight away. She quickly explained what had happened to her grandfather and said it was important he came as soon as he could. From her training she knew that people who had heart attacks often had another one fairly soon after so time was of the essence. She hadn't told her parents; they needed to rest.

"I'll come right away."

Detective-Inspector Cooke was true to his word. Barely twenty minutes had gone by before he and his sergeant were entering I.C.U. Duly capped and gowned, they were shown into the room where Sid was.

The Reverend Trevithick was sitting by Sid's side talking softly with him. When they entered, he looked up.

"Ah, I assume you are the police?"

"We are, Reverend."

Dan walked to the other side of the bed and touched the Sidney's hand.

"Mr Price, I'm the police detective. Is there something you want to tell me?"

The old man nodded slightly. He turned to the Rev Trevithick.

"Bible?"

The vicar put a small Bible on the bed and Sidney put his hand on it.

"Inspector," Sid's voice was barely a whisper and Dan had to lean close to hear. The sick man closed his eyes and his breathing was laboured.

"Y-you need to know that S-Sam Williams did not k-kill the g-girl. I sw-swear on the Bible."

"Who killed her, Sid?"

"G-Gilber…"

"Gilbert Trent?"

The old man moved his head slightly, his eyes closing tiredly. "Yes."

"Did he bury her?"

Again, a slight movement, a shake of his head.

"It was me. I buried her. I had the necklace. I put it in the grave with her. I hoped God would accept it as a proper burial."

The three men in the room looked at each other.

"I'm a witness, Inspector," said the vicar. "It seems you've been barking up the wrong tree."

Dan sighed. It looked like his hand had been forced. He wanted to question Sid further but he couldn't bring that kind of pressure upon the sick old man.

Sid opened his eyes again and put his hand out to Dan.

"It's the truth. I swear on the Bible. God knows. He knows Sam did not kill Rosemary. He loved her. He loved her all his life."

"But why did you bury her? Why hide her death from her family? Don't you think they had the right to know?"

The eyes closed again and tears appeared in the corners. The old man nodded.

"T-to pro-protect Sam. He wouldn't have coped It was terrible, truly terrible. Trent raped her and killed her. I buried her to protect my friend."

"Where did Trent go after that?"

Sid's mouth moved but no sound came out. His face took on a grotesque expression and the machines he was connected to emitted a loud continuous sound. A team of people burst into the room.

"You all need to go!" someone ordered and they excited quickly. Glynis hurriedly groped for her phone and pressed speed dial.

"Mum, Dad, Granddad's just had another heart attack. I think he's going to die!"

In spite of the efforts of the team, Sid did indeed die. They said it was mercifully quick. By the time Elwyn and Mary arrived, he had been gone for over half an hour.

Chapter 24

Unaware of the happenings at Hereford hospital, Paul Gamble made his way from his home in the village to Sutton Court. When Cessy called him last evening she had been upset. He had wanted to come over right away but she said that she didn't want Sam to talk about it any more that evening. But she implored him to come first thing in the morning so of course he agreed.

The weather belied the sad happenings taking place, for it was already bright and warm. The birds were singing and he heard the hum of a plane as it flew far above, making a white trail in the sky as he left his car and headed for the front door of the nursing home.

Cessy greeted him at the door.

"Good morning, Cessy. How is he?"

"Well, as you may imagine, he's not brilliant. He had a good night, thanks to the sedative I gave him but of course it's on his mind again now that he's up and about. He's had his breakfast, although he didn't manage much. Quite honestly, I'm afraid this is going to set him back. He had been doing well until this all started."

"I'm very sorry about it; I can hardly believe it. How on earth can they think Sam is capable of murdering a girl?"

"I really don't know. I'll take you to him."

"By the way, I've had a message from Glynis this morning, apparently, Sid Price was rushed into hospital last night with a heart attack."

"My goodness, poor man. What on earth is going on?"

" I don't know. But Glynis said it happened just after he heard that the police think Sam committed the murder."

"Shock."

Cessy nodded.

"I think it would be wise not to mention it to Sam. I don't think he'll cope with anything else."

"You're right. I won't mention it. It's going to upset him when he does hear. Those two have been friends since they were boys."

"That's a long friendship. Anyway, here we are."

Cessy knocked briefly at the door and opened it slightly.

"Is it alright if we come in, Sam? Paul Gamble is here."

"Ah, Paul. Yes, come in, do."

"Go on in then Paul. Would you like a drink? Coffee? Tea?"

"Not just at the moment, thank you, I've not long had one. Maybe later if I'm still here. Would you mind doing me a favour please? Would you call my secretary at my office and let her know where I am? Ask her to cancel any appointments I had for this morning and I'll be in touch later. I didn't get the chance to call her before I left home, it was too early to get her at the office and I don't like to call her at home. In any case, she was probably on her way to work. She's like me, she doesn't use a mobile phone."

"Of course. Do you want me to tell her where you are?"

"Yes, tell her I'm here seeing a client, an emergency."

"Will do."

Cessy left the room and Paul walked towards the elderly man sitting in an armchair by the window. Sam looked pale and drawn.

They grasped hands for a moment and Paul sat down.

"My dear friend, what is going on?"

"The police think I committed a murder getting on for seventy years ago."

"Who do they think you murdered?"

"A girl I was going out with when I was a teenager. Her name was Rosemary Baxter, Joseph Baxter's sister. She was a wonderful girl and I loved her. It is her remains that were found in the meadow."

Paul nodded thoughtfully. "I heard about that. Now, I'm sorry but I have to ask you this, did you kill her?"

"No, I most certainly did not."

Paul studied his friend's face carefully while Sam looked back at him steadily.

"I believe you. Now, would you like to tell me about it? Why do the police suspect you?"

Sam began his story and Paul listened carefully.

****

Back at Hereford police station, Dan and Grant were discussing the happenings at the hospital.

Dan was not in the best of moods. He paced the floor of his office while Grant sat and watched him. This was not like his boss; usually the detective inspector was even tempered and calm.

"Dammit, Grant! There's something about all this that's not right."

"Don't you believe Mr. Price's confession, sir?"

"I don't know."

"He swore on the Bible, with a priest present."

"Yes, he set it up nicely, didn't he?"

"Do you really think he planned that? Surely he was too ill to orchestrate it. He was going to tell the vicar but we came along in time to hear it too."

"That's true. I suppose we have to believe him but I can't help wondering why he was the one who buried her. Did he see Trent kill her? How come he had the necklace that Sam Williams had given to Rosemary and she had given back to him when they broke up – why did Sid have it? It just doesn't add up, Grant."

"No sir, I can see that."

"We need to look further into this Gilbert Trent bloke. Where did he go after the murder? Where did he come from? Did he commit those other murders? We have work to do, Grant! But first, we have to see what Samuel Williams has to say about what his friend Sid Price told us."

Chapter 25

Cessy greeted the two policemen at the door of Sutton Court. She frowned as she let them in.

"Do you really have to bother Sam again? Haven't you put him through enough already?"

"I'm afraid I do, Mrs Milton. Mr Price disclosed some information to us before he died and it's important that we talk with Mr Williams again."

"We haven't told Sam that Sid is dead yet. Mr Gamble, Sam's solicitor, is with him right now."

"Good. I'm glad the solicitor is here. Can we go through now?"

"Well, I'm not going to stop you, Inspector. Please be gentle when you tell Sam his best friend has died. They have been friends all their lives you know."

"So I understand. Don't worry, I'll be as gentle as I can."

They followed Cessy down the hallways and into the nursing wing to Sam's room. When the door was opened, Dan saw the solicitor sitting near to his client. Paul Gamble stood up and shook hands with the two officers.

"I'm Mr William's solicitor, Paul Gamble."

Dan nodded and waved at the chair to indicate that the tall, thin man should be seated.

"Mr Williams, I'm sorry to be the bearer of bad news. I understand that you haven't yet been told about your friend, Mr Sidney Price."

"What about Sid?" Sam, startled, sat up.

"I'm afraid he had a heart attack and died, Mr Williams. I'm very sorry."

Sam sank back into his chair, his head bowed for a few minutes, then he looked up.

"When? When did he die?!

"Today, around eleven. He had a heart attack last evening and was rushed to hospital and then he had another this morning, which was fatal. He died very quickly."

"Poor Sid. He's had it tough since that accident of his. He hated being stuck indoors and reliant on his family. It's a happy release, I daresay. It's strange that he came to see me only the day before yesterday."

"Yes. What did you talk about?"

"Oh, this and that. We hadn't seen each other for a long time and we had a lot of catching up to do."

"Did you talk about the body that was found?"

"Of course we did. Of course we talked about Rosemary and the fun we had when we were young."

"Nothing specific?"

"No."

"We have to tell you that Mr Price spoke to us before he died. He confessed that he had buried the body."

Dan watched as shock registered on Sam's face again. The old man's hands shook.

"What else did he say?"

"That Gilbert Trent killed Rosemary."

Sam nodded and started to sob. Paul Gamble got up to comfort his friend.

Dan went over to the button to summons staff and pressed it.

The door opened and a woman looked in.

"Please can you get some coffee or tea for Mr Williams? He's had a shock."

The woman, Kate, agreed and disappeared.

Not long later she was back with a trolley laden with drinks and a plate of biscuits. She handed mugs to all the men, fussing around Sam and making sure he had what he wanted.

Dan and Grant settled down with their drinks to wait until Sam was ready to talk again. As he helped himself to a biscuit, Dan had a random thought of Lucy and her scones and experienced a little pang of regret that these weren't her cooking. Oh well, a biscuit would do. He dunked his rich tea biscuit into his drink and watched the elderly man and his solicitor.

Gradually, Sam settled down and became able to talk again.

"Did you know that Gilbert Trent killed Rosemary, Mr Williams?"

Sam sighed and nodded.

"You've known all these years and you never said anything?"

"Yes."

"But you didn't bury her?"

"No."

"Who buried her?"

"Sid."

"You didn't help?"

"No."

"How did you know about it? Did Mr Price tell you?"

Sam looked down at his hands and gave a slight movement of affirmation.

"Why did he bury her? Why not leave her so that her family would know what happened to her?"

Sam shook his head.

"Have you never felt you should tell anyone?"

The old man shook his head.

"Why not?"

"I didn't want to get Sid into trouble."

"Why do you think he buried her?"

"Because of me! Sid buried her because of me."

"Why? Because it would upset you to see her dead?"

"Possibly. I certainly would have been. But he buried her to protect me."

"To protect you? Why?"

"Everyone would think I killed her because I was jealous. I couldn't prove I didn't do it."

"So where was Gilbert Trent?"

Sam shrugged.

"He disappeared?"

"Yes."

"Did Sid see Gilbert Trent kill her?"

"I don't think so."

"But he told you she was dead and what happened?"

Sam bowed his head again.

"I was so upset. I loved her."

Dan stood up.

"I don't think we need to bother you any more, Mr Williams. Once again, my condolences on your losses; your wife and your friend."

"Thank you."

"Right, Grant, let's go."

Dan shook Paul Gamble's hand again and laid his hand on Sam's shoulder for a moment, then strode from the room, followed by his faithful sidekick.

Cessy was sitting in the reception as they came near the front door. Dan nodded to her.

"All cleared up, Mrs Milton. We shouldn't have to visit Mr Williams again. Good day to you."

"Good day to you too, Inspector."

Cessy watched the two police officers go out of the door, then headed down towards Sam's room to find out what had gone on and see if her charge was all right.

****

"Still the little matter of the necklace, Grant. I suppose it could have been a different one in the grave but it doesn't quite ring true. I think our Mr Williams hasn't been entirely honest with us. But we can afford to leave it for the time being. We need to find out who Gilbert Trent really was, and where he went after leaving here."

Dan was thoughtful as they drove away from Sutton Court. Grant was driving the car this time so that Dan could write notes. As they drove past the lane that led to River View, he looked at it longingly.

"You want to see the lovely Mrs Baxter? Or sample her cooking?" teased Grant when he noticed the look.

"Quiet, man!" growled Dan and Grant laughed.

"Don't worry sir!" laughed Grant. "You may get lucky and find another excuse to sample Lovely Lucy's baking."

"It's a good thing you're driving or I might just have to give you a bunch of fives."

"Ooo, police brutality!"

Dan flapped his hand at the sergeant's head. Grant jerked his head out of the way, not even wobbling the car.

In spite of the frustrations of the case, the DI and his sergeant arrived at the station in a happy mood.

Chapter 26

"Right. We're going to look into the other rapes and murders that happened the year or so before Rosemary Baxter was killed, see if there are any similarities."

"How, sir? Ask the various area police forces to look into it for us?"

"No, we are going to investigate personally, with their cooperation of course. These cases are very old but we might get lucky; we might find people who remember something. We'll request the case notes on each one. Fancy seeing other parts of the country, Grant?"

"I'm up for it, sir. What shall we start with?"

"Let's go ask Google before we start travelling; it's surprising what we can glean from that. Get young Jenkins in, he's good at that sort of thing."

"Sir."

Grant went off to look for Jenkins and Dan sank in the chair behind his desk. This case was really bugging him; his thoughts kept going round and round. His detective's nose told him there was more to it than met the eye and, by hook or by crook, he was going to find out what.

****

Sam felt a weight lift off his shoulders. He was desperately sad that his childhood and lifelong friend, Sid, had gone, but was thankful that Sid had managed to tell the Inspector about his part in Rosemary's passing. He realised Dan Cooke was not entirely happy with what he'd been told but Sam now felt he could get on with life. Concentrating on recovering his strength, he devised some exercises to help to rebuild his leg muscles. He walked around the hallways of Sutton Court at intermittent intervals.

Cessy and the other staff were pleased with his progress and supported him in his efforts. It was as if he had renewed energy. Cessy was convinced it was because there was no longer the shadow of accusation hanging over him.

Lucy came to visit, also pleasantly surprised at how well he was getting on.

"I want to get home, Lucy," he told her. "I'm missing my bungalow and I'm not used to living this kind of life, being waited on hand and foot and not having much point in getting up every morning. It's no wonder so many elderly folk fade away when they are in residential homes. Not that I'm criticising this place, Cessy and Neil are great at devising all sorts of things for us to do but it's not the same as being at home and being independent."

"I'm sure it's not, Sam. I don't blame you. But don't leave too soon. Make sure you really will be able to cope when you go home. I'll come and see you of course, to make sure you're ok."

"You're a good lass. As soon as I'm strong enough to walk to the village shop, I'll be out of here."

"That's good. Do you fancy a little stroll outside in the garden?"

"Oh yes, I certainly do!"

"Come on then. It's quite warm out so you'll only need a cardigan or a light jacket."

As they were strolling outside in the lush gardens surrounding Sutton Court, Lucy asked,

"Have you seen my walled garden?"

"No, I didn't know you had one."

"It was part of the garden belonging to the Court but my aunt bought it a few years back because Cessy and Neil couldn't keep it going properly – and they wanted money for renovations. Come and see it, we're nearly there anyway."

As they talked, they had been heading towards the river, but turning to their left they came upon a stone wall with an arched gateway. Lucy guided Sam through the gate into her pride and joy, the walled garden. They sat down together in one of the little shady nooks.

"I remember this now. It's on the boundary between the Court and River View. It used to make me smile when I thought how different our farm was to the gentile mansion next door. I've never really seen it before but it was never looked after properly, even in my day."

"Of course, I forgot you used to live at River View. Was it your family that sold the farm to Aunt Bea?"

"No, we sold the farm in 1952 to a family called Dunn but they only farmed it for a few years. It was them who sold it to your aunt. I think that their hearts weren't really into farming. They came from Birmingham, had this idea that they wanted to be farmers but I imagine they found it harder than they bargained for. The father got sick and wasn't able to work and the sons didn't want to carry on so they sold it, bit by bit. Joseph Baxter was the first to buy land from them to start his garden centre. It took off so well that he bought the row of cottages his family lived in. The other cottages had were empty and becoming dilapidated so I think the Dunns were glad to get rid of them. Then, a few years later, they sold the rest of the farm. The house and surrounding fields that you now own they sold to your aunt and uncle and the land where my bungalow is to a builder. For some reason the original builder only put up a couple of houses and the rest of the land stood empty for a few years until another company took it on and put up the houses on my estate."

"So, most of the land that is the village used to be part of your farm?"

"Yes. The village wasn't much then at all, although there was a village hall even in those days that held dances and other events and pretty much everyone from the villages round about would come to them. It was somewhere to go."

"That was a big farm."

"Yes. It was a lot of work, especially when my father was away at war. Come to think of it, I don't know how we managed. We did have land army girls to help us, which made a big difference but of course once the war was over they all went home. Sid's dad came back and he sort of managed both farms, ours unofficially, to help my mother because it was too much for her. I always worked very hard, as did my brother. A couple of men worked for us once they were back from the war. There were so many men who needed work but we could only afford to take on the two. Mr Price was really good, a real help, and so was Sid. We had always helped each other on our farms while our fathers were at war. I would help him with something then he'd come over and help me. We continued to do that once Mr. Price came back.

My mum didn't want to carry on though, so five years after Rosemary died, she sold the farm. Mr Price's farm is over the river, as you know and he didn't want to take on any more land because of the distance by road. I guess selling River View Farm was ultimately the means to Sutton-on-Wye becoming a substantial village and I'm pretty sure the Dunns made more money by selling the land than mum did. But Jim and I were ok; we were able to do work we wanted to do, and mum was happy as Larry in her cottage."

"So it all turned out well. I'm glad about that, because I adore River View and can't imagine living anywhere else now."

Sam patted her hand.

"Good. The house always had a pleasant feel. In some ways I was sad to leave our home but I'm happy it has a family who loves it and children who will grow up in it. It's a great place for children with the pond and all, although you must be careful and watch them in the pond."

"Of course I'll be careful, don't worry."

Sam stood up.

"I think we must wend our way back, it's almost time for tea! Young Sylvie has been baking cakes, I don't want to miss them. She doesn't often have time to do it now she's at catering college. She's doing well though, I understand."

"I'm not surprised, she showed great aptitude for it a couple of years ago when she was helping me. She'll / go far, I think."

They strolled back at Sam's pace towards the house and Lucy said goodbye to him at the door.

"Must get home and rescue Sheila from John," she grinned.

"Thank you for coming to see me, my dear, and for taking me to see your lovely walled garden. It's a special place."

"Yes it is and I have Aunt Bea and my Kenny to thank for that."

Lucy kissed the old man and hurried back towards the walled garden. Sam watched her until she was about to go through the gate and waved as she turned to wave at him. Then he turned and stepped inside Sutton Court and headed for the dining room in anticipation of sampling Sylvie's cakes.

Chapter 27

"We'll start with this one not far from Coleford as it's the closest. See if they have any records of this incident, the murder of the girl called Agnes Ramsey. Call them, Grant, and ask them to look up the files if they still have them and tell them we'll be down tomorrow morning."

"Righto boss, will do."

"Oh, and find out whether there's a station in Rhuddlan, North Wales. There was a murder there too around that time. She had a Welsh name, Carol, Ceris, no, Catrin Lewis. See if you can get them to locate records for that one."

"Guv."

When Grant had left the room, Dan sat, chewing the end of a pencil, deep in thought. The trouble was, he mused, it was so long ago that any surviving witnesses would be old and maybe senile. It was going to be hard to find anything. However, he had to try.

The next day saw Dan and Grant driving through the beautiful countryside of southern Herefordshire and through the Forest of Dean. Dan tried to relax as Grant drove. There was no doubt about it, they lived and worked in a lovely part of the country. It only took them about an hour and a half to get to Coleford and eventually they found their way to Lords Hill, on which stood the police station. They were welcomed by Inspector Crombie.

"I'm fairly new here but we have a wonderful sergeant who knows how to lay his hands on most things. Come into my office and you can read the notes, although they're a bit sparse."

They followed the Inspector through to his modern office. It had a smallish window but halogen strip-lighting illuminated it well. On the desk was a brown paper folder labelled 'Agnes Dewberry'.

"You may use my office, I need to see to an incident but if you have any questions, ask for Sergeant Hart, Bob Hart. He's been here donkeys' years, there's little he doesn't know about these parts."

"Thank you, Inspector, it's very good of you to let us encroach upon your patch."

"I assume something has happened to make you want to look into this old case?"

"Have you heard about the skeleton that was dug up in a Herefordshire village?"

"Yes indeed, is it connected with that?"

"It may well be. We are looking into a few cases of the murders of young women around 1945/46 to see if there are similarities. There may well have been a serial killer around at that time."

Crombie nodded.

"I see. Well, gentlemen, I wish you well in your search. We will help you if we can, just let us know."

"Much appreciated."

Crombie departed after shaking hands, and Dan and Grant pulled up chairs to begin their perusal of the brown folder.

The first thing they saw was a black and white photograph of the girl, Agnes. Even though the photo had no colour, they could see she was stunning; long, dark hair that fell in soft waves around her face, her eyes were wide and shapely with long lashes, lips full and softly smiling.

Dan felt a lump in his throat as he looked at her; she could easily have been mistaken for a film star, but her life had been cruelly cut short by some brutal maniac. There were a couple of other photographs; one of a hedgerow with a body underneath although only an arm and part of the torso could be seen and another of the girl after she had been pulled free of the hedge; clothes torn, part of her chest revealed, her once lovely hair awry and matted, the beautiful eyes wide and staring.

"Poor thing." Grant voiced what Dan was thinking. This was part of the job Dan never quite got used to, seeing what terrible things people could do to another human being. If this had been a few years later, there would have been more pictorial evidence of injuries. He was glad there wasn't. In this last photo one couldn't see what had actually happened to her, apart from the stocking tight around her neck.

Next was a written account of her injuries; bruising on her face, arms, shoulders, inside the thighs, and on her body. She had obviously been gripped and punched and beaten severely, then raped and strangled with her silk stocking, the other of which she was still wearing. She wasn't yet sixteen.

"Poor kid," Dan shook his head after reading the sordid details. "What kind of a sadistic monster would do something like that to such a young girl - come to that, to anyone?"

"One thing I know for sure, sir."

"What's that?"

"I'm pretty sure it wouldn't have been Samuel Williams."

"You're right there, Grant."

They continued to read the statements of people who had talked to the police. The inquest's verdict was rape and murder by persons unknown.

"If only they'd had DNA in those days, Grant. That monster wouldn't have got far and he would have been caught and hanged."

"He would have deserved it too, Gov. Although I think I would have liked to chop his bits off first."

"They did that kind of thing back in the dark ages.We're not as barbaric as that, Grant."

"No sir, but in my opinion some buggers deserve it."

"I can't help but agree with you. Now, looks like we have to go out to the area and see if we can find anyone who might remember this. The girl had a younger sister and brother; I wonder if we can find out if they still live hereabouts."

"How about asking Bob Hart, sir?"

"Good idea, let's see if we can find him."

Bob Hart proved to be an older man nearing retirement but surprisingly adept at using a computer. Within moments he brought up the brothers and sisters of Agnes Dewberry.

"Hmm, Eric is dead, died last year. Raymond was killed in the war, as reported in the newspaper article about Agnes. David emigrated to Australia back in the nineteen-seventies and the remaining sister, Elsie, got married and moved away. Not sure where she is."

"Are there any residents in the area who might remember the murder?"

"You could try a house-to-house. We could lend you a few officers to help."

"That would be wonderful. Could you put that in motion, please?"

"Certainly. I'll get onto it now. Coffee? Anything to eat? We usually get one of our PCs to go out for grub around this time. There's a great baker's shop just up the road."

"Yes, I could do with something, I'm sure Grant could too."

Grant nodded; he certainly could!

****

The afternoon and evening's search of the area where the murder of Agnes Dewberry had happened proved fruitless. What had been mostly farmland back then was now a substantial village, rather like Sutton-on-Wye and there were many newcomers.

They did find a few elderly people who said they'd heard something about it but they knew no details and were too young to have been around at the time; it was simply a story about the village that had been handed down.

Discouraged, they returned to Hereford after thanking the Coleford police for their help. Bob Hart suggested that they could go on local television to appeal for anyone who might have information. Dan agreed it was a possible move but he had other similar incidents to look into first.

"Don't know about you, Grant, but I could do with a good, hot shower and a drink in front of the telly. I'm bushed."

"Me too, Guv, although I don't have your home comforts to await me."

"Never mind, Grant, I'm probably going to get it in the neck for being so late home, at least you haven't anyone to nag you."

"Go on with you, sir. I know you wouldn't swap your Linda for the bachelor life."

"You're right. Here's my place. Pick me up in the morning, will you? My car's still at the station."

"Of course, sir. Goodnight."

Grant drove off the moment Dan was out of the car. He could hear a can of lager in his fridge calling him and he was anxious to answer it.

Chapter 28

Upon Dan and Grant's arrival at work the next morning, PC Jenkins informed them he had found other cases of missing women about the years 1945/46 and even further back. The war aside, when people obviously went missing and unaccounted for, all the victims were country girls and all under the age of twenty. Some details were hazy, made all the more clouded by the presence of strangers to the various areas because of the war. But each case was meticulously investigated.

"I don't think we can look into some of these, they happened too long ago and there won't be anyone alive who we could talk to, even worse than the situation we have here. We are stretching things a bit, hoping there might be someone to help us with the ones we have. Were none of the bodies found in those cases?"

"Three were, and two many months later apparently, but the other four were never found."

"Do we know if they were sexually assaulted?"

"One of the women was killed when a bomb dropped on Norwich but no one knew she had gone into the city so she remained unidentified for a while. She was identified by her jewellery and a birthmark on her body; there wasn't a lot left of her."

Dan shuddered. "Horrible. So she wasn't a victim of our rapist. Any others?"

One was a young woman named Martha White, who lived in North Yorshire."

"How was this Martha White killed, do we know?"

"Strangled, sir."

"Hmm. Looks like a possible candidate. What about the third girl that was found?"

"She was from Nottingham but was found in a bed and breakfast place in Whitby. The landlady told the police she arrived in a car with a man but when her body was discovered, the man had disappeared without trace. No-one heard anything at all. The woman was discovered by a waitress who had been sent upstairs to knock at the couple's door when they didn't appear for breakfast. At first the waitress thought she was asleep but when she went in and touched her, she realised she was dead. She only went in because the husband wasn't there and she thought it was odd. The woman, Sylvia Grimmond, had also been strangled."

"What year was that?"

"It was just before the war in full swing in 1939, sir. It's the oldest such case I've found."

"Hmm, perhaps it was his first venture. He got her to pretend she was married to him so they could have a 'dirty weekend' at the seaside and something went wrong and he killed her."

"Perhaps she snored, sir." Jenkins remarked.

"Not really funny, Jenkins," although Dan allowed a small smile. "You've done good work. It looks like we've found a trail for our man. After that first one, when he performed his brutal work in the comfort of a bed, he went on to do it wherever the opportunity presented itself. They have several months in between and always in different places across the country. I wonder what was in his life that stopped him doing it more often, also how did he afford a car, for it seems he had one? He must have been well off to have a car and get the petrol to go so far. I wonder how he managed that during wartime?"

"At the moment I have no idea sir. We may never find out."

"Hmm. I know it seems fairly impossible but I have a feeling we are going to find some answers, Grant. Get onto Rhyl police station and tell them we are coming up there tomorrow and get them to find us somewhere to stay overnight."

****

"Smell that sea air, Grant." Dan opened the car window and breathed in deeply. It was nearing the end of April and, although the skies were blue, a chilly wind blasted in.

"If it's all the same to you, boss, I'd rather not." Grant concentrated on guiding the car through the busy streets of Rhyl, following the guidance of the satnav. Eventually, they pulled up in the car park of the police station and alighted, slamming the car doors behind them.

The reception was empty and so they rang the bell that was beside the glass window. Eventually, a desk sergeant ambled into the reception area, sandwich in hand. He opened the sliding window.

"Oh, hello there. Can I help you?"

"Good afternoon. We are Detective Inspector Cooke and Detective Sergeant Grant. We have an appointment with your chief."

They held up their identity cards for the man to see.

"Right."

The window was slid shut and the sergeant went out of the room, leaving Dan and Grant looking at each other with raised eyebrows.

A few minutes later, a side door opened and a young officer came into the small space where they waited.

"Would you come this way please, sirs?"

They followed the officer along a corridor painted pale green and stopped at a door while he knocked. At the call of 'come in,' he opened the door and said,

"Here are the detectives from Hereford, sir."

"Ah yes. Come in, come in."

A man stood behind a large oak desk. Ruddy of complexion, he had short, curly, grey hair and a friendly smile. He held his hand out to welcome his visitors.

"Good afternoon. I'm Inspector Ashton. Welcome to Rhyl."

"Thank you. I'm Detective Inspector Daniel Cook and this is Detective Sergeant Graham Grant."

"Pleased to meet you." They shook hands. "Do take a seat and tell me how we can help you."

Dan explained briefly about the case and what they had found so far.

"We understand there was a similar case here, late in the year 1945, near Rhuddlan. A young woman called Catrin Lewis was found raped and murdered in a barn."

"Long time ago," remarked Ashton. "It's going to be hard to find anyone who could talk about it now."

"It may well be," replied Dan, "but we are going to do our best. Do you have anyone who could help us in our search?"

"Well, no, not really, although we do have patrols that go out that way. We could send one couple, I suppose."

"That would be very good. We are grateful for any help we can get. But first, would it be possible to read the records of the case, if you have it?"

"Hmm." Inspector Ashton pressed a button on his intercom. "Get me Drake, will you?"

A few moments later, the door opened and a very attractive WPC came in.

"Ah, Drake, there you are. These gentlemen are detectives from Hereford. They are interested in an old case, out near Rhuddlan, in 1945...um...Catrin Lewis. Rape and murder. Do you think you can lay your hands on it?"

"I'll do my best, sir." She had the musical voice of a Welsh girl. All three men watched her retreating form with interest. They discussed the case in further detail while they waited for her to return.

"Would you like some refreshment while we wait? I'm sure you must be hungry, having just travelled."

"We are rather."

Ashton pressed a button again and the young P.C. who had shown them in opened the door.

"Ah, Jones. Would you mind popping over the road for...what would you like? Pie, pasty, chips, ploughman's? And some decent drinks, none of that peewater out of that damned machine."

They made their choices and the young man left. Considering he had to go across the road, he was back remarkably quickly with the pies and coffee in a thick cardboard tray. They all ate with relish, even Ashton, who admitted he'd already had a pasty earlier.

"Good, aren't they?" Ashton smiled. "My wife's aunt runs the shop and she makes everything they sell. Lucky we're so near them."

Dan and Grant agreed they were good and they were relieved that their stomachs, which had begun to rumble, had been satisfied. Just as they were finishing their pies, the delicious WPC Drake returned, holding a folder.

"I think this is it, sir," she said in her musical voice. "I had quite a time finding it but I knew it had to be there somewhere."

"Thank you, Drake. Well done."

"Um...sir, I live in Rhuddlan. I may know some people who might be able to help."

"Oh, that's interesting," Dan pricked up his ears. The girl might be key to finding them help. "Would you be interested in helping us?"

"Oh yes, sir," She allowed her eyes to stray to Grant, who was trying not to be obvious watching her. "That is, if it's alright with you, sir?"

"Thank you, Drake, that would be very good. Get ready to go with them, would you?"

"Yes sir." She left the room, after giving Grant a half smile. Dan was amused to see that his sergeant's ears had gone red, a sure sign he was embarrassed. He detected something here!

"Right, can we just look at these reports before we go out there?"

"Of course, help yourself."

The Inspector turned to his computer and busied himself while Dan and Grant engaged themselves in the papers within the folder. Unlike the girl in Coleford's file, there was only the one photo of the dead girl, taken when she was alive; there were none after her death. But the coroner's report was chilling in its similarity to that of Agnes Dewberry. The poor girl had been found in a disused shepherd's hut during a massive search after her frantic parents had reported her missing. Almost everyone in the neighbourhood joined in the hunt and she had been found by one with a dog. The dog had gone sniffing around the old hut and had brought out a piece of torn material in its mouth. The owner had gone in and found the body. By then, she had been dead for two days.

Catrin had spent the evening out with a couple of girlfriends. They had walked home together and the others had arrived home but not Catrin. Apparently, it was not unusual for Catrin to spend the night with one of her friends so they weren't concerned. It wasn't until the next day when it became obvious that she had not stayed the night with any of them, that her parents raised the alarm. Another night passed and then the mass search began. It had taken five hours to find her.

In spite of all enquiries, no one seemed to know anything. Eventually, the case was put away, unsolved.

After an hour examining the reports and all the statements thoroughly, Dan stood up.

"I think we've seen enough. We should get over to Rhuddlan. Is the WPC coming with us or will she meet us there?"

"She's gone over with her partner. They'll meet you at the castle, she said."

"Right. Thank you very much, Inspector, you've been a great help. If there is anywhere to stay in Rhuddlan, we'll spend the night there."

"Very good. That makes sense. Let me know how you get on."

Dan and Grant shook hands with Ashton and went out to their car. The desk sergeant barely raised his eyes from whatever he was reading at reception.

Chapter 29

Rhuddlan Castle was hard to miss. WPC Drake was there in a police car with her partner, PC Burns.

The castle was still imposing, even though more ruined than many Dan had seen. According to the, notices at the entrance, local groups did live performances within the castle walls; there was to be a presentation of Macbeth later in the summer.

Interesting though it was, Dan didn't have time to linger.

"Well, we'd better get on with it."

WPC Drake stepped forward.

"I had a thought as we were driving here, sir. My granddad has lived here all his life. He might know something."

"Do you think he would see us?"

"I'm sure he would, sir. Shall we take you to him?"

"That would be as good a place to start as any. If he's lived here all his life, he might know others we could ask."

"We can leave the cars here as it's only just a few minutes' walk away and it's hard to park near his house."

The four walked down the road from the castle and along to the right. There was a row of pretty cottages, practically under the shadow of the castle.

WPC Drake knocked on the door of the first cottage. After a few moments, the door was opened by a small, plump elderly woman whose faded blue eyes twinkled as she saw who had knocked.

"Jenny! Aidan, it's our Jenny come to see us! My, you do look good in that uniform, Cariad. Who is this with you?"

"Nanna, this is Detective Inspector Cook and Detective Sergeant Grant, from Hereford, in the West Mercia Constabulary. They are investigating some old cases and I thought Granddad might be able to help us. You know Pete, don't you?"

"Oh yes of course, hello there, Pete, lad. Detectives? Oh my! Come away in, I daresay you could do with a cuppa? Come and meet my husband. He doesn't walk too well, you know. He's in here."

The cottage had a lovely feel, warm, cosy and welcoming. Dan noticed a stair lift running along the edge of the staircase. They turned into the first door, the front living room. This was a pretty room, old fashioned with crocheted covers on the arms and backs of the chairs and a colourful rug in front of the fireplace, on which was curled a large ginger cat, who barely twitched an ear at the arrival of the newcomers.

"Aidan, bach, we have visitors! These are detectives from Hereford. Our Jenny thought you might be able to help."

The thin elderly man sitting in the armchair, zimmer frame by his side, looked up with a puzzled expression on his face. His grey hair was in no way thinning and his face was lined and tanned like a piece of old leather. The hands that lay on the blanket showed the tell-tale signs of arthritis. However, his greeting was friendly and as warm as his wife's.

"Come on in, sit yourselves down. I've never been asked to help the police before. What have I done?"

"I'm sure you haven't done anything, sir. We're here to look into a murder that happened many years ago and we were hoping to find some older residents who might just recall it. Jenny suggested you might be able to help us as you've lived here all your life."

"A murder, eh? The only murder around here that I can think of is that girl, Catrin Lewis."

"That's the one."

"Why are you enquiring about that? Bit late in the day, I'd say."

"Well, a body has recently been found in a village in Herefordshire and we have good reason to think they may be connected. We think there was a serial killer about at that time. What can you tell us about Catrin? May I ask how old you were at the time?"

"Ten. I was about ten. I remember Catrin because I was best friends with her younger brother, Thomas. It was terrible when she went missing. After what happened to her, he wasn't allowed out on his own for ages so I used to go round to play with him because he wasn't allowed to come to my house."

"Where is he now?"

"Oh, he emigrated to America years ago. He got married and they went about two years later. I missed him a lot because we were still mates."

"Can you remember if there were any strangers around at the time?"

"Well, people come and go everywhere, don't they? At that time, there were a lot of men looking for work just after the war had ended. They were difficult times."

"They were indeed. Grant, do you have those photos?"

Grant reached into his case and brought out an envelope which he handed to Dan. The Inspector took one out and showed to the old man.

"Do you recognise that car in the background of this photo? Was there a car like this around at that time?"

The elderly man took the photo and then picked up a magnifying glass which was on a small table near him. He examined the picture carefully.

"Yes, I remember this car. It was parked outside the tavern, the Castle Inn, one day. Tom and me, we noticed it because we were crazy about cars and we didn't see many here then, especially like that. I'd say it had been made in the nineteen thirties; it would have been a fashionable vehicle in those days, expensive. I recall that we hung around it, hoping we might get a ride but the bloke came out of the pub and told us to go away. He wasn't very nice really. We watched him drive away in it."

"Can you describe him at all?"

"Yes, he wore an expensive suit and had black, slick-backed hair. Good looking, I suppose, in a smarmy sort of way. I didn't like him at all; there was something about him that made me go cold."

"Would it surprise you if we tell you that we have reason to think that man was Catrin's murderer?"

"It wouldn't surprise me at all, Inspector. I thought he was a nasty piece. I asked the pub landlord what the bloke's name was. He cuffed me round the ear and told me not to bother Mr Tunstall."

"That was his name then? Tunstall?"

"Yes. Apparently his name was Gregory Tunstall. I don't usually remember names but I remember that because Tom and I thought it was funny that his name started with the same letters that were on his car – GT 314."

Dan took the photograph back and looked at the number plate. He could clearly see the 14 and part of what he now realised was the 3.

"You have a remarkable memory, Mr Drake."

"Yes, well, you know what it's like as folk get older. We can remember what happened seventy-odd years ago but can't recall what happened yesterday."

"Well, I'm grateful that you can remember that long ago, Mr Drake. When we came here, we imagined we would have to spend many hours tramping around Rhuddlan, trying to find someone who might help us, and right away your wonderful granddaughter brings us to you! I think the gods are with us."

"So it seems. And I'm happy to help. I would imagine this bloke, Gregory Tunstall will be dead by now but I would also think it's good to be able to put the pieces of the puzzle together. It's strange that the police never found him at the time but I think he left the pub where he was staying before the murder so they probably didn't think he had anything to do with it."

"That seems to have been his trick. We think his first murder was a young woman who was found dead in a B & B in Whitby; supposed to have come with her husband but he was nowhere to be found afterwards. We know of at least three other young women who have suffered similar fates over a period of six years in different parts of the country. Our boy must have thought the war was a gift so he could carry on his wicked ways in different places in the country. We have yet to find that out. Now, thanks to you, Mr Drake, we have the whole registration of the car and hopefully that should lead us to whoever owned it. We have a great deal to thank you for."

"My pleasure, Mr Cook."

"Here we are, dearies," Mrs Drake's voice sounded cheerfully as she carried in a tray. Grant leaped up and took it off her. "Oh, thank you, my dear. Just pop it down there. I'll be right back."

She left the room and reappeared moments later with a large cake, which she put down on the table near the tray. She busied herself putting out the cups and saucers and started to pour out tea.

"Jenny, bach, be a love and fetch some plates, would you?"

"Of course, Nanny." Penny jumped up from her chair and returned with a pile of six plates that matched the china cups and saucers.

"Now, who'd like a piece of my fruit cake? I just made it today. Somehow I knew that I needed to make one."

"I think Nan is a bit of a witch," Penny said, putting her arm lovingly around her grandmother. "She always seems to know – and her cakes are wonderful."

"Oh, get away with you!" Nanny Drake flapped her hand at her granddaughter and began cutting up the cake and placing the pieces on the plates which Jenny handed them. She lovingly cut up her granddad's piece into manageable bits. His hands shook as he picked one up to put in his mouth.

Dan secretly watched the old man and inwardly felt grateful that they had found him in time to catch his memories, for who knew how long he might be around? He liked this couple and their pretty granddaughter. He could see that Grant liked her too. He had been thinking of driving home that evening as they had found what they'd come for already, but changed his mind. They would stay overnight and return to Hereford the next day.

"Do you have any idea where Grant and I could stay the night?" he asked. "My, this cake is very good."

"Thank you, my dear. There's a B & B just down the road, opposite the castle. It's run by one of our daughters, Jenny's aunt Pamela. I'm sure she won't be full up as it's early in the season. Shall I give her a ring for you?"

"Yes, if you would, please."

The old lady went out of the room and they heard her voice, muffled by the closed door, and while they waited they enjoyed the tea and cake and chatted together about life in the village. She came back into the room.

"All set up for you, dears, two rooms, bed and breakfast. She said she would do you an evening meal if you would like."

"We don't want to put her to any trouble. Perhaps we can get something to eat in a pub or something?"

"The Castle Arms do a good meal," said Peter. He got up "Well, the chief said Jenny and I could go home once our business here is done, so is that okay with you, sir? Do you need us for anything else?"

Dan stood up. "No, I don't think so. We've achieved more than I hoped for already, thanks to Mr Drake here. Thank you for being willing to help us." He held out his hand to shake it.

"No problem sir, I wish all our jobs were as easy as this – and ending with delicious cake! Thank you, Nanny Drake."

"No trouble at all, lad. Give my best to your mum."

"I will that. I'll pick you up in the morning, Jenny, as your bike is at the station."

"Thanks, Pete. See you in the morning."

"Goodbye then. Goodbye, Granddad Drake, bye, Nan, Goodbye, sirs." He shook hands with Dan and Grant and followed Nanny to the door. When she came back, she said,

"Nice lad. Known his family for years, watched him grow up. Our Jenny couldn't do any better."

"Oh Nan! Don't go matchmaking. Pete and I are partners at work and he's like a brother to me, I couldn't think of him in that way," chided Jenny gently. Then to Dan and Grant, "I'll show you where my aunt's place is, I have to walk past hers anyway."

Dan went over to the elderly man and shook his hand gently.

"Thank you, sir. We're very glad to have met you and for the help you've given us. It will be invaluable."

"My pleasure, my boy! I'm happy to have been of service to you."

"Goodbye, Mrs Drake. Thank you for your wonderful cake and the tea, just what we needed."

"You're very welcome," she replied in her sing-song voice so like her granddaughter's. "Jenny's friends are always welcome here, the kettle is always ready."

Jenny kissed her grandparents and the three left the homely cottage. The B & B was only a few minute's walk away and they were soon at the door.

"Jenny, would you like to join us in the pub for a meal? Or maybe a drink afterwards?" Grant asked.

The girl hesitated.

"Mum will already have my dinner ready but I could have a drink later. I'll meet you in the Castle Arms at eight."

Grant watched as she strode down the road, admiring her slender back view.

"It seems evidence isn't the only thing we've found up here in Rhuddlan," Dan remarked drily. Grant smiled sheepishly.

"You have to admit she's rather something."

"Indeed she is. Come on, let's get booked in here and then we can get over to the Castle Arms to eat."

Chapter 30

The landlady of the B & B was friendly and the rooms comfortable. She was quite happy when Dan and Grant told her they would eat at the Castle Arms.

"Oh yes, they do good food there and it's a nice place. Well, I'll leave you to settle in but if there's anything you need, just phone 5 and it will get straight through to me."

"Thank you. It all looks very nice."

Grant was thankful to go to his room, to relax for a while. He got a bottle of water from the table, opened it and, taking his shoes off, laid on the bed. He put the television on and clicked lazily through the channels, most of which were Welsh. He found an English-speaking channel, but found his thoughts drifting off to a softly-spoken Welsh girl with a lovely figure and incredible eyes. He wondered if she would let him keep in contact with her, for he knew that he had finally found a girl he was really interested in.

He and Dan had arranged to go to the Castle Arms at seven. He looked at the bedside clock; it was six-thirty, time for a quick shower. He had a change of underwear and shirt so he would put that on. Pity he didn't have anything more interesting to wear but at least he'd be clean.

The shower was lovely, a real power-shower, the water was hot and constant. Tempted to stay in longer, thoughts of good, hot food followed by the meeting with Jenny, persuaded him to be swift.

How good it was to feel fresh and clean. Travelling always made him feel more smelly by the hour, although he probably wasn't. It would be good to sleep there in the comfortable bed.

He dressed, dried his hair and shaved his five o'clock shadow then stood in front of the full-length mirror in the bedroom.

"You'll do, Graham, my lad. Go get'em – or rather, go get the girl!"

At that moment, Dan knocked on his door.

"You ready, Grant?"

He opened the door. Dan had also obviously showered and changed.

"Don't know about you but I'm looking forward to this food," said Dan.

"Me too. Let's go."

The two men ran lightly down the stairs and out the door.

*****

A short way down the street, the Castle Arms was pretty much as one would expect in a place with such a name: large beams across the ceiling, a big fireplace with a huge lintel and shiny brass coal-shuttle and poker set, heavy green curtains with tasselled tie-backs and diamond-glass paned windows. Photographs of the castle adorned the walls, including an artist's impression of what the castle would have looked like before it fell into ruin. Tables and chairs were in dark oak, with long, padded leather seats along the walls. It should have looked dark and oppressive but somehow wasn't. The young woman who served them had a wide and friendly smile. The menu offered a good variety of food but both Dan and Grant decided to go for substantial British fare. Dan went for a steak pie and chips and Grant a chicken pie with chips.

As it was still quite early, the pub was quiet and the two found a pleasant table near a window overlooking the castle.

The young barmaid brought their drinks over and promised their food wouldn't be long. She was true to her word, for they had their meal in ten minutes and they both enjoyed their tasty meal and watched the pub gradually fill up. By eight o'clock the place was busy. Grant watched the door anxiously for Jenny. Would she turn up?

Dead on the dot of eight, the door opened again and in walked a young woman, her long dark hair falling in waves around her face. She wore a red blouse under an open black jacket, and tight blue jeans and walked elegantly in her black high-heeled shoes, holding onto a red shoulder bag. Grant couldn't believe his eyes; she was lovely in her uniform, now, she was stunning. He stood up and waved as she was obviously searching for them. She smiled and walked towards them. Dan gave a low whistle. 'Wow!'

"Hands off, this one's mine – sir," was Grant's whispered response.

"Hi," she said, smiling shyly. Grant hastened to pull out a chair for her.

"I was worried you wouldn't come," he said as she sat down. She smiled and put her bag on the table.

"Drink? I'll get this round," Dan offered

"Just orange juice for me, please," Jenny said. "I'm not much of a drinker."

"Half a lager, please, boss."

Dan went off to get the drinks. When he came back, they made small talk for about half an hour then Dan said,

"Right, I'll leave you two to it. I'm tired and I want to call Lynn. See you in the morning, Grant."

"Okay, boss, see you at breakfast."

They watched Dan walk out, then Grant moved to the leather seat by the wall and patted the space next to him. Jenny moved to join him.

"Tell me about yourself," invited Grant. For the next hour, they chatted, deeply involved in each other.

"Do you fancy going for a walk?" he asked after a while.

"In these shoes?" giggled Penny.

"Hmm, you have a point."

"We could pop down to my house and I could put on some trainers."

"Okay. Would you like to?"

"Absolutely!"

They went into her house and he hovered in the hallway nervously until she came back, this time wearing trainers and a warmer, zipped jacket, minus the handbag. As they were leaving, a woman came out of a room and stopped short.

"Hi, Mum. This is Graham. He is one of the detectives from Hereford that I told you about. We're going for a walk."

"Hello Graham," said Jenny's mum. Graham could see where Jenny's looks came from.

"Good evening, Mrs Drake."

"Enjoy your walk."

They strolled around the town; Graham hadn't much idea of where they were going and he relied on Jenny to show him the interesting spots. He was totally engrossed in her; she was lovely to look at, enchantingly animated when she talked and he could listen to her voice for hours.

They finally sat on a seat on a small green. With great regret, Graham realised the evening would have to come to a close because he had to drive back to Hereford the next day and needed to get some sleep and he was actually a little chilly. He drew Jenny closer to him.

"Can we keep in touch, Jenny? May I come to see you again?"

"Of course you can, I'm on Facebook and I'll give you my phone number."

"I've only just met you and I don't like to rush things, but you're a very special girl, Jenny. I'm glad we came here today."

"I'm glad too."

He turned to look in her eyes, then took her tentatively in his arms. They kissed, ever so gently. Then he took her hand.

"Come on, you're cold. I have to get you home and although I don't want to leave you now, I have to get some sleep so I don't fall asleep at the wheel tomorrow."

They stood up and, hand in hand, and stopping to kiss occasionally, made their way back to Jenny's house.

At her door, they kissed again. Graham loved the taste of her lips on his; he recalled the line from the old song that went 'kisses sweeter than wine' and knew what it meant for the first time in his life.

"Don't forget me, Jenny," he whispered.

"I won't. I'll never forget you," she replied tenderly.

He watched her as she opened her door. Before she shut it, she blew him a kiss. He smiled and turned to walk away, realising he wasn't entirely sure which way he had to go but he reasoned that if he kept the castle in sight, he would find the B & B eventually. As it happened, it was straightforward. He turned a corner, saw the Castle Arms and knew exactly how to get back.

Later, as he lay in bed, he smiled as he recalled her voice, the sweetness of her kiss and for the first time in many years, he felt he was in love.

While was thinking of Jenny and how he felt about her after only one day, his thoughts turned to Samuel Williams and all of a sudden he understood how poor Sam was entirely wretched, knowing that someone had snuffed the life out of his first love even after all these years, because he was sure he would feel the same if something like that happened to his Jenny. He became determined that he and his boss would do everything they could to get justice for Rosemary Baxter.

Chapter 31

While Dan and Grant were travelling back to Hereford from North Wales, the village of Sutton-on-Wye were gathering to say their farewells to Sidney Price. Many people packed into the church ready for the service to be conducted by the Reverend Trevithick.

The good vicar had told the family there was no need for others to know what Sid had confessed before he died and it would definitely not be mentioned at the funeral service. Elwyn and Mary followed the coffin, which was covered in flowers, down the aisle of the church and their sons and their wives followed, as did Glynis and Alison.

Everyone agreed the service went well. The Rev Trevithick had done his best to make it as personal as possible. Sid did believe and had attended church sometimes before his accident but that was before the Rev Trevithick had come to the village. He had visited Sid occasionally and had become well aquainted with him. Sometimes he'd dropped in to play chess with the senior Price, but the Reverend would be the first to admit that he didn't know Sid as well as he might have done. However, the Elwyn and his family didn't blame him for that.

After the service everyone filed out to follow the coffin to the churchyard. Sid was being laid to rest with his wife Dorothy, who had died ten years before of a stroke. Mary had looked after them both for a while.

Afterwards, people walked over to the village hall, where Sheila and Lucy had helped Mary to prepare loads of food for the 'wake'. The residents of Sutton-on-Wye were good at such gatherings. They all knew each other well and enjoyed the chance of a get-together, even if it was a funeral. They also liked the opportunity of free food made by Lucy, because her cooking was phenomenal and much sought after.

Being sociable didn't come easy to Elwyn and he was still distressed about his father's admission that he had buried Rosemary Baxter's body. For the life of him he couldn't work out why his dad had done that. Sid had always been straight and honest and it just didn't fit in with his character. After an hour, Elwyn had had enough, and needed to get out.

Mary knew him so well that, without him saying, she was aware he had to leave. She patted him on the arm and said,

"You go, love."

He kissed her briefly and gave her a quick squeeze and left the hall. With Lucy not far away, Mary coped fine; being busy with her guests was keeping her mind off things for a while. Elwyn, on the other hand, needed the quietness of his fields and the animals to sooth him and she knew he would soon be busy working on the farm.

Sam was present at the funeral but he had kept to the back of the church and stood afar off during the internment. He hadn't intended going to the hall, but Lucy had insisted and had taken his arm to help him. He loved Lucy and hadn't the heart to tell her he didn't want to, because he felt to blame for his friend's death. If Sid hadn't been worried about Sam, he wouldn't have had his heart attack. Cessy had insisted that Sam was not to blame, Sid's heart had been bad for some time and the attack probably would have happened anyway, if not at that moment, then sometime soon.

Before the others laft, Sam slipped out and made his way slowly back across the road to the churchyard. Now, with no-one present, he stood at his friend's graveside, looking down at the coffin with the handfuls of earth scattered on top and bowed his head.

"Sid, my friend, I love you as a brother and I love you for what you did for me. Rest in peace."

"Come on, Sam, I'm taking you back to Sutton Court." He turned to see Cessy standing beside him. "I think you've had enough for one day. Let me take care of you."

"Thank you, my dear. You have been so kind to me throughout all these terrible happenings. I can't thank you enough."

"We love you, Sam. You've had to contend with so much lately. I'm happy to be able to help you. You will be able to return to your own home soon but in the meantime I intend to continue to look after you. Come now."

They hooked arms and walked slowly to Cessy's car which was parked close to the church. They drove to Sutton Court, which took only minutes. Sam was thankful to sink into his familiar chair near the window in his room and watch a quiz show on television to help take his mind off the sombre business of attending his best friend's funeral.

****

Dan and Grant made good time on their journey back to Hereford. Dan was elated that they had been able to get so much useful information from Jenny's grandfather.

"We have two names for our murderer now, Gilbert Trent and Gregory Tunstall. But I'm sure they are the same; the car is the common denominator. In fact, I'd be surprised if his name is anything like that. I expect he made up names to go with the GT on the car. What I want to know is, what happened to the car? Where did it end up? We need to concentrate on the car for now. Find out who it belonged to, if there are any reports of it being stolen or whether it went back to its owner. I have a strong feeling that car did not belong to our guy with the slicked hair."

"I think you're right, sir. I'll get Johnson onto it when we get back. If anyone can find the car, he can."

"So, what about you and Jenny then? Are you going to keep in touch with her?"

"Certainly am. I'm not going to let her go easily."

"All the girls in Hereford and you have to fall for a Welsh girl."

"Well, you have to admit, gov, Jenny is pretty special. You have to go a long way to find a special girl sometimes."

Dan couldn't help but agree.

"It's going to be difficult to see her much."

"I'm sure we can work it out, sir."

Dan said no more, but couldn't help wondering if his sergeant would apply for a transfer. He hoped he would not for they worked well together. However, now was not the time to worry about that, it was early days yet for the pair. His concern was how he was going to move this case forward. Were they likely to actually find Gilbert Trent/Gregory Tunstall? He was unlikely to be alive, as by all accounts he was a good few years older than the girls he killed. Sam and Sid were eighty nine so the killer would be almost a hundred. Dan knew they hadn't much chance of finding him alive.

'I know what I'd like to do to him if only I could get my hands on him,' he thought, although of course he wouldn't because it would be the end of his career, but that didn't stop him wanting to...

****

Mary was right that Elwyn would have gone back to work on the farm. He called upon one of his younger farmhands and the two of them made their way to the meadow to erect the fence he'd been intending putting up when he found the body. He'd been given permission by the police to go ahead but he'd not had the chance because there had been so much going on. Now was as good a time as any.

The two men worked hard in co-operation with each other and did not talk much. Mike knew that his boss wasn't much of a talker.

Elwyn couldn't help thinking about his father digging that hole to put the lass in; he couldn't get his head straight, it didn't fit in with the rest of his dad's character.

'It just goes to show that you don't always know someone the way you think you do,' he thought, but somehow it hurt that he hadn't known something about his father until the day he died and even then he had found out second-hand through their Glynis.

He worked himself hard. Work had always been his solace and they had quickly erected the new fencing on one side of the gate. They would do the other side the following day. Elwyn's herd was in another field, kindly allowed by Lucy, until the new fence was completed. It was the field that was usually used as a car park when the village had an event on but it had plenty of new grass. It wouldn't be far to drive them up the lane to the meadow. He would be glad when things were back to normal.

"Come on, Mike, let's pack up and go up to the house for a cuppa, I'm gasping. The misses should be home by now."

The men cleared up and set off over the picturesque stone bridge that spanned the river where it was narrow and which joined the two properties.

"Hmm, look at that, I've not noticed it before. Remiss of me, I should have done. How could I not have realised?"

Mike looked to where Elwyn pointed to the far side of the bridge. A tree had grown close to the structure, so close that the men could see that the stonework was being prised apart in places by the roots and by the trunk pressing into it.

"Sometimes, when you're so used to seeing something, you stop seeing it or at least you don't realise it could be a problem."

Elwyn nodded.

"That'll have to be my next job, to get rid of that tree, it'll be knocking down that there bridge. Can't have that. Soon as we have that fence up and the cattle in, I'll be tackling this job."

"Who does the bridge belong to, boss?"

"Do you know, I'm not awfully sure. The question has never come up before. I'll have to have a word with Kenny, see if he knows. Come on, I'm so hungry, me stomach thinks me throat's been cut."

Chapter 32

Sam was looking forward to going home. Arrangements had been made for a carer to come every morning to make sure he was okay and coping. Sue next door promised to keep an eye on him, as did Lucy, who assured him she would stop by often.

He spent one last weekend at Sutton Court and on the Monday morning was up bright and early, ready to be off as soon as he decently could.

Not that he wasn't grateful to Cessy and her staff . They had been wonderful to him and he was glad that she'd been there to help him through the difficult time of feeling like a suspect and then losing his dear friend Sid so soon after his Emily. He had to admit that it had turned out to be much better than being on his own this past month since losing his beloved companion. Now, though, he was ready to tackle life on his own. He had plans of the things he wanted to do, like visit his niece and nephew's families, one in Leeds, the other in Suffolk. He would travel by train as he didn't feel he could drive those distances alone at his age. Sam had strong opinions about not driving when you get too old, and he was too old at eighty nine. He had no wish to endanger other road using by being too slow in making decisions. He was looking forward to being in his own place again for a while before he went away. He also had to see about Emily's things but wasn't sure he was ready to do that yet. Lucy would help when he felt he could tackle it.

"Well, Sam, good morning to you," Cessy came in after she'd knocked. "Are you ready for home? We are going to miss you."

"Oh, I think I've caused you quite enough trouble!"

"You've been no trouble at all. Are you ready for some breakfast?"

"I am indeed, ma'am."

"Let's go then."

They linked arms as they strolled down the hallway together, Sam only using only one stick.

"I must make a good breakfast, it'll be coffee and toast for me in the future," he joked.

"Go on with you! I know you can do better than that; you had to do everything for you and Emily for some time."

"Oh yes. It's a matter of whether it's worth it when it's only for one. But don't worry, I don't intend to starve myself to death!" he laughed.

Lucy turned up at ten thirty to drive Sam to his home, not far but too far to walk, especially with his belongings. As Neil helped him into the passenger seat, Lucy stowed his bags away in the boot and they drove away with Sutton Court's owners waving after them.

The bungalow in Dorothy Avenue was warm, inviting and dust-free. Obviously, Lucy had been in and given it the once-over to make sure it was all ready for him, and a casserole was cooking in the slow cooker.

"Mm, it smells divine and the house looks lovely. Thank you so much, my dear."

"You're welcome," said Lucy and gave him a hug. "Do you fancy a cuppa?"

"I do indeed. But let me at least put the kettle on." Sam moved carefully towards the kitchen and Lucy heard the tap running followed by the click of the kettle being switched on. She sat at the small kitchen table and watched while Sam gathered teabags, put them in the pot ready and got two mugs down from a cupboard.

"Do you have any plans for the future?"

"I'm hoping to visit my brother's family. I have a niece in Suffolk and a nephew in Leeds. I would like to see both – not at the same time, of course, they're in different directions. Perhaps go to one, come home for a break and then go to the other. I'll have to see how they are placed."

"How will you travel?"

"By train. I'm too old to drive all that way now. In fact, I've already got rid of my car. I'm of the firm opinion that old people shouldn't drive."

"I think I agree. Driving is getting more and more demanding these days. The roads are quite frightening now," replied Lucy and then, "Thank you," as Sam handed her a mug of tea. "Mm, I'm ready for this."

"Me too."

"Would you like a biscuit? I got some in for you."

"Yes, please."

Lucy got up and took a packet of chocolate digestives out of the cupboard.

"My favourites," grinned Sam.

"Mine too. I also made you some Bakewell tarts and some small, individual fruit cakes. They are in the tin on the worktop there."

"Brilliant. I love your cakes. Thank you, my dear."

"No problem. I'm always baking as you know. I'll call in or phone you every day to make sure you're okay and Sue next door will look in on you in the evenings."

"You're all too kind. I'm sure I'll soon be fine without all you women running around after me – although I rather like having women running around me, especially attractive ones like you!"

"Daft man!"

Lucy kissed him affectionately.

"I must go now or poor Sheila will think I've run off with you and left her holding the baby."

"I can't thank you enough, my dear. I'll be fine now."

"Good. I made the casserole in the slow cooker so you won't have to lift it from the oven. You can just ladle out what you want."

"Wonderful. Thank you."

"I'll see you tomorrow then. Bye for now, I'll see myself out."

"Bye Lucy and thank you again. Take care how you go and give your little lad a big hug from me."

"I will. Cheerio."

With that, she was gone and the house was silent. Sam switched the radio on. He liked to listen to Radio 4 and it filled his little home with cheerful chat, dispelling the loneliness that threatened to descend.

****

"I do hope Sam will be alright," Lucy said to her husband as they sat together after baby John had gone to bed. Kenny slipped his arm around her.

"Try not to worry; he's a capable man, my darling and he looked after Emily very well."

"That's my worry – he had her to look after, now he has nothing. Even his best friend has died. When you've looked after someone, life can feel empty."

"Well, love, I know you do your best but you just can't look after everyone."

"I know, but my heart aches for him. I can't imagine what it must be like to be all alone. He hasn't got anyone belonging to him anymore. He said he was planning to visit his brother's son and daughter and their families if they were willing."

"That'll be a good thing. I hope they say he can go."

"Me too. Talk about looking after everyone, I'm really concerned about Elwyn too. He hasn't been right since his dad died. Can't put my finger on it, or say for definite what tells me that because he's never talkative but somehow I just know something is bothering him."

"Well, he's not your responsibility, darling. I'm sure Mary knows how to handle him."

"Yes, I'm sure you're right. I do need to stop worrying about everyone. I'll grow old too quickly doing that," Lucy laughed.

Kenny took her in his arms.

"You will never be old, in my eyes you will always be young and beautiful, my wonderful Lucy."

"Oh, you're soppy! But I'm pleased you are. I love you so much, I'm always glad that Aunt Bea led me to you. Just think how terrible it would have been if I'd never met you."

"Don't think about it! Your Aunt Bea was a wonderful woman. I'll never forget the day I first met you – and that time when we sat under the weeping willow by the river on the day of the summer fete. How I longed to fold you up in my arms and make everything better for you. I'm so happy I can do that now, hug you and kiss you whenever I want. My life with you is so special and I hope it will go on and on for many years."

Lucy rested her head on his shoulder, with his arms around her and thanked God that they had each other and the prospect of a wonderful family life together. But it didn't stop her feeling sad for Sam or completely suppress the niggling concern for Elwyn.

Chapter 33

Johnson turned up trumps with the car. The car pre-dated the DVLC, but eventually he discovered that it belonged to a Lord Smethwick who had a grand mansion in Devon, the house now in partnership with the National Trust.

"We should go down there," said Dan. "We may be able to pick up some information."

"Right sir. Tomorrow?"

"No, Monday. The wife won't be happy if I'm away for the weekend. She's planne trip to the theatre and drinks with friends and a Barbeque on Sunday if the weather holds."

"Bit early in the year for barbequing, isn't it?"

"Yeah but you know how she is when she gets a bee in her bonnet; you can't shift her. It will probably end up with me barbequing out on the patio under an umbrella in the rain while everyone else is inside. It's happened before and I've no doubt it will happen again!"

They laughed; Grant did indeed know what Dan's missus was like because he'd been at their house while Dan had to barbeque in the rain. He'd wondered why the stuff couldn't have been cooked inside. His boss had explained that it was because cooking inside just didn't give the right, burned charcoal taste…

****

Letterton Hall was on the edge of Dartmoor. Contrary to the day before when it had indeed rained (much to Dan's disgust), the sun made a weak effort to put in appearance although, by the time they reached Letterton, the sky was grey and overcast.

They drove up to the tall, iron gate which was shut. A big notice to one side, said: 'LETTERTON HALL, Open to the Public, Tuesdays, Wednesdays and Saturdays, March – October, 10a.m. – 5p.m.'

"Damn! I never thought to look when it would be open. I assumed that a National Trust place would be open every day during the season."

"I read that the present-day Lord Smethwick still lives here, sir, and the National Trust is in partnership with him and will take it over when he dies because he has no heirs; he is unmarried."

"Hmm, I wonder if there's a way we can contact the owner direct. Let's find somewhere to eat first. Come on, we've had a long drive, we need to relax a little before we set to. I'll contact Jenkins and see if he can come up with contact details for Lord Smethwick."

That's just what Grant liked about his boss, he was practical and not wound up about wasting time; he knew when food or a break was needed.

They found a little country pub with the endearing name of The Woolly Lamb and ordered steak and chips.

"At least this is a decent steak, unlike the charred meat we had yesterday," commented Dan as they ate. "Why my Linda can't see that no one likes to eat meat like that is beyond me."

"Perhaps she's hoping you'll get better at it if you have more practice." It was an idle comment from Grant but it made Dan stop and think...

Before they had finished eating, a message came on Dan's phone from Johnson, giving a phone number for Lord Smethwick.

"Right. That's the number we've been waiting for, Grant. I'm going to give him a call. Won't be long."

"Shall I order coffee?"

"Yes. I'll be right back."

Soon after the coffee had been brought to their table, Dan returned with a satisfied look on his face.

"Lord Smethwick will see us. He told me another entrance to the estate other than the usual public one. I said we'd be with him in half an hour."

"Great. Here's your coffee."

"Thanks."

Even though the coffee was hot, they still made it to Letterton House within the half-hour.

Grant drove along a gravel drive to what was obviously the back of the great house. As they pulled to a stop, the wheels crunching on the stones, a door opened and the two detectives had their first sight of Lord Smethwick. He looked nothing like a 'lord' to them; he was very tall and wide and his hair reminded Grant of a certain well-known politician. Underneath the mop were beetle brows over small eyes – or maybe the brows just gave the onlooker the impression that his eyes were small – and a nose that had obviously once been broken, for it was crooked with a sort of hump in the middle. His lips were full and Grant's thoughts traitorously pictured a sink-plunger.

"Well, helloo there, gentlemen, how perfectly lovely to have visitors! It's always so quiet here when the house is not open – mind you, then I get fed up sometimes with people tramping all over the place – not much privacy you know – and one fears for one's pelargoniums."

Lord Smethwick had a booming voice and a hearty handshake.

"Where did you say you're from? Come away in, I'll get my faithful Mrs Brown to make a cup of tea."

"We have just had lunch, sir. Perhaps a bit later?" Dan said.

"What's that? Oh, yes of course – just had jolly old lunch meself. We'll wait a bit then."

Dan and Grant followed the elderly Lord into the house and along a hallway painted plain magnolia and sporting all kinds of photographs. He led them into a room that was surprisingly modern.

"Used to be the servants' wing, you know. Had it made into a private apartment for meself when we decided to open to the public. I will take you round the house if you're interested."

"We'd like that, wouldn't we, Grant?"

"Oh, erm, yes, very much sir." Grant felt he had to agree but wasn't altogether sure he was really interested in these sorts of places. His mum loved them and he and his brother had often been dragged around them and they all sort of merged in his memory. When you've seen one stately home, you've seen them all, in his opinion. But he realised he couldn't object.

The brown leather chairs were comfortable and Grant felt a little sleepy after the driving and their good pub lunch. He hoped he would be able to stay awake.

"Would you like the tour or questions first? You've come to ask me something, haven't you? You did say you needed my help, although I'm completely mystified. Where did you say you come from?"

"Hereford, sir," Dan said patiently; he'd already told him on the phone.

"Ah yes, Hereford. Beautiful place, was there years ago. 'Spect it's changed somewhat since then."

"I would imagine it has, sir."

"So, what are two detectives from Hereford doing here to question me?"

"You may have heard that a few weeks ago, a skeleton was discovered buried in a field in a Herefordshire village?"

The Lord frowned.

"Not sure that I did, no."

"Well, our enquiries are to do with that body, sir. Apparently it had been there for some seventy years –"

"Seventy years! My goodness. But what has that got to do with me?"

"Not directly you, sir, but maybe with your family. Do you recognise the car in this photograph?"

Dan handed Lord Smethwick the photo of Rosemary with the car in the background.

"No, why should I? Pretty girl."

"That's the dead girl, sir."

"Is it now? Shame."

"It is indeed. She was only sixteen."

"Far too young to die. I'm assuming she was murdered?"

"Yes, it seems she was strangled, sir."

"Terrible, terrible. Bad do, that."

"Yes sir. We think we know who killed her."

"Do you now?" The Lord was startled. "How can you know after all this time?"

"We believe a man called Gilbert Trent killed her."

"Never heard of him."

"We have reason to believe that wasn't his real name."

"Ah. Go on."

"The car in the photograph is the car that he had. It's a 1932 Model T Ford and the full registration is GT 314. Records show that this car was owned by Lord Geoffrey Shackleton. He bought it brand new. It is not listed under anyone else so he never sold it. We are here to ask if you can tell us anything about that car, sir."

"Lord Geoffrey was my father. He had an important role during the war. Died in 1984. I am the last of the line. When I die, the title will probably go to some obscure several-times-removed cousin or something. Wish I'd got married.

"Spent a lot of time abroad, you know. All those dusky maidens, too busy with them you know; left it too late really – who's going to want an old boiler like me, eh? I bet there's a few of my offspring around the world (he winked cheekily) but none who can legitimately claim the title or the estate, more's the pity. Now I come to think of it, I did hear tell of a car that went missing. Father was still upset about it years later. Come with me."

He led them into the main house. This was so different from his luxurious apartment. It was typical of a stately home with huge windows, heavy curtains, highly polished old furniture, uncomfortable-looking silk-upholstered chairs and huge portraits on the walls. All the eyes seemed to follow them as they walked through the rooms and Grant shuddered. He didn't know how anyone could live in a place such as this.

They came to what was obviously a library, for it had floor to ceiling glass-fronted cases full of old, leather bound, books. There was a desk with several photographs standing on display. Lord Smethwick picked one up and handed it to Dan.

It was a photo of a handsome man wearing a sporty outfit standing by a Model T car. He leaned casually on the side of the car. Another photograph showed the same man sitting in the driving seat, waving.

"My father."

"And the car," stated Dan. "Is this the car that went missing?"

"Yes, I believe so. Father was heartbroken. He loved that car because it was his very first."

"Do you know when or how it disappeared?"

"Hmm, I think there may be something in here."

He opened a drawer and rummaged around in some papers. Finally, he drew out a folder and put it on the desk and opened it. It appeared to be full of newspaper cuttings. Taking a pair of spectacles from his top pocket, he started to sort through them, peering at each one carefully. Eventually,

"Ah, here we are. Read that."

Dan took the cutting. It had a picture at the top and the headline read: 'Mysterious Disappearance of Lord's car and Chauffer.' It went on to say how Lord Smethwick's Chauffer had taken the car home because he was to fetch Lady Smethwick's mother from Gloucestershire the next day and was setting off early in the morning. Her own car had broken down and was in for repair. The chauffer had indeed set off early in the morning but he had not arrived in Gloucester and had not been seen since. They were appealing for information.

The picture was of the car and Lord Smethwick, in fact, the one they had been looking at on the desk. Also pictured was the face of the chauffer, Henry Smithson. He had a superior grin on his face and dark, slicked-back hair.

Chapter 34

"I think we might have found our man," murmured Dan to Grant, who nodded.

"Looks like it, sir. It matches the description we have of him, both from Sam Williams and Mr Drake."

"Do you know if this man was reported missing at the time?"

"I'm sure he probably was, after all, it was in the newspaper. I can't say personally because I was only a lad at the time. Now I come to think of it, I do remember the car and the chauffer. Beautiful car, it would be a collector's item now. It was black but the wheels had red middles, with a spare on the side above the footplate. I didn't like the chauffeur, he put on airs and graces and made out he was better than the other servants. He wasn't popular with them and he hated me and any other kids that were around. Not many missed him. I'm sorry to say we were more upset about the car. Would you care to see the rest of the house while we are in this part?"

"That would be good, thank you," responded Dan, giving Grant a nudge when he saw the expression on his sergeant's face.

There followed an hour of conducted tour, together with history of the family. Dan and Grant did their best to be as interested as they could; in fact Dan was because he liked history. Grant was not so thrilled and often let his mind wander as Lord Smethwick talked. It was a beautiful house and some the tapestries and furnishings were exquisite; Grant had to admit to himself that it was impressive.

"I expect you're ready for that cup of tea now?"

They sighed with relief when the elderly peer said, "I expect you're ready for that cup of tea now?" for it meant the tour was over.

In fact, they had done a circle of the house which had brought them back to the servants' quarters where Lord Smethwick lived.

Mrs Brown was a cheerful, round lady with grey hair tied in a bun and brown eyes that smiled warmly.

"Here we are, sir."

She brought in a wheeled trolley with teapot, cups and saucers, milk jug and sugar bowl. There was also a plate of assorted small cakes and another of small sandwiches.

"Afternoon tea, an old tradition of the upper classes which I am loath to dispense with. There's something about triangle sandwiches I always find inviting, don't you? Do help yourselves, gentlemen."

The two detectives helped themselves to a selection of sandwiches from the plate. When Grant bit into his white triangle with its egg and cress filling, to his surprise, he had to agree with the elderly man.

"Do you think our missing chauffeur is a murderer, then, Inspector?"

"It's highly likely. Surprisingly, we have descriptions of him from two witnesses and this photograph of Henry Smithson fits what we've been told. It seems that the girl in Herefordshire was his last murder, for we haven't found any others of similar ilk after that but we have no idea where he went when he left there. It is also a puzzle how he managed to be in various parts of the country at different times. He's been in Yorkshire, Lincolnshire, North Wales and in the Forest of Dean, besides Hereford. We wonder how he did that, especially during wartime."

"Ah well, I think I can help there. My father was in Intelligence, stationed in or visited various parts of the country during the course of his work and given extra petrol allowance so he could use his own car – and of course as his driver, Henry Smithson went too. People like my father were driven by forces personnel Henry was drafted into the appropriate regiment so he could drive for Father. It would have been easy for him to be in different parts of the country."

"Ah, I see. That explains a lot."

"I'm appalled that Henry Smithson was a murderer. I didn't like the chap – but a murderer! I can't believe it. How awful for his wife and children." He clapped himself on the head. "I'm such an old duffer! Of course I know the man – and his family! The old grey cells are a bit slow these days, you know."

"He was married?"

"Oh yes. It was unusual for servants to be married but my father gave permission for Smithson to marry his girlfriend when he got her pregnant. She wasn't very old either, only about seventeen, at the time. He came from a very big family, you know; he had a brother and about seven sisters. My father actually had two of the girls here in service and the brother was a gardener. Nice family really. There was a big upset when Smithson got the girl up the duff and Dad insisted that he marry her. She had a son who died soon after he was born. Smithson was upset; said he hadn't needed to marry her. She went on to have another three, two boys and a girl as she seemed to get pregnant every time he had leave. When I was young I used to believe she was like that all the time because I never saw her when she wasn't pregnant. I think she was glad when he went missing, she never married again.

"My father supported her and the children did alright. One son became a mechanic and had a garage in Truro and the other one joined the Navy first then ended up in the Merchant Navy and lives in Plymouth. The daughter married a local man and still lives in the village."

"Does she indeed?" Dan's ears pricked up. "Do you think she would see us?"

"I'm sure she would if I asked her. She's just over seventy now but you wouldn't know it."

"One last thing before we go, could we have a copy of that newspaper report please? It would be very useful to have a picture of the car and the man. We might have to put out an appeal on the television; see if we can find anyone else who might help us."

"Of course, no problem. There's a photocopier in the office."

They followed the elderly man through another hallway and into a room, or a set of rooms, that were obviously offices. The large photocopier sat in a small room of its own that had shelves running along one wall. Grant tucked the copy away in his case.

"I'll just call Doreen to check she's okay with you coming over and then give you her address. Won't be a tick."

He used the office phone.

"Hello? Hello, Doreen? Ron Smethwick here. Would you be so good as to see two detectives who are down from Hereford? Asking about your father. No, I don't suppose you can but they would still like to see you. Will you be at home for a while? Oh, good. I can give them your address. Don't worry, they are very nice chaps. Yes, I'm still on for Thursday. I will see you then and I'll send these detectives over. They'll be with you very soon. Goodbye, my dear."

He turned. "She says you can go over, although she doesn't know what she can tell you."

"That's fine. We just like to go over everything we can. We can't thank you enough for your help, Lord Smethwick."

"Oh, do call me Ron. Lord Smethwick is so stuffy, don't you think?"

"Thank you, sir, er, Ron. Would you like us to contact you if we manage to find out anything?"

"Oh, yes indeed." The old man rubbed his hands together in glee. "This is quite exciting, isn't it? I never dreamed that our dear old car would be mixed up in something like this."

"I suppose it is – that is, if we ever get to the bottom of it."

"Well, if you ever manage to unearth the old car, I'd like to see it."

"Of course – it will belong to you, won't it?"

"I suppose it would, yes. Never thought of that. Jolly, what?"

The elderly Lord walked with them to their car.

"Goodbye, sir, and thank you again." Dan shook Ron's hand.

"Goodbye and good luck. Do keep in touch – and do call in if you're down this way again."

"Thank you, we might just do that."

Grant shook hands and nodded a goodbye to Lord Smethwick and the two detectives got into their car. Grant drove off gently, remembering they were on loose gravel and he didn't want to cover the old man with dust.

Dan saw that Ron was still watching them and waved his hand in a salute out of the window and saw that the lord waved back and then stepped inside the house.

"Well, that was interesting, don't you think, Grant?"

"Very. Good that we now have a picture of our prime suspect. I wish we could find out where he went after he killed Rosemary Baxter and why he didn't kill any more."

"Well, we assume he didn't. Nice old boy, Lord Smethwick."

"Yes, not really like a member of the aristocracy exactly."

"Something of a 'free spirit', I think, although many were like that. They had the money to be."

"He obviously doesn't have money now."

"Death duties. Crippling," commented Dan. "That's probably why the National Trust is in on it."

Grant nodded; he was concentrating on the satnav guiding him to Doreen's house. Once off the grounds of the big house, they traversed a winding road, so typical of Devon and suddenly it widened out and became a pretty village with a duck pond on a green and cottages with thatched roofs.

Doreen lived at number three, Cherry Tree Lane and they soon found it after turning up another narrow road. The cottages were all detached and standing in their own pretty gardens. Each one was well attended and charming in their individuality. Number three had a neat lawn with a standard, weeping rose bush in the middle of a round cut into the centre of the lawn and the beds surrounding the grass had a multitude of flowers in all heights and colours that blended perfectly and gave out a heady aroma. The house itself had a porch with yet another climbing rose growing around it – the whole scene presented a perfect, chocolate-box picture.

When they knocked at the door, it was answered by a straight-backed woman who looked much younger than her seventy one years. Dan and Grant were both struck by the astonishing thought that this woman was almost the living image of Henry Smithson.

Chapter 35

Doreen Chandler invited the two detectives in. She led them into a pleasant sitting-room that had a window at the front and French doors leading to the back garden. This gave plenty of light to the room, which was surprisingly modern with skim-plastered walls painted in a very light green and the three-piece suite was cream and green. A green rug lay on the laminated wood floor in front of the modern fireplace that housed a log-burner.

"Do sit down. My husband is out in the garden, do you need him too?"

"I don't think so, although we have no objection to him being here."

"I'll give him a shout and he can choose whether he comes in. Would you like a cup of tea or anything?"

"Thank you, but we've just had afternoon tea with Lord Smethwick."

Doreen chuckled. "Yes, he likes to hang onto some of the old ways. He's a nice man though, as was his father before him."

"I understand his father helped your mother when your father disappeared."

"Yes. He was good to us and watched over us until we were able to support ourselves. I didn't know my father, Inspector, I was only a baby of about seven months old when he disappeared so I don't really see how I can help you."

"We're just trying to build a picture of what he was like, what kind of man he was, Mrs Chandler, so anything you can help us with will be useful. Did your mother ever say anything about him, or do your brothers remember him at all?"

"My eldest brother, Henry Jnr, died last year and my other brother, Albert, is in a home. He has Alzheimer's."

"I'm sorry to hear that. Did they talk about him ever?"

"Well, Albert was only three and Henry was seven so he did remember him. From what I could gather, my brother didn't see much of him and when he was at home he had to be quiet all the time. Father didn't like kids, I don't think. Henry seemed to think he'd got something in particular against him. As for Albert and me, he barely took any notice of us. Of course, I didn't really know it, being only a baby. When Mum was much older, she talked with me quite a bit about the past. Although she never said so in so many words, I think he forced himself on her and she became pregnant when she was only young and Lord Smethwick made him marry her. She told me he used to hit her. She always said she was glad he never came back, although she often wondered what had become of him. She would say that if he ever dared to show his face here again, she would show him the door but of course he never did. She said she never heard from him ever again."

"That's sad. Did she never try to find out what had happened to him?"

"I don't know. I don't think so. Lord Smethwick did, he reported him missing and the car stolen but I am pretty sure he never heard anything. The police had it put in the papers but no one reported seeing Father or the car."

She crossed her legs and continued,

"From what Mum said, my father could be very charming and lots of girls and women liked him. She said she really fancied him at first and he was good to her and went out of his way to ingratiated himself to her. But when she didn't want to lay with him, he got nasty and forced her (at least that's the impression I got). She told me she didn't want to marry him because by then she knew what he was like but she felt she had to because of the baby.

"It was shameful to have a baby and not be married so she went along with it. Then when she lost the baby, Father was mad with her for losing it, accused her of being careless, which she had not. He was angry that he'd been trapped into marriage.

She was glad when Lord Smethwick arranged for him to be his chauffeur when he was on special duties during the war because he had to be away from home most of the time. But of course, he came back to her every time he was on leave which resulted in Henry, Albert and me. Having heard all Mum would say about him, I'm not sorry I didn't know him, although the curious side of me would like to know what happened to him. I don't suppose we will ever find out."

"You never know. We have uncovered things that we never thought we would to do with these old murders. It's surprising what you can find out when you're really determined. We have so many more things to help us nowadays, such as the internet and DNA. It's amazing what we can find out."

"I'm getting the idea that you think my father was a murderer, Detective Inspector. Am I right?"

"Who knows? The interesting thing is that all his victims were very young, only about sixteen or seventeen years old."

Doreen got up from her chair and stared out of the French windows. She stood there for a few minutes. Dan and Grant waited for her to speak. Eventually, she turned round.

"It almost seems as if he is punishing them for what he did to mother – or rather, what he thinks she did to him. She was young, only seventeen, when he got her pregnant and she'd never been with a man before. I think that might have cracked him somehow and he went out to punish other girls for what happened to him. Crazy."

"It's a distinct possibility," replied Dan, thoughtfully. "That may have been the case. The first one he pretended to be married to and left her dead in a bed in a boarding house but after that he just left them in fields, under hedges or in abandoned huts. It seems to indicate that he had less time and had to be careful not to lay a trail by taking them to boarding houses; too much risk of witnesses.

"Oddly, it seems that he spent some time courting the girl in Hereford, causing great heartache to the lad who loved her and she was preparing to go away with him. But he killed her instead. After that though, it seems he disappeared into thin air and the car with him."

"It's very strange," remarked Doreen.

At that moment, Doreen's husband came into the room from the kitchen. The two detectives stood up.

"My dear, this is Detective Inspector Cooke and Detective Sergeant Grant. This is my husband, David."

The men shook hands. David Chandler was good looking in a rugged sort of way. He was tall and bald with blue eyes. His hands were big and rough; obviously a man used to manual work.

"They've come to talk about my father, dear."

"Oh, good luck with that one. We don't know a lot, do we? I've heard other folks say he was a Jekyll and Hyde sort of character. He could be charming one minute and turn nasty the next. He put on airs and graces because he was his lordship's chauffeur and Lord Smethwick arranged it so he could continue during the war. But from what I have gathered in the past, he wasn't widely liked."

"People can be very discerning. He's turned out to be a murderer, by all accounts, so these detectives tell me."

"A murderer eh? Bad, very bad." David drew a pipe from the pocket of his cardigan and stuck it in his mouth, although he didn't light it.

"He's trying to give it up," remarked Doreen.

Grant smiled in sympathy; he had given up smoking several times over the past couple of years!

Dan stood up. "Well, I think that's all we can do for now. Thank you for being so honest with us, Mrs Chandler. It can't be easy to learn that your father might have been a killer."

"Well, it's a bit surreal but as I never knew him, it doesn't really hurt exactly. I think it might not have surprised Mother. I grew up with my grandfather, mother's father, who was more of a father to me and Lord Smethwick as another grandfather so I really didn't miss my father. I don't feel like he belongs to me in many ways. But I would like to know if you find out anything else about him, what happened to him."

"We will keep you informed. Thank you for seeing us. We will leave you good people in peace. Do you know of anywhere we might get beds for the night?"

"Oh yes, if you go down the main road about a mile, you will come to a pub that does Bed and Breakfast. It's called 'The Three Horseshoes'.

"Thank you very much. Goodbye now."

As they drove off in the direction of The Three Horseshoes, Grant said,

"Well, it appears that Henry Smithson wasn't a nice person and certainly his family were glad to see the back of him."

"That's right. We have made some progress though. We have a picture of the car and Smithson so I think the next step is to put out an appeal for information on the television because it needs to go countrywide."

"I agree. I don't think we will get any further without. We have been to the places where the girls were murdered, except for Whitby for the first dead girl. Oh, it looks as if we have found our place to stay."

"Hopefully they will have rooms," replied Dan as he gazed at The Three Horseshoes' front. It was attractive, made of the soft stone similar to surrounding buildings, diamond-paned windows and hanging baskets all along the front, filled with cascading petunias of vibrant colours. "But most of all, I hope they have a great chef and a dining room, 'cos I'm starving."

Chapter 36

The Three Horseshoes proved to be a comfortable place to stay and their host friendly and easy-going. They were the only guests, and as they ate their full English breakfasts they were able to take their time. The aptly named Mrs Jolly cooked for them cheerfully and then as they were finishing with toast and coffee, she sat down to chat with them. She had a pleasant Devonshire accent and, although she looked as though she'd had too many of her own English breakfasts, she had a pretty face and laughed easily.

When they told her why they were visiting the area, she was excited and amazed.

"Fancy you being able to find out so much after all these years," she said. "And I thought nothing much happened in these parts, although of course we're right on the edge of the moor and sometimes things do go on there. But generally it's quiet around here."

"Well of course, he never committed any murders in this area – as far as we know. He kept it away from his own doorstep, so to speak, and his officer's position meant he had easy access to other parts of the country."

"Fascinating."

Dan rose.

"Well, Mrs Jolly, it's been lovely staying here. You are a wonderful cook! But we must away now and face the road, although I'd much rather stay here to sample more of your wonderful food."

"Very kind of you to say so. I hope we hear more about this and you know where we are if you need to stay here again."

"We do indeed. Perhaps I'll bring my wife down, she'd love it here."

Mrs Jolly smiled widely.

"Oh my! It would be lovely to have you."

"We will just get our things and then I'll be down to settle up with you."

"Right you are. I'll see you in a jiffy."

It was a tiring journey, the roads were slow, but the two men were not in a terrible hurry to get home so they took it easy. Beautiful as Devon is, Dan and Grant were glad to be back in Hereford the day following their discoveries down south.

****

The appeal went out on the following week's programme 'Crimewatch'. Elsie Rowe always watched the it, horrified at the crimes they featured; life always seemed so quiet round her way. She loved living with her daughter and family on the Gower Peninsular in her beautiful house overlooking Oxwich Bay. She had moved into a 'granny flat' on the side of the house while Jill and Alan, Marie, Adam and Jacob lived in the main house. The arrangement suited everyone; Elsie had her privacy but Jill could keep an eye on her.

After collecting Marie from a friend's house, Jill popped her head round the door to tell her mother she was home. The programme had been on for a while and as Jill came in, Elsie heard the words:

'Now, we have an unusual case to put before our viewers. Herefordshire police are seeking anyone who might have known this man, seventy plus years ago.'
'Several weeks ago, in February, Herefordshire farmer, Elwyn Price, discovered the skeletal remains of a body in a meadow when he was going to erect a new fence. The body was found buried not far from the gate to the field."

(Scenes of re-enactment of a man digging and coming across a skull in a hole). Herefordshire police forensics finally identified the body as that of seventeen year old Rosemary Baxter. She had never been reported missing because her family believed she had run off with her then boyfriend, a man much older than herself, named Gilbert Trent. He drove a car, a Model T Ford.

Miss Baxter's brother, Mr Joseph Baxter, was only eight at the time of her disappearance but he still remembers it clearly.'

(Joseph Baxter being interviewed in his home) "Yes, I remember Gilbert Trent very well. I believe Rosemary had her head turned by the fact that an older, mature man was interested in her. She'd been seeing a local lad but broke off the relationship when Trent started to pursue her. My parents believed she'd gone away with him. She told us that she was going to be married and I watched her pack her case and saw him put it in the back of the car. She was very excited and promised she would get in touch once they had settled in London, where they were going to live."

(Interviewer:) "So, Mr Baxter, I expect it was a shock to you to find that the body in the field was that of your sister?"

"It was and it wasn't. I long since thought something had happened to her. I'd searched the records to see if I could find the marriage or birth of any children but there was not a trace of her after that evening she left to go with Trent."

(Reporter) *"Hereford detectives have followed evidence of other rapes and murders across the country and have traced the owner of the car. It was owned by Lord Smethwick, father of the present Lord and Gilbert Trent has been identified as Henry Smithson, Lord Smethwick's chauffer. It was thought he used other names in different places, all inspired by the GT on the car's licence plate."*

"They believe that this man was responsible for the horrific rape and murders of several women around the country, among them being Agnes Dewberry, who lived in the Forest of Dean and Catrin Lewis, who lived near Rhuddlan, North Wales.'

"Agnes!" exclaimed Elsie. "My Goodness! Jill, come and listen."

Jill hurried in and perched on the arm of her mother's chair. By this time, the screen showed the newspaper photographs of the car and Smithson.

"I saw that car – and him!"

The presenter carried on: 'The police believe that Rosemary Baxter was his last victim. After her murder, both the man and the car disappeared completely, so we are putting out this appeal to all our viewers across the United Kingdom. Did this man turn up in your town or village? Or did you ever see this car mysteriously abandoned anywhere? It is a 1932 Model T Ford, black, open-top, with red centres to the wheels, the licence plate GT 314. Henry Smithson, who was also known as Gregory Tunstall, was in his late twenties and had black, slick-backed hair. If there is anyone out there who might know the whereabouts of the car or who might have any information for the police, please get in contact using the number at the bottom of the screen."

"We must get in touch with them, Jill dear. That must be the man who killed my sister Agnes."

Chapter 37

Much to Dan's surprise, they had many phone call and email responses to the appeal on the Crimewatch programme. The telephonists were expert at weeding out hoax calls of which inevitably there were a number. Others were obviously mistaken identity from viewers who hadn't been watching carefully and thought they'd seen someone looking like Henry Smithson at the age he was in the photo. Considering he would be about a hundred years old, that didn't seem likely! All possibilities were passed on to Dan's office, where they underwent another sifting process.

Grant wiped his hand across his eyes tiredly; he couldn't read any more.

"I'm fetching some coffee, boss, would you like one?"

"Yes please." Dan never took his eyes off the screen as he clicked through the many messages. Without doubt Henry Smithson had been seen in various parts of the country, notably where girls had been murdered, but also by men who had been working with Lord Smethwick in Intelligence during the war. Quite a few very elderly people asked others to get in touch for them to say that they either knew Henry the chauffeur or had seen him around the home villages of the murdered girls.

When Grant returned with the coffee and two donuts, Dan took one absent-mindedly.

"It seems our Henry wasn't as invisible as he wanted to be, Grant. I can't think how the police of the day didn't find him. The interesting thing is that nobody saw him after 1946."

Grant took a bite out of his donuts.

"It really looks like our man disappeared into thin air after that. Maybe he left the country?"

"That might have to be the next line of enquiry, although quite how we can find out, I'm not sure."

"Oh, this one is interesting, boss! There's a woman here who says her mother is Agnes Dewberry's sister."

Dan looked up. "Is that so? Where are they?"

"Near Swansea, I think, sir."

"Right. We'll go and see her tomorrow. We've done enough for today and I need to inform my wife. Get the team to finish going through these messages for me."

Dan drank back his coffee and left the room. Grant drank his more slowly and continued to click through. However, after a while, he switched off the computer and headed towards the door. His eyes felt like they'd turned inside out.

****

It couldn't have been a better day for their visit to The Gower. It took longer than they'd thought, but eventually, Dan and Grant arrived at the beautiful house overlooking the bay. The door was opened by a woman of around forty, with a youthful appearance and a friendly smile.

"Hello?"

"Good afternoon. I'm Detective Inspector Cooke and this is Detective Sergeant Grant from Hereford police. You contacted us about Agnes Dewberry?"

"Oh, that's right. Do come in. It's my mother you need to see. She's elderly but she has all her buttons. I'm Jill."

Inside the light, airy hallway, they followed the woman through the house until they came to another hallway with a door at the end. Jill knocked on it and opened it, calling cheerfully; "Mum! There's two detectives from Hereford here to see you!"

"Oh, bring them in, love," came an answering voice.

Dan and Grant went through into a wonderful room with large windows with French doors that looked out towards the sea and another looking towards the front garden. The woman that greeted them, an older version of her daughter, and came towards them without any of the usual signs of encroaching old age, although she must have been pretty old. Bright eyes sparkled in a wrinkle-free face that had rosy cheeks and a smiling mouth. She wore an eye-catching dress and her movements reminded one of a dancer, so light was she on her feet.

"Good afternoon, Ma'am. I'm D.I. Dan Cooke and this is my sergeant, D.S. Grant."

"How do you do, gentlemen. I'm Elsie Rowe." Her handshake was surprisingly firm. " Do sit down. It's a beautiful day, would you care to sit on the patio and enjoy the sea view? Jill will bring us tea shortly."

"Thank you, that would be great. I do love the sea. What a beautiful place you have here and a wonderful situation."

"It is, isn't it? My husband built this house to my specifications and then we had it extended to make this granny flat for me when my daughter felt she wanted to keep an eye on me." She gave a delightful tinkly laugh. For an elderly woman, she was remarkably attractive. Opening the French doors, she led them towards a round table with an umbrella in the middle and four chairs. For a few moments all three were content to sit and breathe in the fresh sea air.

"Mrs Rowe, we would like to hear what you can tell us about your sister and Henry Smithson."

"Well – oh, here's our tea! Thank you so much, Jill dear."

Jill put the tray of mugs down on the table and handed them round and placed a plate of biscuits there for them, then sat in the fourth chair and took her own tea.

"Agnes was nearly three years older than me. She was sixteen, almost seventeen and I was fourteen...

When she got to the bit where her sister had run off and not returned home, Elsie's voice broke and Jill reached out to lay a comforting hand upon hers. Elsie covered Jill's hand with her own. For the first time she trembled.

"I don't think I can tell you more than you already know but I felt I had to contact you when I saw the Crimewatch programme so you could make contact with one of my sister's family. None of us ever got over the shock of how Agnes died, especially as we had already lost my brother Raymond in the war, it was so hard for our parents. When I look back, I still find it hard to come to terms with it. We had been so close until he came along and suddenly she didn't have time for anyone else."

"Thank you, Mrs Rowe, for talking with us. Just one more thing, can you remember what the boyfriend called himself?"

"Oh yes indeed. His name was George Tilbury."

"Ah. Another GT. Thank you very much for seeing us, Mrs Rowe, you've been very helpful."

"If you find out any more, Inspector, will you let me know?"

"Of course. Goodbye now, Mrs Rowe."

The two men followed Jill from the patio. Grant glanced back at the old lady still sitting by the round table. Now, she seemed much older than she had before.

****

Tempting as it was to stay on the Gower for the night, Dan and Grant decided to return home.

Their visit to Elsie, although pleasant, had not really helped their investigation. They already knew the details, although now they had seen it 'from the inside', listening to Elsie. How sad that the girl had been so besotted with the man that she ran out to find him after her father paid the man to stay away from her. At least it explained how she came to be out that night. And she'd had a relationship with him. Elsie was certain it was the same man and car; the name she had given them confirmed to them that Agnes' murderer was indeed Henry Smithson.

In the next few days, they talked with others who had made contact but none could give them any further ideas on where Smithson had gone after he left Hereford. It seemed they'd hit a brick wall.

Chapter 38

Sam made little effort to contact his nephew or niece. He couldn't be bothered. He was content to potter around his house and garden, particularly his greenhouse where he spent hours, watering and re-potting and generally wasting time, talking to his plants.

But still, he reasoned, *did it actually matter?* Was it really essential that he should take himself off somewhere else when he was content in his own home? No, he was alright. He had Susan next door and Lucy who still popped in and the village shop within easy walking distance. Besides, he couldn't leave his plants, could he? One part of him realised that lethargy had set in; without his Emily nothing seemed to have much point. He had lived for her and looked after her lovingly through her illness. At one time he'd had a good job as a teacher and headmaster; he and Emily had lived well with plenty of money, although they weren't extravagant. They had loved their dancing and their one indulgence had been the dresses Emily had worn for the ballroom. When he'd become a headmaster, it became more difficult to find time to go dancing but somehow they found opportunities to continue with their shared love.

At some point he would have to clear out Emily's things but he just couldn't bring himself to do it. Besides, when he caught sight of a bright pink corner of something poking out of her side of the wardrobe, or perhaps a sky blue piece, it made him feel she was near.

If he was really honest with himself, he didn't want to leave the home they had shared; he wanted to be left alone with his memories. Although sometimes his memories travelled too far back – back to the memories of Rosemary. But if he saw her beautiful, smiling face drift into his mind, he did everything he could to shut her out. He didn't want to remember that terrible time – and yet, and yet, he knew that as long as he lived he would never forget it, for who could ever forget something so truly awful?

****

"You know, my love, I'm rather worried about Sam," Lucy said to Kenny one evening.

"Why, my dear? I thought he was better now."

"Well, his leg is better, yes. But he's not happy. He said he was going to visit his nephew or niece but I'm sure he's done nothing about it."

"There's nothing to say he has to go, is there? Perhaps he's just not ready to socialise yet after losing Emily and then being laid up."

"Mm, that's true," mused Lucy. "But I'm not sure he should be shutting himself away like he is. He barely goes out of the house, except to his greenhouse."

"If he's taking an interest in his plants, that's a start. Why don't you invite him here? He might enjoy visiting his old home."

"Oh yes, that's an idea! I'll do that."

Lucy extended the invitation to Sam the next day. His eyes lit up.

"Thank you, my dear, I'd love to visit River View and see what changes have been made to it since I lived there."

"I'll pick you up tomorrow, about eleven then. I always cook lunch for Kenny. We eat around half past twelve. I thought it would be better for you to eat then rather than later. Then you can spend the afternoon with me and John. Perhaps have a stroll around the garden or down by the river?"

"That would be very nice, my dear, thank you. I'll look forward to it."

Surprisingly, he did look forward to it. He realised he hadn't had anything to look forward to for a good while, discounting leaving Sutton Court for home. It would be good to see his old home again.

Lucy turned up the next day on the dot at eleven. Sam was ready, looking smart in light grey trousers and a white polo shirt with royal blue trims around the collar and the short sleeves. He carried a light zippered jacket over his arm.

"It can sometimes be chilly by the river," he grinned when Lucy looked at his arm.

"That's true," she agreed. "Good thinking."

"Oh, just a moment," Sam disappeared into the house and came back carrying two bunches of flowers. He gave one to Lucy.

"These are for you, for being so good to me."

"Oh, thank you." Lucy took them and kissed him on the cheek. "They will look lovely on the kitchen window-sill."

Although burning to know, she didn't ask who the other bunch was for. She carefully stashed her flowers in the boot of the car and Sam put his in too.

John was in his child seat in the back and when he saw Sam he clapped his little hands and giggled with glee.

"Hello there, young man."

Lucy soon pulled up by the kitchen door of River View. She lifted John out and he ran towards the door, which she unlocked and they went inside. Sam looked around the kitchen and nodded appreciatively while bending down to fondle Clarry, who greeted him with enthusiasm, her whole body wiggling as she wove around him. Once she'd had her greeting, she settled down.

"Very nice," he said. "It looks so much better now. In my young days it was very basic with a range, a butler sink and a big wooden table, where Mum did all her baking and we sat and ate at. This is so bright and lovely with all the fitted cupboards and everything. All mod cons, as they say. How my mother would have loved to have a kitchen like this! Mmm, it smells lovely too – is that newly baked bread I can smell?"

"It certainly is! I still bake bread every day for us and for Madge's shop. The villagers love my bread, Madge always sells out. Here, would you like a slice? John will want one to help keep him going until we eat our meal."

Sam sat at the table and watched Lucy briskly cut slices from a loaf she took from the pantry and put one on a plate for him and another on a plastic plate for John, who was now sitting in his high chair. She spread butter on John's piece and little dabs of Marmite on it ("We all love Marmite") and cut it into fingers and handed John one, who immediately started to stuff it in his mouth. Sam spread some butter on his slice and ate with relish.

"This is wonderful bread. I must ask Madge to send me some in her next delivery."

"I'm glad you like it. Now, I must just get this cottage pie in the oven and then I'll take you round the house – when John has finished messing around with his Marmite fingers."

As she was talking, Lucy was busy at the stove and Sam smelled onions being cooked and heard the sizzle of minced beef being put into the pan. It reminded him of how his mother used to make cottage pie in this very kitchen; how many times had he smelled that very same aroma? His mother's cooking was plain but very good; they ate well, even during the war, because she grew her own vegetables in the triangular-shaped plot at the side of the drive. He supposed they had been lucky in many ways but he did so wish that his dad had come back from the war like Sid's dad had...

He was brought back to the present when Lucy cleaned John's face and hands with a damp flannel, collecting the bits of mangled bread off the tray of the high chair and putting them on the plastic plate on the table while she lifted her son out.

"He's falling asleep. I'm going to lay him in his cot for a nap, Sam. I'll be right back."

"Don't worry my dear, I'm perfectly fine."

The tour of the house was surreal to Sam. Lucy's Aunt Bea and Lucy herself had made the rather plain farmhouse into a charming home for a modern family. While they had kept all the old features in place, the whole house seemed lighter and brighter with the comfortable chairs and brightly-coloured cushions and curtains that made it all seem very cheerful but homely. Gone was all the dark-wood furniture and brown chairs of his day; that in itself lightened the rooms. Nevertheless, there was something about the house that, although it looked different in many ways, it seemed as if it spread arms around him and welcomed him back to his old home. It touched his heart and brought tears to his eyes as he felt the comfort of some unseen presence and yet it wasn't scary or worrying.

Lucy noticed. She brought him back to the kitchen.

"You can feel it, can't you?"

Without questioning her, Sam nodded.

"I feel it too. This house knows who belongs to it and welcomes them when they come. It did the same when I came, although I'd never lived here before. I had been here to visit Aunt Bea of course. But it's like the house enfolded me – and it's just done the same to you."

Sam looked at her; somehow, he knew and understood. She continued,

"I used to think it was Aunt Bea. In fact, I do see her, quite often. But then I realised that she'd felt it too when she came here. This is a house that needs to be loved and in return it loves those who do. I know it sounds silly, but I believe it."

"I think you're right. It's the spirits of all those who've gone before us, who have lived here. Sometimes, when I was a boy, after my father died, I was convinced that my dad was still here, watching over us and even more so after – after Rosemary..."

His voice faded away, his sentence unfinished. Lucy touched him arm in sympathy, absent-mindedly looking at the clock. Then she registered the time and exclaimed,

"Oh, my goodness, look at the time! Kenny will be here shortly and I haven't put the vegetables on! Good thing they're already prepared, they won't take long."

As she spoke, Lucy lit the gas under the saucepans that were sitting on the top and she gave a nod.

"There! They should be just in time for Kenny. Oh, I left the flowers in the car! I must get them. Shall I bring yours out too, or are you taking them somewhere later?"

"No, please would you bring them in?"

She nodded and disappeared out of the back door, Clarry scuttling after her. A few moments later, Sam heard the slam of the car boot being closed and Lucy came back, the flowers in her arms. She laid them on the worktop.

"Would you like me to pop yours in water until you are ready to take them?"

"Yes please."

Pouring water into a bucket, she put Sam's flowers in, still wrapped in their paper. Then she found a vase from a cupboard and deftly arranged her own bouquet. She fiddled about with them until she was happy with them and popped them on table as the door opened and in walked Kenny. He greeted Sam pleasantly and kissed Lucy's cheek as she fished knives and forks from a drawer.

"Hello darling, sit down, I'm just getting the pie out of the oven." Lucy busily set the cutlery out as she spoke and then headed to the oven.

"She's such a good lass," Kenny said to Sam as they sat at the table.

"You're a lucky man," commented Sam.

"I am indeed. She's not only beautiful but a great cook too! What more could any man want?"

"I thought you loved me for my wit and charm?"

"That too, but the food comes first!" joked Kenny. "Actually, I've been lucky all my life because my mum is a great cook too."

"She is that," agreed Lucy, "No wonder you're getting a bit tubby."

"Tubby? I am not tubby! What are you talking about, woman? Look at this muscle!" He flexed one of his brown arms.

Lucy patted his stomach. "What's this then?"

"That's relaxed muscle," he grinned sheepishly.

Sam smiled, enjoying their banter.

"Where's my little man?"

"He went down for a nap a bit later than usual."

"Oh. Well, I'll try to get home a tad earlier than normal so I can spend a little time with him then."

"That'd be very good. Now, I will have to put some cottage pie by for him but we must get on so you can get back to work."

"She's a slave-driver this one! Never lets a man have any peace, always shoving me back off to work," Kenny remarked to Sam while they watched Lucy put the food on the table.

"Well, you have to work hard to keep me the way in which I'm accustomed."

"There! You see, she only wanted me for my money!"

Lucy punched him lightly on his arm.

"Ow! She hit me!" Kenny gripped his arm as if in pain, then laughed and helped himself to some cottage pie, followed by mixed vegetables, fresh from the steamer.

The meal was a happy affair; Sam was quite sorry when the delicious meal was over and Kenny had to go back to the nursery.

"Perhaps we could go for a little stroll later?" asked Sam. "It's been a long time since I walked the river path."

"Of course, John would enjoy that. He'll be up soon and when he's had his lunch we'll go."

"I could do with a short nap myself. Would you mind awfully?"

"Of course not. Go settle yourself in the lounge. Both the chairs are recliners, so put your feet up. I'll get on with a few things while you're napping."

Sam took himself off and Lucy hummed as she worked in the kitchen, deftly washing up and tidying everything away neatly. She quickly made some cheese scones and popped them in the oven for later with a cup of tea after their walk. John's voice sounded through the baby monitor and she fetched him down. Sam was fast asleep in a comfy chair and they crept past By the time John finished his dinner, the scones were ready to come out of the oven and Sam had awoken from his nap.

He joined them in the kitchen.

"Oh, hello there! Do you feel refreshed?"

"I do indeed, thank you."

"Would you like a cup of tea now or when we come back from our walk?"

"Oh, I think later, I'm still full from that wonderful meal."

"That's good. I've made some cheese scones to have with our tea later." Lucy waved her hand at the scones, now cooling on a wire tray.

"Lovely, I love cheese scones. Haven't had one in ages."

"Something to look forward to then. Come on then, young man, let's get you cleaned up and your nappy changed. Then we're going for a nice walk."

Lucy lifted the small boy from his high chair and carried him out of the room. Sam took the flowers from the bucket, laid them on the worktop and emptied the water down the sink. When Lucy and John came back, the little lad was wearing a cute pair of red shoes, a blue cap with Thomas the Tank Engine on and his reins; they were all ready.

"Do you have a plastic bag or something I can wrap the stems of these flowers in, please Lucy? I want to take them with me."

"Oh yes of course."

She handed him a bag from a cupboard and he carefully wrapped it around the bottom of the flowers.

It was a particularly beautiful day for a walk by the river. The sun shone on the water as it rippled and danced on its way to Hereford. Birds sang in the trees and they saw a flash of bright blue as a kingfisher swooped into the water and up again in a trice, a small silver fish in its beak. John was very excited; it was a good thing Lucy was holding tight to his reins because he wanted to be down near the water!

They arrived at the gate to the meadow where Rosemary had been found, and it was here that Sam put the flowers, propped up against the gate post.

"This is where I always met her," he explained to Lucy. "I would wait for her or she would sit on the gate while she waited for me."

"Is that why Sid buried her here?"

"Yes." Sam said no more and Lucy didn't ask. She waited patiently while he stood with his head bowed for a few moments and when he turned to walk on, she caught a glimmer of a tear rolling down his cheek. Without a word, she tucked her arm through his and squeezed it. He responded by leaning his head towards her, returning her sideways embrace.

If Lucy had more questions, she did not probe; he needed this time for own thoughts. In any case, it wasn't her business. She just loved Sam and cared about him and wanted to comfort him.

John was at his entertaining best on the rest of their stroll and soon had both adults laughing at his antics. Delighted at everything he saw, from the trees to the smallest insect he spotted on the ground; he stopped suddenly and bent double to watch an ant as it hurried about its business.

Sam had only wanted to lay his flowers, and couldn't walk much, so they only went as far as the gate to the grounds of The Nursery House and back.

Upon their return, Lucy settled Sam into an outside chair and brought out tea and scones. They sat together, contentedly eating and drinking while John played with a trolley of bricks by their side.

"Very pleasant," remarked Sam. "This garden is beautiful. So different to the farmyard it was when I lived here. We never sat out like this, having tea."

"Aunt Bea created the garden. She absolutely loved this house and so do we."

Sam nodded and smiled.

"I'm glad to think that my old home is loved and I'm so happy that it's you that owns it, Lucy. You've been a wonderful friend to both Emily and me since you came. It's hard to remember you've only been here a few years, it seems like you've been part of us for ever."

"I feel like that too, strangely, although you know I lived in London for about three years before coming here. If Aunt Bea hadn't left River View to me I would never have come, I'd never have met my Kenny and been part of this wonderful community. I have a lot to thank her for."

"Some things are just meant to be, I always think."

"Would you like to stay and have dinner with us?"

"Oh no, I don't want to outstay my welcome! I've had a lovely day and am happy to go home shortly. When Kenny comes home it's your family time and I don't want to encroach upon that."

"But we would love to have you, of course you wouldn't be encroaching."

"No, I'll go home. I actually don't think I could eat another big meal after that very nice lunch."

Seeing that he had made up his mind, Lucy didn't try to persuade him further. Not long after, she popped John into his car seat and, after giving Sam two more cheese scones in a clean ice-cream box, she drove him home.

She helped him out of the car and watched him unlock his door. She made him promise he would come again to River View, then drove off as Sam waved to her from his doorway.

*****

Sam made his way into his snug sitting room and sat down heavily. Although he had promised Lucy, he probably wouldn't go to River View again. Today's visit was a pilgrimage in a way; to see his old home and to pay tribute to the girl he'd once loved.

His home was no longer the same and although he'd loved the changes to it, he wished in some ways he'd not seen it. Now, his memories of the house would be clouded by the knowledge of the present. However, he truly was glad that it was Lucy's home and she was happy there. She meant a lot to him and he wanted her to be content, wrapped around by that extraordinary house and in the love of her husband and child.

He looked across at his favourite photograph of Emily that still sat on a small corner shelf. She was young, beautiful and smiling, her shoulder-length hair blowing slightly in a breeze. Taken on their honeymoon, there was sunny blue sky behind her as she stood on a beach in Cornwall, tiny waves lapped gently at her feet.

He had only ever loved two women in his life, Rosemary and Emily. His love for Rosemary had been heart-stoppingly beautiful, a time of new discovery, full of innocence and delicate as a flower. There was no doubt she had broken his heart when she had dumped him. But Emily was a whole different matter. It had been many years before he loved again. He'd had girlfriends but he'd always measured them by Rosemary and each one came out wanting.

Now he realised that love wasn't like that; if you loved you didn't measure, didn't compare, you just loved.

He'd met Emily at university and the moment he set eyes upon her he'd loved her. All the rest of their lives together he never considered anyone else. She didn't have Rosemary's incredible beauty but she had qualities that made her perfect for him.

He knew eventually that what he and Emily had was far and away superior to what he'd had with Rosemary but he also realised that was what life was about. It was a journey of discovery of oneself and each experience built up and helped the understanding. Yes, he had been truly blessed to have found Emily. His life with her certainly hadn't *felt* like a punishment from God...

Chapter 39

It was about a week later when the message came through. Dan was pretty fed up. He'd read through the files and looked at all the emails and phone responses to the Crimewatch programme but there was nothing else he was able to pick out that would be any use. He ran his fingers through his thick hair, making it stick out in disarray. He was about to press the intercom to ask for a coffee when a knock came at his door.

"Come in," he growled and looked up to see Johnson, holding a piece of paper which he presented to his boss.

"What's this?"

"It's a message, sir, from a Mr Blackwood. He says he has the car you've been looking for."

"What?" Dan scanned the paper and looked up. "Find DS Grant please. Tell him we're going to Shropshire."

*****

"There it is! Castle Farm, up there on the left."

The Satnav had brought them straight up the A49 which ran from Hereford to Ludlow. Castle Farm, where Dave Blackwood lived, was not far from Richards Castle, just over the border of the county.

Grant turned onto the narrow road that the signpost said led to the farm. Eventually, they came to a large gate, on which there was a nameplate 'Castle Farm, Proprietor D. Blackwood.'

"Looks like we've found it."

Dan pressed a bell button on the gate and waited. A disembodied voice answered, 'yes, who is it?'

"Detective Inspector Cooke, Hereford Police."

'Ah, yes, come in.'

The huge gates swung open and Grant drove up the drive to the large house surrounded by outbuildings. A tall, well-built man stepped out of the main door just as the car stopped. He wrung the hands of the two detectives.

"Hello, I'm David Blackwood. Do come in. My wife Margaret is here too."

They were shown into a large room that was comfortably furnished, if not modern. A wood burning stove squatted in the inglenook fireplace but not lit. A woman came through.

"This is my wife, Margaret. Do sit down."

"Thank you." The two detectives sat on two upright chairs and he couple sat on the sofa.

"You say you have the car we are looking for?"

"Well, yes, I have an apology to make to you. We didn't see the programme when it went out. We always record programmes for when we have time to watch. A farmer's life is a busy one!" Dave laughed. "Margaret and I didn't see it until last evening – and I must confess it did cross my mind to keep quiet. I've had the car a long time you see."

"Where did you get it?"

"Well, that's the odd thing. I inherited this farm from my uncle. He had no children, you see and as I'd always shown an interest in farming and used to help him often, he left it to me when he died. He died in an accident, so it was sudden, like. When I started to examine what I'd inherited, I found the car under a tarpaulin in the corner of one of the barns. My uncle had a thing about old cars, he used to drive one and often went to vintage rallies, but I never saw this one before. I hunted through every piece of paper here, and although I found registration and ownership papers for his other vehicles, I never could find a thing to do with that one. He'd never shown it to me and no one seemed to know anything about it so I just kept it. Being interested in vintage cars myself, it's a hobby and a sideline of mine. But when I saw the programme, I recognised the number straight away."

"Can we see it?"

"Certainly, it's what you're here for, isn't it? Follow me."

They followed the farmer out the back and across a wide yard to a large building with big sliding doors. Mr Blackwood opened the doors and they were amazed at the sight that met their eyes. The building had many vintage vehicles of all sorts from different eras and was set out like a car museum.

"As I said, it's a sideline of mine and the main reason why I have big security gates at the entrance to my farm. Some of these vehicles are worth quite a bit and I wouldn't like them to be stolen. Until this moment, GT 314 has been my most prized car and by far the oldest."

They stopped by a beautiful vintage car, shiny black, the wheels with red middles and the leather upholstery buffed and comfortable looking. Dan couldn't believe his eyes; he never for one moment imagined he would find this car looking so pristine. He was very taken with it and it seemed so was Grant for he ran his hand lightly along the bonnet.

"Beautiful, isn't it? Model T Ford, 1932, in good working order too. I've restored all these cars but this one didn't need much work, it was in remarkable condition when I found it. Now, I suppose it will have to go back to the owner, unless he'd be willing to sell it to me or allow me to keep it here under permanent loan."

"We'll speak with him about it," said Dan. "There's no point in letting forensics have a go at it; your work will have destroyed any evidence there might have been."

"Yes, well, I'm sorry about that, like, but I had no idea it didn't really belong to my uncle."

"Of course you didn't. I don't suppose there was a case or trunk of clothes in it?"

Dave shook his head thoughtfully.

"No, sorry. I've not found anything like that in the house or on the premises anywhere either. We've been here over thirty years now."

"Mm. Yes, well, thank you for contacting us, Mr Blackwood. I'll leave the car with you for now but will contact Lord Smethwick to ask what he wants to do. If it's alright with you, I'd like the Crimewatch team to put out another bulletin about this. Would you mind if they came to film the car?"

"Not at all. Just ask them to let me know."

They left the huge barn and Dave closed the massive doors. They walked around the side of the house back to the car and shook the farmer's hand.

As Grant drove down the narrow lane to the main road, Dan said thoughtfully,

"Well, although we've found the car, I'm afraid it just means we have yet more questions to answer."

Chapter 40

Lord Smethwick was thrilled when he heard his father's car had been found.

"It's been on a farm in Shropshire all this time, you say? Well I never! Do you think Mr Blackwood would mind if I go up to see it?"

"Well, technically, it belongs to you, sir. Mr Blackwood was hoping to come to some agreement with you over it. 'Crimewatch' are going to do another feature on it so perhaps you might like to be part of that?"

"Indeed I would! How exciting!"

"I'll be in touch with you to let you know when they're going to film at Castle Farm. Perhaps you can come up then."

"Right you are, I'd be delighted. Shall I tell Doreen?"

"Well, I was going to call her but if you would like to pay her a visit, it would indeed help."

"Anything to oblige. I'll wait to hear from you regarding the programme then. Goodbye for now."

Dan chuckled as he put down the phone.

"He's happy as a sand boy! This must be the most excitement he's had in a long time."

"You're probably right, sir. I've been thinking..."

"Oh no!" Dan grinned. "What were you thinking?"

"Well sir, perhaps we should put this out on the local news in Herefordshire and Shropshire. Castle Farm is only just over the border from Herefordshire and I'm sure that the car didn't appear there by magic. Not everyone watches 'Crimewatch' but they might watch the local news. Someone might even know how the car got there or might remember seeing Henry Smithson in the area. If his car was there, he would have been. I can't believe nobody saw him at all. I do believe it's worth a try, sir."

"Hmm, yes, I agree. After all, we found Penny's granddad when we didn't expect to, and Agnes' sister Elsie from the Crimewatch programme. Old folk do tend to watch the news, don't they, especially the local news? It's almost like a religion with some of them."

"You're right, sir. Shall I get onto the television people in both areas?"

"Yes do. We'll aim to air it the day after the Crimewatch appeal and arrange to film at Castle Farm at the same time."

"Sounds good to me. I'm glad you thought of it, sir," Grant laughed at his boss.

"You can always rely on me, Grant."

Dan clapped his sergeant on the shoulder and Grant went to put their plans into action.

****

The date was set for the filming. Lord Smethwick travelled up to Castle Farm the day before, by arrangement with Dave Blackwood. The Lord came up by train and taxi.

The two men hit it off immediately and as soon as Lord Smethwick's bags had been brought in and he'd made his acquaintance with Margaret Blackwood, ('Do call me Ron, Lord Smethwick is so stuffy') they went off to the large barn to see the car.

Ron's eyes opened wider when the huge doors were opened to reveal the vintage vehicles inside.

"My word, Dave, old chap, you have quite a collection!"

"I do, but it was your car that started me off. I restored it and went from there. I restored them all."

"Did you now? Wonderful, wonderful. So where is the old girl?"

"Here she is."

Lord Smethwick was astounded when he saw the Model T.

"Is that really her? By jove, you've made a grand job of her! She looks like a new car."

"Well, she was in quite good condition when I came across her. She'd been covered up and was in the dry. Her tyres were flat but her upholstery and bodywork were good."

"Is she roadworthy?"

"She is indeed. Only, I can't take her out onto the road because I have no papers for her. But I've driven her around my yard."

"I'd love a spin in her."

"Well, I'm sure that can be arranged."

"Jolly good." Ron rubbed his hands in glee.

"Would you care for something to eat? You've had a long journey and I'm sure you must be tired. Margaret said she'd have dinner ready by six and it's getting on for that now. We have a big day ahead of us tomorrow; the film crews are going to be here at 8.30a.m."

During the meal and evening, Ron was like a boy in his excitement and enthusiasm about the next day's events and the car being found.

"I never thought I'd ever see it again," he remarked, "and I certainly never thought I'd see it looking so marvellous."

"What will you do now you've found it?" Dave couldn't hold back any longer; he had to know.

"Well, hmm, I'll have to think about it. Let's get the filming over with tomorrow and then we can talk about it properly."

Dave felt he couldn't push any further after that so he swallowed back his anxiety and offered his guest a drink instead. The rest of the evening, Dave and Margaret found that their guest was a very entertaining fellow and it was bedtime before they knew it.

****

The day after the filming, Lord Smethwick took his leave of Castle Farm. Dave was to drive him to Ludlow station and so his bags were duly stored away in the farmer's Range Rover.

"Thank you so much for putting up with me m'dear," he said to Margaret.

"You're welcome any time," she said. "Just give us a call when you want to come again."

"That's very kind of you. Goodbye then."

"I don't know when I've enjoyed myself more," the elderly Lord said to Dave as they drove.

"That's good."

"I'm going to leave the car with you. There's no point in me taking it home because I won't use it."

"Well, you could sell it, I suppose, it would fetch a good price, I should think, especially in such good condition."

"Maybe. But it's part of your collection now and I think it should stay there. Perhaps I can come up sometimes and have a little drive of it occasionally."

"Certainly, you're welcome any time."

"Perhaps the mystery of how it came to your farm will be cleared up one day."

"Well, perhaps, but I'm not holding my breath. Time will tell, I suppose."

Soon, Lord Smethwick was on the train that would take him to Devon and even before that, Dave Blackwood was driving back to his farm. Both men were well satisfied with the outcome of the elderly peer's visit.

Chapter 41

Sam watched the programme.

"Now for our next item. You may remember that we put an appeal out two weeks ago for information on a man called Henry Smithson and a 1932 Model T Ford that he drove. As a result of the programme, the sister of one of the murdered girls has been found and she positively identified Smithson as someone she had seen around the time of her sister's death. Also, surprisingly, the car he drove has come to light. It has been restored and is in a private collection on a farm in Shropshire. Lord Smethwick, to whom the car belongs, came up to Shropshire to see the car and meet the man who has restored it."

There followed a film of an elderly man and a burly farmer beside a very smart-looking open-top vintage car.

Interviewer: 'Mr Blackwood, when did you come across this car first?'

Mr Blackwood: 'When I inherited this farm, thirty-odd years ago, I eventually found it under a tarpaulin in one of the outbuildings. I had no idea where it had come from. I assumed it had belonged to my uncle who owned the farm before me, although I never found any paperwork about it. As I have an interest in vintage cars, I decided to restore it.'

Interviewer: 'Didn't it occur to you to contact the vehicle licensing office to try to find legitimate paperwork for it?'

Mr. Blackwood: 'No, I'm afraid I didn't. As I said, I assumed it belonged to me as it was here on the farm and as I wasn't going to take it out on the road, I didn't think it mattered.'

Interviewer: 'But when you saw our programme you contacted Hereford police.'

Mr. Blackwood: Yes, I got in touch with the police because I recognised the number plate.'

(The camera focussed on the number plate for a moment, then went back to the interviewer.)

Interviewer: 'Lord Smethwick, how did you feel when you were told the car had been found?'

Lord Smethwick: Well, of course I was over the moon, dear chap! Couldn't believe it after all these years. I was only a lad when it went missing, but I remembered it well.'

('I remember it well too,' thought Sam with a shudder.)

'Henry Smithson was my father's chauffeur, you know, and it was jolly inconvenient when he absconded with the car.'

Interviewer: 'I can imagine it was. Thank you, Lord Smethwick and Mr Blackwood'

The Interviewer now turned back to the camera and his voice continued while the film switched to a reconstruction. It showed a similar car with an actor who looked remarkably like Henry Smithson setting off from Letterton Hall and driving up the road, while the narrator told about the events of the disappearance of Smithson.

Narration: We are now asking again, is there anyone out there who remembers seeing this man and his car at any time after he left Letterton Hall in the spring of nineteen forty five and again after his sojourn in Sutton-on-Wye? Do you have any information as to how the car got to Shropshire? Was he seen in Shropshire or anywhere else? Perhaps he decided to dump the car because it could identify him? Did anyone see him do that? If you have any information, please call this number, we are waiting to hear from you.'

Feeling churned up inside, Sam switched off the television. He knew the actor wasn't really Smithson but the likeness was such that it had the effect of making him feel nauseous. It wasn't like him to drink but he dug around in the sideboard and found half a bottle of whiskey. He poured himself a glass and sat down to drink it, his hands shaking as he raised the tumbler to his lips. The liquid burned his throat and gullet on the way down. It wasn't doing him any good but he poured himself another.

By this time his hands had stopped shaking so much and his felt a little woozy. After he'd finished his second glass, he made his way to bed, hoping the alcohol would help him sleep and wipe out the bad dreams he was sure he would have after seeing Gilbert Trent/Henry Smithson's face before him on his television screen.

****

The following day a man walked into Hereford police station and said he had some information about the old car on the news.

The man, whose name was Jack Moseley, was immediately shown into Dan's office. Grant was there too and the two detectives shook hands with their visitor and invited to sit down.

"I was visiting my sister in Hereford and I saw the news last night," he began. "I live in Worcester but when I was a lad I grew up in Richard's Castle. My best mate was Rickie Blackwood who lived at Castle Farm."

"Ah...do go on, Mr Moseley." Dan leaned forward, one elbow on his desk, chin resting on the back of his hand.

"Well, I thought I'd come to tell you that the car just appeared one day in one of Rickie's dad's fields."

"It appeared?" Dan frowned.

"Yes. Rickie and I used to play in that area a lot. There are woods on the edge of the field. Well, one day the car wasn't there, the next day it was. In fact, we were the ones who found it. We ran to find Rickie's dad to tell him. He was very cross, there was a crop of wheat in the field but it turned out that not much damage had been done, because it was only just inside the gate."

"Didn't he try to find out where it had come from?"

"That I don't know. All I know is, it appeared on the farm and on the farm it stayed."

"And you never saw any strangers around?"

"Not that I remember, no. I was only a boy, as I said, but I think I would remember if I'd seen a strange man. We didn't get many strangers in those parts."

"I see. Well, thank you for coming in to see us, Mr Moseley."

"Not at all. I just wish I could be more help. That Smithson bloke sounds like he was a nasty piece of work. I'm glad he never saw my sister, she was sixteen then and very pretty."

"Indeed. I don't suppose you're still in touch with Rickie Blackwood?"

"No. He died in a car crash many years ago and not long after his mother died of cancer. They all said it was the shock from losing Rickie. He was their only child, you see. Poor Uncle Harry – that's what I called him – really went through a bad time. Good community there though, all the people rallied around him. But all the friendship in the world can't compensate for losing your wife and only child, can it? He was never really the same after that and he let the farm slide rather. His nephew Dave had quite a job getting the farm back into shape."

"He seems to have done a good job of it, the farm looks prosperous. Would you leave your contact details with us so we can contact you if we want to talk with you again? And if you recall anything else you think would help, please don't hesitate to get into contact with us. This number will get you directly through to me."

When Grant came back from showing him out, Dan said,

"So the car just appeared there. Extremely odd."

"Yes sir. It does rather look like Smithson dumped it because it was too conspicuous. After, all, many people had seen him in Sutton-on-Wye. It seems that he stayed there rather longer than he usually stayed anywhere."

"You're probably right. I don't think we're going to get any further with this. We've hit another brick wall. We've done our best for Rosemary and Joseph Baxter but maybe we won't find out anything else."

"Well, sir, you just never know. On the face of it, it seems you're right."

"Yes. But I'm not happy, Grant. This nose of mine tells me there's still something not quite what it seems."

Grant looked at his boss. His chief had intuition with things like this. Perhaps, he mused, something might yet turn up...

Chapter 42

The remains of Rosemary Baxter were released for burial once forensic experts were sure the bones could not tell them anything else. The Baxter family were to hold a funeral and what was left of Rosemary would be laid to rest with her parents in the churchyard.

The appointed day dawned grey and drizzly. Joseph Baxter felt that the weather matched his mood. It seemed surreal to be finally holding a funeral for his sister who had died many years ago and so had not been in his life since he was eight. Although he was sad that her life had been cut off at such a young age when she had barely had time to flower, at least he knew now what had become of her and was able to bid her a proper goodbye.

Lucy, bless her, joined his wonderful daughter-in-law Sheila produced a mountain of food for afterwards. Knowing the village as they did, they expected a large attendance, so the village hall was once again going to house the after-funeral gathering. In one way, they would have liked to have a quiet event with only the family present but they knew the village would want to show their support.

And indeed they did; when Joseph and his family followed the coffin into the church, all the seats were filled.

The Reverent Tony Trevithick had planned the funeral with Joseph and it was beautiful, with readings and poems and a choir from the local primary school sang 'All Things Bright and Beautiful'.

At the conclusion, the Rev. Trevithick said,

"Rosemary Baxter was a beautiful young woman who had everything to live for. But her life was cruelly snuffed out. All the hopes and dreams she might have had were terminated in a few minutes. Her family were led to believe she was living a life elsewhere, happy with the man she'd fallen in love with. Instead, she was lying under the earth close to her home, the rights of her family to grieve properly for her, taken away. Now, there is only Joseph left, but we, as his friends and neighbours in this remarkable village community, are all here to support him and morn with him. This service has been a joyful celebration of her life but it was for us because she moved on to her heavenly home many years ago. Our Lord told us that to take a life is a grievous sin, so we can rest assured that, even if Rosemary's killer escaped justice in this life, he will not escape the judgement of God.

We say to you, Joseph, we love you, we support you and may God bless you and your family and may your heart be peaceful, knowing that your beloved sister is enfolded safely in the arms of Our Lord. In the name of The Lord Jesus Christ, Amen."

As Joseph walked out of the church behind the coffin with Tom, Sheila, Lucy and Kenny, he spotted Sam sitting at the back, head bowed, tears running down his cheeks. His kind heart went out to him and he stopped and held out his hand.

"Sam, you and I are the only ones who knew and loved my sister. Come, walk with us."

"I shouldn't…"

"Yes, you should. Come."

Sam got up shakily and the two elderly men walked side by side from the church and across the churchyard to the gaping hole in the grass. When it was time to throw soil on the lowered coffin, Joseph handed some to Sam and they both threw in their handfuls.

When everyone else had gone, Sam was still at the graveside until he realised that the men were waiting to fill the hole. He walked slowly down the path to the road. There was no way he wanted to eat with people talking and laughing around him. He needed the quiet of his home.

*****

Lucy Baxter watched Sam linger by the graveside, then walk off, looking shaky as he leaned on his stick.

She hurried to her car, parked near the roadside, drove up to him and rolled down the window.

"Get in, Sam, I'll take you home."

Sam got in with some difficulty.

"You shouldn't be wasting time with me, you have lots of guests to be with."

"Don't be silly. I can afford a few minutes to pop you home. I knew you wouldn't want to come to the village hall. I have a bag with some food for you to eat when you feel like it."

"You're a wonderful girl. I'm very grateful."

It only took minutes to get to Sam's house and Lucy saw him in safely with his food and left him. She knew he didn't want company; she understood that Rosemary's funeral affected him probably even more than Joseph.

*****

When Lucy returned to the village hall, Kenny's face relaxed into a smile and he hurried to her side.

"There you are! I've been looking everywhere for you."

"I took Sam home. He was very shaky. I didn't linger, I just saw that he went in safely. I'm sorry you were worried but I had no time to let you know."

He squeezed her arm lovingly.

"You're forgiven – you and your soft heart. Will he be alright, do you think?"

"I hope so. It's all been too much for him, what with Emily's illness and passing and now all this about Rosemary. I'm hoping that he'll have a chance to settle down now it's all over."

"It's all been very dramatic . It looks like it was a big factor in Sid having his heart attack too. Granddad has coped quite well but he looks quite haggard at times when he thinks no-one will notice. This whole business has taken its toll on him, I'm sure."

"It's affected the whole village. You just don't expect something such happenings in a sleepy country place like this. I'm hoping this funeral will help Granddad Joseph to have closure. However, I have a feeling that Sam will be affected for the rest of his life."

When they arrived home, to be greeted effusively by John, who was being watched by Sylvie, she offered up a grateful prayer of thanks that she had been blessed with a lovely man who adored her and always treated her and all his family with kindness and consideration. She couldn't begin to imagine what it had been like to be married to Henry Smithson or be the daughter of a man who had been revealed as a rapist and murderer. She couldn't help reflecting and wondering, what was it that happened in a man's – or a woman's life, come to that – that would turn them into someone who wanted to kill other people?

Chapter 43

Elwyn Price and Kenny stood side by side looking at the stonework on the bridge.

"Hmm, we'll have to do something about that or it'll crumble before we know it. My cows won't be safe going over that afore long," remarked the farmer.

"That tree's going to have to come out; it's the roots that's doing it."

"Aye, you're right there, lad."

The picturesque stone bridge over the river Wye was old, there was no doubt about that, but it had always been sturdy. But the stonework on Elwyn's side of the river was being torn apart by an oak that Kenny estimated was around eighty years old. Probably self-seeded, the tree with roots, now thick and showing above ground had been allowed to grow unheeded and, being too close to the bridge, had become a danger to it.

"Well, it's my problem as it's my side."

"The first thing to do is to chop it down as far as we're able, then dig out the roots. That'll be a job and a half but it's got to be done. I have stuff to kill the roots at the garden centre but they will take time to die."

"Can't really wait for that, can we? Some of the stones are looking very lose. My cows going across there could be the end of it."

"I'll get a couple of my men to fell the tree first and we'll see how to go from there."

They nodded in agreement. Kenny headed over the bridge and Elwyn strode over his field in the opposite direction.

Later that day, Joe and Roger set to work on the tree. They cut off some boughs first so they could control it when it fell; it was tricky because the tree grew on the sloping bank of the river and they didn't want to risk it falling into the water. It definitely wasn't a straightforward felling job.

The sound of their electric saws filled the air; birds flew, squawking in protest, and small animals scurried unseen through the long grasses to find new cover. It took the two men the best part of the afternoon to get the tree down but the main trunk was easier than they'd anticipated. Elwyn and Kenny were back in time to see the tree come down. Elwyn had brought his tractor and they wrapped chains around it and drove away as the poor, beleaguered tree fell to the ground, effectively drawing it away from the river.

"Look at that! It was hollow!" said Joe.

"So it was," replied Kenny. "Another gale like the one that blew down the meadow fencing and it would have come down anyway – and probably pulled down half the bridge while it was at it! Just as well we've done it now. Good work, lads."

Elwyn and Kenny inspected the stump that remained.

"Tomorrow I'll get my lads to help dig out those roots. We can perhaps do some of it with a small digger but we'll have to be careful, we don't want to damage the bridge, although we'll have to take some of it apart and rebuild. I'll get my builder mate Will to come over and take a look tomorrow."

"I'm much obliged to you, Mr Baxter," the farmer said.

"Isn't it about time you called me Ken? After all, we've always been neighbours."

"Right you are – Ken. Your lads have done fine work today. I'll bid you good day now. My Mary will have the meal ready."

*****

The next day, Joe drove over the bridge with the small digger belonging to the nursery. This was to do most of the work but the most delicate parts would be done by spades and hand trowels. Kenny and Elwyn came to supervise the work as Roger arrived with more tools. They watched while Joe manoeuvred the digger; it was precarious because of the river bank but he was good at his job and soon had much of the earth around the stump scooped up. He dug around the crumbling tree bottom, making piles of muddy earth behind him. When he got to the bridge side of the tree, he was extra-careful in his efforts not to disturb the stonework further. Surface roots yielded and he moved to tip his load on his other side. As he did so, he heard a yell.

"Stop!"

Joe stopped the machine and watched as the other men stared at the earth he had just deposited. Kenny was pointing to something white sticking up. It looked like a bone.

Elwyn was the first back at the river bank and was peering into the hole the digger had just made between the tree stump and the bridge.

"Oh crap," he muttered, "not again."

****

Grant was in the office alone when Johnson came through with the message.

"Seems they've found another skeleton in Sutton-on-Wye, Sarge. Under a bridge, apparently."

"Is that so? Interesting. DI Cooke with want to know about this."

"But he's on a day off, sir."

"I know that, Constable, but he'll want to know, trust me."

As he dialled Dan's number, Grant smiled. His boss's nose was usually right and so it was proven again. Although it had been several weeks since they hit their last brick wall, he knew that the DI still mulled the case over when he wasn't busy. The detective sergeant had no doubt that this last find was connected to the previous one and he had no compunction in disturbing his boss on his day off, knowing that if he'd waited until the next day to inform him, his own head would be on the chopping block.

Chapter 44

Grant was right. Within minutes of his boss receiving his phone call, Dan was kissing his long-suffering wife goodbye and rushing off in his car towards Sutton-on-Wye. As he pulled up on the forecourt of River View, the kitchen door opened and there was Lucy, as usual looking impossibly young, wearing a very becoming flowery summer dress and with her hair in a pony-tail, little John resting on her hip.

"Hello again, Mr Cooke," she smiled. "This is becoming a habit."

"It is indeed, Mrs Baxter," Dan returned the smile. "Not that I mind coming here in the least. It seems that Sutton is strewn with bodies. Perhaps we should dig up all the fields and every empty space while we're at it, who knows how many more we'll find!"

"Don't you dare!" Lucy laughed. "We can't have my fields turned into mud with the village Summer Fete next month."

"In that case, we'll wait for each body as it is discovered then. It'll give me an excuse to come here again."

"You don't need an excuse, you're always welcome. Your team isn't here yet so would you like a piece of fruit cake that I made yesterday?"

"I would indeed! I can never resist any of your offerings, you know that."

He followed her into the house and watched her put the child down and move about her kitchen. When she handed him the plate with the slice of cake on it, he thanked her and took a bite. It was gorgeous.

"So, where was this one then, how was it found?"

"It's under the little stone bridge on the other side of the river. Kenny and Mr Price and two of the nursery workers were digging up a tree stump. The tree's roots were growing into the bridge and prising the stonework apart so they felled it. The body was in between the bridge and the stump. Elwyn is not happy about it." Lucy laughed. "He now thinks that every time he digs a hole he's going to find a body! I think it's put him off digging for life."

"Oh dear, poor Mr Price." Dan broke off as Grant appeared in the open kitchen doorway.

"I thought you would be here," Grant grinned. "The team have arrived, sir."

Dan popped the last bite of cake into his mouth and put the plate on the table.

"Thank you very much for that. It was delicious."

"No problem; you know where you're going this time, don't you? My husband is there, waiting for you."

Dan felt a momentary pang of guilt; he'd been dallying in Lucy's kitchen eating cake while her husband and Mr Price were waiting by the bridge. Oh well...

Dan and Grant strode quickly along the river path, their team following. It took but a few minutes to reach the bridge, where he could see on the other side that four men and a small digger sat waiting.

Between them, the four men explained to the detectives how this body had been found; it was pretty much the same as Lucy had told him already. Elwyn was, as Lucy said, fed up.

"I suppose this means that we won't be able to carry on repairing the bridge," he growled.

"We'll be as quick as we can, Mr Price," Dan assured him. "We don't need your men to stay; we know where you are if we want you."

The four men nodded.

"Is it okay if we take the digger away too?" asked Kenny.

"Yes, thank you."

Joe climbed into the cab and drove it over the bridge, Kenny and Roger following while Elwyn headed in the opposite direction. The team moved in to do their work.

An hour or so later, Lucy appeared with a large plastic lidded jug and some disposable cups and poured chilled home-made lemonade out for the thankful men. As she walked away, a wolf-whistle sounded and she turned as Dan cuffed a young officer on his neck. 'Sorry miss, don't know what came over me,' the young man apologised, red-faced.

"Apology accepted, officer," Lucy smiled and walked away.

"Don't you ever do that again," growled Dan. "I won't have common behaviour in my team, understand?"

"Yes sir." The young officer's face was even redder as he turned back to his task.

"Young upstart," said Dan, still annoyed. "Don't they teach them to behave better in Training?"

Grant grinned; he guessed that Lucy brought out the protectiveness out in the DI and that Grant could understand completely. She always looked so vulnerable but he guessed she was actually a lot tougher than she appeared and she had a kind heart to boot. She was also one heck of a good cook.

As he mused about Lucy, Grant's thoughts drifted to Jenny. They had daily contact through Facebook and he had been up to see her recently. The more time he spent talking with her, the more he wanted her to be his. He had to decide what he was going to do; should he ask for a transfer to North Wales to be near her?

Although he wanted that so much, he also acknowledged that he and Dan were a great team. Dan was the best chief he'd worked with and he would miss that if he moved away. However, he couldn't ask Jenny to leave all her family.

The time was soon coming when he had to make a decision, for he knew that Jenny wanted to be with him as much as he wanted her to be.

Right now, he had to think about the job in hand. He watched as the bones were gradually brought up out of the hole and laid out on the table under the 'tent' that had been hastily erected. It seemed to him that these bones were generally larger and didn't seem as delicate as Rosemary Baxter's.

Eventually, Dan had a word with the team leader and, after much nodding of heads, he walked away, calling Grant to join him.

"We can't do anything here. We'll leave them to it. I'll see the pathologist tomorrow."

When they arrived at River View, Lucy was outside with John on the lawn. Still wearing her floral dress, she now wore a wide-brimmed sun hat. The little boy wore a t-shirt and shorts and he also wore a hat. The two of them sat together in the shade of a tree, looking at a book.

"A very pretty picture," murmured Dan and Grant agreed. The men strode across the lawn.

"Grant and I are going now, Mrs Baxter. We can't do anything; our team are experts so we're leaving them to it. I feel that we're coming to the end of our investigations with the finding of this body."

"Oh, do you think so?"

"Yes, although it will raise even more questions."

"Who do you think it is then?"

"We won't be sure until forensics have done their tests but I feel, deep inside of me, that we have found Rosemary Baxter's murderer, Henry Smithson, or, as he was known here, Gilbert Trent."

Chapter 45

"I popped in to see Sam this afternoon," Lucy told Kenny that evening after John had gone to bed. "He's off to stay with his nephew in the morning."

"Good for him," replied her husband. "Let's hope it does him some good."

"Yes, he said he was fed up being there alone without Emily and hoped it would help him feel better. He also mentioned something about the possibility of selling his home and going into sheltered accommodation to have others to associate with."

"Sounds like a plan. It's hard to be alone, especially when you're that old and a man."

"Do you think it's harder for men than women?"

"Not really, no. But many women cope on their own. Men seem to be more emotionally dependant. But I'm sure it's very lonely for women too."

"He's given me a key to the house; he wants me to pop by now and then to make sure everything is okay with it and with his greenhouse. Apparently, Sue next door is away on holiday so he couldn't ask her. His greenhouse will be fine for a few days, he's set it up with a self-watering system."

"How enterprising of him! In that case, once a week will be fine. Did he say how long he would be away?"

"No, he was a bit vague. He said it depended on how long they could put up with each other! And that he may go straight on to visit his niece."

"Looks like he could be away for a while. I hope he's left details of where he is going?"

"Oh yes, he said he'll leave his nephew's and niece's contact details on the table in the kitchen."

"Did you tell him about the new body?"

She nodded. "He didn't seem very interested. He was full of thoughts of his impending visits he even had his case packed in the hallway."

"Let's go to bed early tonight, I'm tired. It's been a stressful day. Poor Elwyn is worked up about not being able to get on with repairing the bridge and I do feel for him. It won't be an easy job and time is of the essence; we need to get it finished before winter sets in again."

"It is a worry. But Detective Inspector Cooke said that they'd try not to delay too long. He seems pretty sure that the body is Gilbert Trent, you know."

"Does he? I wonder why? His car was found in Shropshire so he must have gone that way. How could he have driven his car there if he was dead? Oh no, it has to be someone else; perhaps a tramp that got gradually covered by nature."

"Perhaps you're right, my love. I did forget about the car. Now I come to think of it, it's not really likely to be him – a dead man can't drive a car."

****

The Reverent Tony Trevithick was a troubled man. He was walking back to the Vicarage at around ten thirty that same evening. Two hours earlier, he'd had a phone call from one of his parishioners who wanted to see him. He'd sensed the urgency in the voice so he went straight away. The door had opened immediately as if the person had been waiting behind it, listening for the knock.

Now, as he walked, his mind was in a whirl. He'd just heard the most fantastical story he'd ever heard in his career as a vicar. He didn't know what to do. He was not a Catholic priest and so wasn't bound by the confessional. However, he didn't want to rush into anything that would have bad results.

Instead of going straight home, he let himself into the church and knelt at the altar to pray.

****

Detective Inspector Cooke was at the pathologist's lab and, along with Grant, his faithful shadow, stood by the table that held the bones that had been brought in from the river bank at Sutton.

"Male, Caucasian, around thirty years of age. Strangulation. Multiple injuries to legs and head."

"Before or after death?"

The pathologist shrugged.

"Hard to say. I'd guess afterwards. Strangled first, I think. Been in the ground around seventy years."

Dan looked at Grant.

"Seems I might be right. Buried around the same time as Rosemary. Can't be a coincidence, can it?"

"It would seem not, sir," was the reply.

"Right, Grant, get onto the Devon police to organize a DNA sample from Doreen Chandler. I'll call her myself personally. "

He turned to the pathologist.

"Thank you, Stan. We'll get the DNA sample to you as soon as possible."

"Very good."

Dr Wilson covered up the bones and slid the body into a cold storage drawer.

****

Doreen Chandler was most interested in Dan's news of a second body being found in Herefordshire and was willing to give a DNA sample to help with the identification.

"It looks like someone killed him, Mrs Chandler."

"Whoever it was, we have cause to be grateful to him. It stopped him coming back and disrupting our lives and goodness knows how many more young women he might have killed. However, I'm a bit confused about how the car was found in Shropshire when he was dead."

"I have an idea about that. We know someone who may be able to give us some answers. I've always felt he was holding something back. Maybe he was protecting his friend but I'm sure he knows what happened. But you're right, whatever happened, they certainly did the country a favour. We'll keep you posted."

Grant came into his office as he put the phone down.

"I've made the arrangements with the Devon police, sir."

"Good. Mrs Chandler is happy to co-operate. Right, Grant, get your car keys, we are going out to Sutton-on-Wye."

"Who are we going to see sir? Mrs Baxter?" The Detective Sergeant grinned at the glare on his boss's face.

"No we are not!" he snapped. "We are going to have a little talk with Sam Williams."

Chapter 46

When Dan and Grant pulled up outside the neat bungalow in Dorothy Avenue, Lucy had also arrived in her little blue Polo and was about to go through the gate.

"Hello there, Mr Cooke and Mr Grant," she greeted them pleasantly. "Have you come to talk with Sam again?"

"Yes, Mrs Baxter, and I don't think you should be here when we do."

"Please let her stay, Chief Inspector, I'd like her to hear what I have to say."

They hadn't noticed the door open and Sam standing in the doorway.

"Sam! I thought you were going away today? I was just dropping by to make sure everything was okay."

"I was never going away, my dear – at least, not to family. I have been expecting you, gentlemen. Won't you come in?"

Puzzled, Lucy followed the men into the bungalow and shut the door behind her. They went into the small living room and sat down.

"Before you say anything, Mr Cooke, please let me say that I know the last body is Gilbert Trent. That's because I put him there."

Lucy gasped. "No! Sam, no, don't say that. I don't believe it. Are you protecting someone?"

Sam put his hand out to her and she took it, moving to sit next to him.

"It's alright, my dear. You have been so good to me, you deserve to know the truth. I hoped you wouldn't see me being arrested, because I knew I would be. I told you I was going away so that you wouldn't know until afterwards. I felt it would happen very quickly after Trent's body had been found. Mr Cooke is a clever man, I knew he'd work it out."

The elderly man looked towards the detectives.

"I'm sorry I held out on you for so long. I hoped the body of Trent would never be found. However, I now realise that all things work to the good and I won't be going to my grave knowing I'd committed a crime that I'd never owned up to. As the Reverend Trevithick said at Rosemary's funeral, it's a grievous sin to take another person's life, and I did that. I didn't intend to, but I did."

"Would you tell us about it, please, Mr Williams?" Dan put in quickly.

"Do you want me to go, Mr Cooke?" asked Lucy, half rising from her seat.

"No! Lucy, don't go. Let her stay, please, Mr Cooke."

Lucy sat down again and took Sam's hand. He looked at her lovingly and began his story.

Samuel's Story, Part Two

"Ever since Rosemary gave me back the cross I gave her, I'd been depressed. My friend Sid did his best to get me to carry on, go out with other girls and have fun. I did try, I really did, but it was impossible because Gilbert Trent hung around and I used to see them out and about together.

I tried to talk sense into Rosemary, that he was no good, and much too old for her but she wouldn't listen. She was completely besotted with him and couldn't believe that a sophisticated man like Gilbert would look at her, a young inexperienced country girl. He'd promised her the earth; he promised to marry her and take her to live in this big house he said he had in London. She believed everything he told her.

Whenever he saw me, he sneered at me behind her back and it showed me just what a horrible man he really was, which made me worry all the more.

Sidney was always taking me out, introducing me to girls and I did go to dances and so on. Sometimes he was able to borrow his dad's van and we used to go further afield, although we had to be careful because petrol was still rationed. But his dad didn't use it that much and he didn't mind (I have an idea he somehow managed to get some by black market dealings but I don't know for sure or how).

This one Saturday, I'd seen Joseph earlier in the day and he'd told me Rosemary had packed a case and was going away with Gilbert that evening. He said his parents, especially his mum, was very upset about it. Rosemary had promised to write to them once she was settled in London. They'd pleaded with her, told her she was too young to be married but she'd grown angry and told them that if Gilbert thought she was old enough then that was fine by her and if they didn't let her go with their blessing, she'd run away and they'd never hear from her again.

It was on my mind all day. I dared not try to see her again after the last time but, as every hour passed by, I became more and more upset. I had lots of work to do but my mind wasn't on it. About eight-thirty, Sid came to River View in his van. He thought he'd seen Gilbert Trent's flashy Model T up the lane at the back of our barn. I wondered what it was doing there. Anyway, I wasn't quite ready, so I finished shaving and the two of us went to his van. It was a hot night, especially for the beginning of September and we had the windows rolled down. As we pulled out of the drive, we noticed Gilbert's car was still there. Then we heard a scream. Sid braked hard and we grabbed torches, threw ourselves out of the van and ran towards the end of the lane, past his car and onto the river path.

There were no more screams but as we neared the bridge, we heard muffled sounds. We ran over the bridge and there, before our eyes, was Gilbert pulling up his trousers. Sid shone his torch around and it picked out Rosemary lying on the river bank, partly under the bridge. She looked like a broken doll, her head to one side, eyes wide and staring, her beautiful hair in disarray. Her best dress was torn down the front and the bottom was up round her waist, her lower parts naked, legs splayed and I could see blood. Gilbert saw us and he shouted,

'Ah, lover boy! You can have her now, she won't mind. If you do it now, it'll feel real, she's still warm.' And he threw back his head and laughed.

It was the laughter that did it. A loud rushing noise filled my ears and everything seemed to be red in front of my eyes. I heard an anguished howl and kind of knew I was moving forward. I had something in my hands and I was squeezing, squeezing. Eventually I realised someone had me by the shoulders and was trying to pull me away. It was Sid, trying to pull me backwards. My sight cleared and I loosened my grip and I stared in horror at the man before me, his eyes were also wide open and he slumped back when I let him go.

"You've killed him, man!" Sid exclaimed. I gasped with my hand to my mouth and stumbled back.

"Oh God, I've killed him! Oh, God forgive me, I've killed a man with my bare hands!" I sobbed. Then I went across to Rosemary and pulled her dress down and the front of it together. Sid shut her eyes. I looked at him.

"What are we going to do? We'll have to tell someone."

"No!" he exclaimed. "We can't tell anyone about this – they'll hang you man!"

I stared at him in anguish. "What can we do then?"

"We'll have to bury them!"

"Bury them?" I repeated, stupidly.

"Yes. We have to destroy all the evidence. We must bury them."

"Where?"

"Wherever we can. Here looks okay; the earth is quite soft and we can relay the grass on top so people don't notice. The grass on the bank is always rough."

"I'm not burying Rosemary near *him*!" I spat out the word.

"Okay, we'll take her somewhere else. Where?"

"The meadow. It's not far and that's where I used to meet her. Put her near the gate where the ground is rough. It's never ploughed there."

Somehow, the two of us carried Rosemary across the bridge and into the meadow. Sid crept to our barn to fetch a couple of spades. By agreement, he buried Rosemary because I couldn't face it. I gave him Rosemary's cross, which I'd always worn around my neck since she gave it back to me, and asked him to put it in with her. I hoped it would make up to her for not having a proper funeral and not being laid to rest in a proper burial ground.

While Sid buried Rosemary, I buried Gilbert. But I'm afraid that, before I put him in the hole, I lost my temper with him again because he seemed to be looking at me with his wide-open eyes and shouted at him and kicked him on his head and other parts of his body. I was livid with him for what he'd done to Rosemary and for putting me in danger of being hanged. Then I tipped him in the hole anyhow and covered him up quickly, relaying the grass on the top as we had said.

By the time I'd finished I was sweating and I knew Sid would be too. We were both big, strong, strapping lads; we were farmers after all, but the digging was hard work and it was a hot night.

After that, it was far too late to go out, so we took the spades back to the barn and I walked with Sid to his van. It was then we saw the car.

"We have to get rid of that car! If they find it here, they'll hunt around these parts."

"How can we do that?"

"We'll have to take it somewhere and leave it."

Luckily, Trent had left the keys in so we had no trouble starting the Model T with the handle. Sid drove it with me following in his van. He left it in a field just over the border of the county and we drove back home in the van.

Sid and I made a pact that we would never breathe a word about it to anyone and we were each other's alibis should any suspicion fall upon us. It wasn't until recently when it was obvious that I was being suspected in the murder of Rosemary that Sid spoke up to try to protect me.

However, all these years I've had no peace. I have a firm belief in God and I knew murder wasn't something He looked upon kindly. I often wondered if our inability to have children was a punishment for what I'd done. I've done my best to lead a good life ever since that time; I was a faithful husband and a good teacher and helped numerous children and other people. But all the time the fact I'd killed a man with my bare hands haunted me.

When I was younger, I expected all the time that the law would catch up with me. My only excuse for what I did in covering up the murders was that I was very young and extremely afraid of the noose. When hanging was abolished, the time had gone when I could confess. By that time I was studying to teach and had met Emily and couldn't bring myself to own up. In any case, I didn't want get Sid into trouble. He wasn't responsible for either of the murders; he was only protecting me. I'm sad that the strain of the happenings recently brought about his death."

Sam stopped speaking and silence filled the room. Lucy squeezed his hand and he gave her a tremulous smile.

Dan cleared his throat.

"Samuel Williams, I hate to do this but I am arresting you for the manslaughter of Henry Smithson and for concealing the deaths of the said person and that of Rosemary Baxter."

"No!" Lucy cried, jumping to her feet. Sam put his hand out to her.

"It's alright, Lucy, don't fret. The Inspector is right to arrest me. I must face this. 'Be sure your sins will find you out' goes the saying and it's true. I have been found out and I don't wish to hide any more. I'll take whatever comes. It doesn't matter what happens to me now. My Emily is gone and there is no one else that cares for me, so I'll take my punishment."

"I care, Sam!" Lucy was wild-eyed with distress.

"Look after things for me, my dear."

With a nod she watched dumbly as Grant took Sam's arm.

"I don't think there's any need to cuff him, Grant."

The sergeant nodded, and guided Sam out to the car.

"I'm sorry I have to do this, Lucy," Concerned about her, Dan didn't realise he'd used her Christian name instead of Mrs Baxter.

With tear-filled eyes she asked,

"What will happen to him, Mr Cooke?"

"We'll take him down to the station to sign a statement. I'm afraid we will have to detain him until he goes before the Magistrates' Court, who will probably release him on bail because he's no threat to anyone. He will be tried in the Supreme Court, probably soon because he has confessed and will plead guilty. It'll be up to the judge to decide what will happen then."

"So, he could be home again in a couple of days while he waits for the trial?"

"It's likely."

She nodded. "I'll look after him. It will be hard waiting for the trial."

He put his hand on her shoulder.

"You're a good girl. Sam is lucky to have you for a friend."

"Poor Sam. What a terrible thing to witness; the girl he loved being so brutally treated and then murdered."

"Yes. Strictly off the record, I have a lot of sympathy for his situation and I understand why he acted the way he did. Any man would want to kill the beast who'd done such a thing to a woman he loved. But of course, we can't take the law into our own hands."

"No. No, of course not. But I still feel more sorry for Sam than anything else."

Dan patted her shoulder and left her then to get in the waiting car.

****

As Dan drove the car away, with Grant and Sam in the back seat, the Detective Inspector wished even more than Elwyn Price had that the bodies of Rosemary Baxter and Henry Smithson had never been found.

****

After Sam's confession, there was no need for the DNA testing but it was done anyway, just to be sure Gilbert Trent was Henry Smithson. Needless to say, it was.

"Would Sam Williams really have been hanged?" asked Doreen when Dan called to tell her the results of the test.

"Quite possibly, although there were mitigating circumstances and it was manslaughter, not murder. Murder is premeditated."

"Poor old man! I'd like to bet there were others who really would have liked to do what Sam did. I know Henry was my father, but he was bad, through and through. He deserved what he got. In fact, he actually deserved to hang.

"At least my mother was spared that shame and I'm thankful for that but I don't blame Sam at all. It must have been awful for that boy to see the girl he loved in that state. Poor lad. And poor man, to have carried that guilt all these years."

"You're very understanding."

"I suppose I am. I have no feeling for my father, Mr Cooke, especially now I know exactly what he was. Well, at least we have an end to all the wondering."

"What do you want to do with the body? It's your decision."

"I don't care what you do with it! Throw it on a compost heap for all I care! I'm not paying for a funeral for him, he never did anything for me and he was wicked, Mr Cooke, wicked! I never want anything more to do with him, so just stick him in a hole somewhere, or cremate him."

"Well, I guess I can understand that. Just as long as you're sure. I'm equally sure that the good people of Sutton-on-Wye won't want him there either!"

"No, you're right there. Well, goodbye, Mr Cooke and thank you very much."

"Thank you for your help and understanding. Goodbye."

Chapter 47

Sam went before the magistrates the day following his arrest. He was, as Dan had predicted, let out on bail; they deemed he was not dangerous to the public. He was brought home in a police car and Lucy was there to meet him, having been called by the DI.

He seemed to have aged several years overnight.

"Oh, Sam, are you alright? I've made you some tea."

"Bless you, my dear."

Lucy helped the elderly man over the threshold and into the lounge.

"You sit down and I'll bring it in."

He sat heavily on the sofa and put his head in his hands. Lucy looked at him with concern. She sat next to him and wrapped her arms around him.

"Was it bad, Sam?"

He sat back and sighed.

"If you're asking if I was treated badly, no, I was treated gently. Mr Cooke was quiet and patient. All I did was repeat how everything happened and then I had to sign it. Being locked in a cell wasn't very nice. For the first time I experienced what could happen to me after my judgement. I was afraid of being hanged, but being locked up is almost as bad and I could spend the rest of my life locked up, and what for? For killing the b****d who should have been hung. That twenty-four hours I spent in custody gave me lots of time to think. At the time, I couldn't believe I'd actually killed a man and felt bad about it, shocked I'd been able to. Last night, I saw for the first time that what I did to him actually gave him an easy way out. If Sid and I had run to a phone instead of confronting Trent, he would've had his just desserts. I understand there were other young women he murdered as well as my Rosemary.

"All my life I've felt guilty. Guilty that the Baxters never knew about their daughter's death and guilty that I've hidden what I did for all those years and Sid had to keep the secret too. I never told my wife, so I kept a secret from her, which a husband should never do. What will she say to me when we meet again?"

"I think she will still love you. I think she'll understand."

"Do you? Even though I'm a killer?"

"You're not a killer, Sam. You were young and you reacted to the shock of seeing what he'd just done to Rosemary. You've never killed again, have you?"

"No, of course not."

"Then you're not a killer. You made a mistake and let your anger drive you. You're not a killer by nature, not like Henry Smithson."

"How can a man do something like that? Rape and murder all those young women?"

"I've no idea. Whatever happens to you in the future, you should always remember one thing."

"What's that?"

"That it's probably quite likely that you saved other young women from suffering a similar fate at his hands."

Sam nodded slowly.

"Yes, I suppose you might be right there."

Lucy patted his knee.

"I'll get that tea."

****

Cessy arrived to see Sam the next day.

"Come to Sutton Court and let us look after you, Sam," she said. "You shouldn't be on your own at this time."

He sat and thought for a few minutes.

"Thank you, Cessy, my dear, but I feel I would like to stay here. It might be the only time left for me to be in my own home. After I've been to court, who knows where I'll be?"

She nodded and patted his knee gently.

"I understand. But I am worried about you being here alone."

"Oh, I'm not alone much! Susan pops in and out and Lucy comes every day, bless them. And other people have been too."

"Well, as long as you're sure. But if you change your mind, just call me. You can have a room of your own upstairs and be with other people or not, whatever you want."

"Thank you. I'll think on it."

The days were okay; he could get by. The nights, however, were not so good. He had many wakeful nights, with everything going round and round in his head. When he slept, he had nightmares, about the seventy year old murders and about going to prison. It was constantly on his mind. Although he was always glad to see Lucy and Susan, he became withdrawn and reclusive. Often, when people knocked on his door, he would not answer but wait, holding his breath, until they went away.

He had to wait two months for his case to come up in court. The night before the hearing, he dreamed he was walking along the river path, hand in hand with Emily. Then, as she turned to kiss him, her face turned into Rosemary's and then into a grotesque version of the dead girl's face and he realised he was looking down at her skull in a deep hole. Pain gripped his chest and he lay still and stiff for a while, waiting for his heart to calm down and the pain to ebb away.

It was time to get up and face the day – the day he'd been dreading for over two, very long months.

Lucy arrived on the dot of nine thirty and Sam was ready for his appearance in court at ten thirty. As he was about to get in the car, Susan rushed over and gave him a hug.

"I'll be thinking of you, Sam. Good luck!"

"Thank you, my dear. And thank you for everything. You've been a wonderful neighbour."

She smiled.

"I'll see you later. Bye for now."

Settled in the car as they drove off, he murmured, "I wish I could be as sure that I'll be back later."

Chapter 48

The Prosecution Counsel, Clive Thomson, presented the case to the court. Joseph Baxter had been called to give evidence. He had stated that his sister, Rosemary Baxter, had gone out on the evening of September tenth and not returned. His parents had later discovered she had taken her clothes and personal belongings away in a suitcase. He was shown the cross on a chain and said that his sister had been in possession of a necklace like that but could not be one hundred percent sure it was that one.

Florence Hind swore the necklace was one and the same.

"Rosemary showed it to me after she'd been given it. I saw it close up. I told the Detective Inspector it was the same."

The Defence counsel challenged her.

"How can you be sure it is the same after seventy years? Surely the memory doesn't retain that much detail for so long?"

But Florence was adamant and would not be moved.

When he stood in the witness box to give his evidence, Sam looked around the courtroom and was astonished to see, not only Lucy, but Kenny, Susan, Cessy, the Rev. and Mrs Trevithick, Elwyn and Mary Price and many other people from the village. Many nodded and smiled as his eyes met theirs. Tears welled up and his hands shook on the wooden plinth in front of him as he took the oath.

The Prosecution counsel said: "Mr Samuel Williams, you have pleaded guilty to the charge. Please tell the court, in your own words, what happened on the night in question."

Samuel stood for a moment and then began to speak. There was complete silence in the room as everyone listened to his story. Lucy and the Rev. Trevithick had heard it before but Sam was aware that this would be the first time for Joseph. When he reached the part where he and Sid came upon Trent having just murdered Rosemary, Sam broke down as he described the state she was in.

"Take your time, Mr Williams."

Sam managed to pull himself together.

"I'm sorry, Your Honour. Even after all these years it still upsets me."

"Don't worry, Mr Williams. Are you able to continue?"

"Yes Sir. Um…as I said, she was lying there and he looked at me and made a joke and laughed."

"Can you remember what he said, Mr. Williams?" asked Mr Thompson.

"Oh yes," Sam hung his head. "But it was so disgusting, I wouldn't like to repeat it."

"Tell us, please?" prompted the Counsel.

He took a deep breath. "Very well, if I must. When he saw me, he laughed and said, 'Oh, lover boy. You can have her now, she won't mind. If you're quick, she'll still be warm.' Then he laughed again."

An audible gasp came from the spectators.

"I lost control and went for him and caught hold of him round his neck and squeezed and squeezed. Sid tried to pull me off but I was strong then and I resisted. All I could hear was a roaring in my ears and I felt like I was in a red fog and couldn't see properly. When Sid finally managed to get me to let go, it was too late. Trent was dead."

Samuel continued to tell how they had buried the bodies and drove the car over the county border.

Mr Thompson sat down and Sam's Defence Counsel, Mr John Portland, stood.

"Is there anything else you would like to tell the court, Mr Williams?"

"I was young and afraid, sir, afraid I'd be hanged. I was stupid, I know, and I did wrong. I've worried about it all these years. I'm glad it's out in the open now and sorry we hid the bodies because the Baxter family never knew what happened to their girl. I want to tell Joseph Baxter I'm deeply sorry for what we did."

Sam looked at Joseph, who looked back at him steadily and gave a small nod of his head.

"Thank you, you may stand down now, Mr Williams."

The court watched while Sam was helped back to his seat next to his counsel.

The prosecuting counsel stood up.

"Your Honour, this man, Mr Samuel Williams, has admitted to the manslaughter of Henry Smithson, known in this area as Gilbert Trent. He was a young man then and had a temper. He strangled the man in a fit of temper and then, assisted by his friend, Sidney Price, attempted to cover up his crime by burying the body and that of the girl, Rosemary Baxter, thereby committing another crime of not reporting the two deaths. Unfortunately, Mr Sidney Price is no longer alive to testify but the police do have a statement which he gave them before he died stating that he buried the body of Rosemary Baxter. Whatever the circumstances, Mr Williams should not have taken the law into his own hands; it was for the law to decide Mr Smithson's fate as Miss Baxter's murderer. I therefore ask for the maximum sentence for manslaughter."

He sat down and Mr Portland stood.

"Your Honour, my client, Mr Samuel Williams has indeed pleaded guilty to his crime of the killing of Mr Henry Smithson and to that of hiding the deaths of Smithson and Miss Rosemary Baxter. He did, as he admits, kill Mr Smithson in a fit of temper. However, see again the picture of the young Samuel, upon hearing a scream, runs with his friend towards the sound.

" In front of his horrified eyes, he sees the girl he loves, her clothes torn, her body bloodied and obviously dead and the man who has just perpetrated this wicked act, in the process of pulling up his trousers, having just flung the girl aside. The man laughs and makes fun of the young man's love for the girl by suggesting he should 'have his way with her' while she was 'still warm'.

"I would defy anyone, coming across such a situation and being taunted thus, to be able to just walk away. Samuel was young, barely eighteen at the time and he didn't stop to think about the consequences. The pain of seeing the girl he loved, once beautiful and vibrant, now bloodied and flung aside like a useless rag doll, was too much for him and he did what any man would want to do, he went for the man laughing at him. Clouded by his emotions, he squeezed the life out of Smithson.

Afterwards, realising the reality of what he'd done, and now afraid because of his friend's assertion that he would be hanged, the two young men hid the evidence. Samuel didn't want his beloved to be buried near the man who'd killed her, so Mr Price buried her in the field, by the gate where the two lovers had always met, and Smithson was buried under the bridge where he'd committed his heinous crime. Then, afraid that if the car was found, the bodies might be searched for in that area, they took the car and abandoned it over the border in Shropshire.

"Your Honour, we know Smithson committed similar acts on other young women in various parts of the country. We don't know for sure if he would have been caught, even if the two boys had reported seeing him. He was a master of disappearing acts, by all accounts. Would he have raped and killed again?

"Most likely.

"Samuel Williams has lived with the guilt of his crime for seventy years. He is sorry that he helped to deceive the Baxter family. He is glad to have finally been able to admit to what he did but he is an old man now and may well not have many more years left. But he has spent his entire life trying to atone for what he did by living an exemplary life. When he strangled Smithson, the balance of his mind was very much disturbed after what he'd just seen of the man's victim. For these reasons, I plead for leniency for my client. Thank you, Your Honour."

Justice Peter Clifford announced there would be a recess of half an hour while he considered his verdict.

When the court was reconvened, Samuel was asked to stand.

"Samuel Williams, you have pleaded guilty to the manslaughter of Henry Smithson and to that of hiding the deaths of Smithson and Miss Rosemary Baxter. Obviously, because of your plea, I have to find you guilty. However, I have carefully considered your statement and considered that of your counsel.

"I am sure that any man sitting in this room today would have great sympathy with you over your finding the girl you loved in the state you described and would probably want to do what you did to the man responsible if they found their wife or girlfriend is such a situation. However, we cannot take the law into our own hands. What would our country be like if we all did that? Then, having done that, you hid your crime and his by hiding both the bodies.

"Your friend's assertions that you would be hanged was a real fear, also understandable, especially since you were such a young man but I do feel that, even in those days, you would not have been, since it was manslaughter and not murder.

"Smithson would most definitely have been hanged, because he was a serial rapist and murderer. However, such conjectures on our part are not helpful. I do agree with your counsel that the balance of your mind was profoundly disturbed at the time of the killing.

With all these considerations in mind, for the manslaughter of Henry Smithson and the concealing of two deaths, I sentence you to one year, suspended, with twelve months' probation. This is the judgement of this court."

Samuel looked at John Portland.

"What does that mean?"

"It means you are free to go, Mr Williams."

"Oh! Thank you. Thank you very much."

"Congratulations, Mr Williams. You can go home now and enjoy the rest of your life. The cloud over you is passed and gone."

They shook hands and Mr Portland strode away. Samuel turned and right behind him was Lucy, Kenny and Joseph. Lucy put her arm around him.

"Come on, Sam, let's get you home."

Home! That sounded good to Sam. He saw Joseph and did not know how to meet his eyes.

"I'm sorry, Joseph."

Joseph put his hand on Sam's shoulder.

"I'd like to come over to see you later. Perhaps tomorrow?"

"Oh, erm, yes of course. Any time."

"I'll take you home, Sam," Lucy put in. "Kenny will take Joseph and get back to work."

"Thank you. I do appreciate your support. In fact, I appreciate everyone from our village who is here, I'm so blessed to have such good friends."

"There you go! You're well loved in Sutton and just about everyone thinks what you did wasn't altogether a bad thing."

"Well, I've always thought it was a bad thing and I'm glad it's all out in the open now."

Chapter 49

Lord Smethwick and Dave Blackwood were interested to hear how the Model T ended up at Castle Farm.

"I have a lot to thank Samuel Williams for. If he'd not taken that car away and left it in the field of Castle Farm, I would never have met Dave Blackwood and would not have someone to share my interest in vintage cars. It rather seems to me that Henry Smithson got what he bally-well deserved. What a bad lot he was. Mr Williams did the world a favour," blustered Lord Smethwick down the phone. "I'm sure my father would be very upset if he'd known what his precious chauffeur was up to. A good thing he's not around to hear about it. Poor Pater, he set a lot of store by Henry Smithson, bent over backwards to help him and his family."

"No one would ever blame your father for what Smithson did. And I'm sure Mrs Smithson and her children are grateful to the late Lord Smethwick. I know Doreen thinks a great deal of him and you."

"Oh yes," further bluster, "I know she does, yes, oh yes."

And indeed, Ronald Smethwick often spent time at Castle Farm, especially when Dave was due to take his vehicles to a vintage car show. The Model T was often taken out, sometimes driven proudly by the elderly Lord and sometimes by Dave.

On his second visit to Castle Farm, Lord Smethwick handed Dave a document. The farmer was moved when he realised it was a document transferring ownership of the Model T, registration number GT 314 to him. He looked at the old man incredulously.

"Are you sure, Ron?"

"Oh yes, m'boy. It's only right that you should have it, after all, you've looked after it all these years thinking it was yours. At first, I intended to leave it to you in my will and then I thought, no, you should have it now. Saves any complications later. I am a peer of the realm, dear boy, and as such everything I do is examined and looked at and someone might take it into their head to contest something, although who might be out there to do that, I haven't a clue. I'm the last of the line. Anyway, have it with my blessing, as long as you let me come here and have a drive sometimes."

"Of course. You're welcome any time you like and in fact you can drive any of my vehicles that you fancy. I'll insure all of them for you."

Ron put his hand on the younger man's shoulder; there were tears in his eyes.

"You know, lately I've lived a pretty lonely and pointless existence. Most of my close buddies are either dead or incapacitated. Now, once again, I have something to look forward to. Oh, I know that perhaps vintage cars are a tad pointless but they do give pleasure and it helps us remember the past and keep a bit of it alive. That's not pointless, is it?"

"No, it's not, Ron. Look, why don't you give up that monstrous house of yours and come and live here?"

"It's a good thought but I'm pretty skint you know. I don't have the means to buy even a small house. That monstrous house, as you call it, has pretty much cleaned me out; death duties are death to places like that. I'm lucky the National Trust have rescued it, or it would have been lost before now. I'm proud of the ancestral home but I'm just a lodger there really you know."

"There's an empty cottage on the farm here. I'll have it done up and you could live there. I could do with someone on hand to help me with the cars because I'm a very busy farmer you know." Dave winked secretly at his wife and she smiled her approval. "Why don't we wander over there and take a look, see what you think?"

"That's a great idea. Dinner will be ready by the time you come back," said Margaret.

They took Dave's Land Rover to the cottage. It was surprisingly modern and roomy with one bedroom. It stood in its own small garden that was in full bloom with roses and dahlias and other summer flowers, if in rather chaotic disarray.

"It's been empty for about three months and I have no one else to put in it. I'm afraid the garden is a little wild because no one has tended it for a while."

"It's lovely," Ron was taken with it. "I can't wait to see inside."

It was just as delightful inside and the elderly man felt immediately at home.

"This is just the ticket! I'd love to live here if you're sure, m'boy?"

"Of course I'm sure, or I wouldn't have offered it. If the stairs become difficult to climb, it's a good staircase for a stair lift."

"Wonderful. It will take a while to get up here; I'll have to arrange it legally with the National Trust."

"I will have it painted if you tell me what colours you fancy and it will be clean and ready when you come."

"Oh, I'll be happy with whatever you do."

"I'll get Margaret onto it. She's great at things like that."

It was two happy men who joined Margaret for dinner half an hour later. Lord Ronald Smethwick was all set for a big but exciting change in his life. He could hardly wait.

Chapter 50

Relieved to get home, Sam sank into his favourite chair. Lucy made him a cup of tea and he took it gratefully.

"I've left you a plate of dinner," she said, "Just warm it in the microwave when you are ready."

"Thank you, my dear."

"Now, are you sure you're okay for me to leave you?"

"Oh yes. I'm so relieved it's all over, a weight has been lifted off my shoulders. I'll have a nap and then get my food."

"In that case, I'll leave you to it. My baby will be thinking he doesn't have a mummy."

He caught hold of her hand.

"I can't thank you enough for all you've done for me. You've been a wonderful support and help, I wouldn't have coped without you."

Lucy kissed the leathery cheek.

"No problem. I'm glad it's all over too. You can make plans to visit your family now without this hanging over you."

"Yes, I can do that. Goodbye, my dear."

"Don't worry about the plate, I'll collect it when I call in tomorrow."

"Thank you."

Lucy gave him a cheery smile and went out of the room, shutting the door quietly behind her. Moments later, he heard the sound of the front door being closed and shortly after her car engine started up. Sam put his head back on his chair and was asleep in moments.

****

That afternoon, when Sam answered a knock on his door, to his surprise, there stood Joseph.

"Oh." Embarrassed, he didn't quite know what to do.

"Sam, I'm sorry to bother you today as I'm sure you must be frazzled after your ordeal earlier. I intended calling tomorrow but I had a strong feeling I should come today. So I got young Kenny to drop me off." Joseph was quick to explain. "Can I come in?"

"Oh, erm, of course." Sam held the door wider and stood back to let him in. "Go into the living room. Would you like tea, or coffee?"

"No, I'm fine. I've only just had lunch. Come and sit down with me."

They sat comfortably opposite each other until Joseph leaned forward a little.

"I needed to come. I want to tell you that I understand completely why you did it. When I heard what had happened to my sister, I felt I wanted to kill Trent myself. He got what he deserved, except perhaps he should have been hanged. But there was no guarantee he would have been caught if you'd let him go. On the one hand I wished we had known Rosemary was dead, but on the other hand, I'm glad my parents didn't know. I honestly don't think my mother would have got over it, ever. I long suspected she was dead but I never let them know I thought that."

"I should have told your family. Would it be too awful of me to say that I feel worse about hiding her death than I do about killing Trent? Although of course I feel bad about doing that too. When I look back, it's strange. I can't believe sometimes it was actually me who did it. It's almost like it happened to someone else."

Joseph nodded. "I can understand that. It's to do with the passage of time, combined with the fact that it was completely out of character."

"I suppose that's it."

Silence reined for a few minutes, each of them deep in his own thoughts.

"Anyway, Sam, I came to tell you that I don't blame you or hold anything against you. I'm glad to know what happened to my sister and now she is buried in her rightful place with our parents and has given me closure. As for Trent, or Henry Smithson, I hope he rots in hell."

"So do I. I just hope that I'm not rotting with him," said Sam, gloomily.

"I don't think so. He was out and out wicked. You're not."

"Hope you're right."

"I'm sure I am," was the firm answer. "Rosemary didn't know when she was well off having you for a boyfriend. And you made Emily happy. Wicked men don't have a lifetime of contented marriage. Look at Trent's poor wife and family. You lived an exemplary life after you killed that man and it was something that happened because the balance of your mind was disturbed. Goodness knows, almost any man would want to do the same in your position."

"That doesn't make it right though."

"Maybe not. But it was a natural reaction and you were very young."

Sam nodded thoughtfully. "I suppose."

A knock came at the door. Joseph stood up.

"That'll be Kenny. Now, you must try and put all this behind you. You have been tried in court and been sentenced. It's over. Try to find some peace. Now, I must go, don't want to keep Kenny waiting."

"Thank you, Joseph, I appreciate you coming."

As he walked towards the door, Joseph said,

"Now, you mustn't be a stranger; I'll call on you again when I can."

"I'd like that, thank you."

The two men shook hands at the door and Sam watched Joseph walk down his path and get into Kenny's car. As Sam turned to go back into his house, he felt like the final load had slipped off his shoulders.

****

The next day, Lucy intended popping in to Sam's as she had John with her so could not stay long. When she arrived, the house looked quiet, and all the curtains were closed as if there was no sign of life. She let herself in with her key, holding John by his hand, and called out.

"Sam! It's Lucy, are you okay?"

When there was no answer, she knocked on his bedroom door and could see the lump in the bed. She smiled; he was still asleep. She'd make him a brew and take it in to him. John played on the kitchen floor, motoring his little cars around, while she prepared the tea and popped some bread in the toaster.

When everything was ready, she laid a tray and went through to Sam's room. She knocked on the door calling, "It's Lucy, Sam! Time to get up, sleepyhead."

After setting the tray down on the bedside table, she drew back the curtains and turned to the bed. Something wrong; he was too still. She touched his neck; he was cold. Withdrawing her hand quickly, she went out of the room hurriedly.

With shaking hands, she dialled 999.

****

It turned out that Sam knew he had heart trouble. It had been discovered when he'd his leg operation and he had not told anyone, except Paul Gamble.

The solicitor came to River View one day to bring Lucy a letter, which she opened immediately.

'*My Dear Lucy,*

If you are reading this letter, it means I have gone the way of all the earth. I didn't want to tell you of my heart condition because I didn't want to lay more on your shoulders and frankly, I am hoping I will be gone before I have to face the court, for I fear prison.

I am so thankful my secret came out at last; at least I will leave this earth knowing I have no other shameful hidden sins.

Don't be sad for me, my dear. I have longed to go to my Emily, life is nothing without her. But I want to thank you for all your love and support, all you have done for me. You made me feel loved at a time when I felt completely unworthy. You are a very special young woman and I thank God that you were my friend.

Sam'

"Oh Paul!" Lucy burst into tears and he held her, gently patting her back while John clung to her leg. After a few minutes, she picked up her little boy. He put a finger on her cheek.

"Mummy cy." He patted her face. She laughed then and hugged him. He squirmed and she set him back on his feet.

"Sam loved you very much," said Paul gently. "You know he's left his property to you? He has left some of his money to his nephew, his niece, Susan and a donation to St. Michael's Hospice. The rest goes to you."

"I'm amazed. I'll have to think what good I can do with it."

"Knowing you, you'll think of something. What I am glad about is Sam lasted long enough to stand trial; in spite of his fears, he needed to do that. I understand that Joseph went to see him too and put Sam's mind at rest regarding his feelings about what happened. His heart could have gone at any time but I feel it took him at the right time."

"I agree. I'm sorry he went through all that but it was for the best. I hope he passed peacefully. He certainly looked peaceful when I found him, as if he'd just gone to sleep and never woke up."

"A good way to go," remarked Paul. "I hope I go like that when my time comes."

"Me too. Although I don't want to think about that for either of us just now!"

"I should think not, you have a whole life to live."

Lucy hugged him.

"And you'll be with us for many more years. Who else is going to make sure my cooking stays up to Aunt Bea's standard?

****

The Reverend Trevithick conducted Sam's funeral in the little Parish church that was the centre of the village of Sutton-on-Wye. Again, it was packed out; the village still considered Sam to be their own and wanted to give him their love and support. The few people who decided to stay away were in the minority. Most people wanted to remember the Samuel Williams that they knew, the patient schoolteacher, the loving husband to Emily, the good friend to many of them. Susan Smith was there; she had been very upset when she returned from her holiday to hear what had happened. Cessy and many of the staff of Sutton Court and even some of the residents were there too. In his address, the Reverent said:

"Samuel Williams was a good man. If you think it strange that I should say that, just think of the man you knew, then think of yourselves; are you the same person you were at seventeen? How many of us have wanted revenge for something done to us or to someone we love? Life has a way of shaping and molding us into who we are now. Our Lord Jesus Christ said, 'he who is without sin, let him first cast a stone'. Are we in a position to truly cast a stone at the young Samuel Williams?

For the next seventy years, Samuel tried to live an exemplary life. Every day for seventy years he suffered guilt for what he had done in taking the life of another human being, when he knew that God had ordered us not to kill. No matter that the man in question would have been hanged for his terrible crimes. Never again did Sam let his temper get the better of him. He treated his fellow beings with respect and care. We know that; many of us were recipients of his care. In the Old Testament, in 1st Samuel, chapter 15 we are reminded that 'the Lord looketh upon the heart'. I feel that Sam had a pure heart; he loved and was loved in return. His wife Emily adored him, his friend Sid was a lifelong friend and many of us loved him. An evil man does not inspire love.

"Therefore, we bid farewell to Samuel and we do not regret the love we have for him. We do not judge him, we leave that to God, who is just and fair. We can pray for forgiveness for Samuel so that he can rest in peace, reunited with his beloved Emily. In the name of The Father, the Son, and the Holy Ghost, Amen."

Samuel was laid to rest with Emily in the churchyard. Afterwards, the villagers gathered in the village hall, as usual, to eat the food once again prepared by Lucy and Sheila and to discuss what they knew Sam had done and the tribute that the Reverend Trevithick had just given to him.

"That was quite a talk you gave there, Vicar," Joseph shook Tony Trevithick's hand. "Pretty much what I said to Sam that last day when I visited him."

"Thank you. I don't want you to think I've condoned what Samuel did but I wanted people to try to imagine what it must have been like for him and the fear he felt, both of the law here and of God's law. He lived his whole life in fear and guilt; I can't begin to imagine what that must have been like. Of course, I think I wouldn't kill anyone, but if I'd seen my Helen in that way, having just been raped and murdered and having the killer jeering at me, I can't say that I wouldn't. I don't think any man could if a mad moment took him."

Joseph nodded. "Yes indeed. Shame he did it though, I'd have liked to know that Henry Smithson had been hanged for his crimes."

"Absolutely. He got off lightly where the earthly law was concerned. I wouldn't fancy his chances with God though."

"I realised it wouldn't help me to be angry with Samuel for what he did. I'm glad my parents didn't know Rosemary was dead, especially the way she died. I think it would have killed my mother. Even though she was always sad that Rosemary never got in touch and she waited for the rest of her life, I think it was still better than knowing what a terrible end Rosemary had.

I hope I set Samuel's mind at rest and now I will let the past go."

The Reverend smiled and patted Joseph's shoulder and moved away to speak with someone else.

Chapter 51

"Darling, Aunt Bea keeps telling me something strange."

"What's that?"

"She keeps saying, 'go up into the roof space'. Don't you think that's odd? Why would she want us to go up there?"

"Perhaps there's something wrong with the electrics. I'll have to bring a ladder in, it won't be easy to get through that small hole. I'll do it after dinner tonight – must get back to work. Bye for now, my darling."

Kenny kissed her lovingly and ruffled John's hair as he sat in his high chair, busily squeezing a piece of toast.

"Bye, young man."

Clarry came to the door to see him off the way she always did. He bent to give her a pat.

"Bye now, Clarry girl!"

She treated him to a doggy smile and he was gone.

That evening, after John was in bed, Kenny brought a ladder in from the barn and carried it up the narrow stairs and set it up against the trap door to the roof space.

"Do be careful love."

"Don't worry, I'll be fine. Just hand me the torch when I get up there, would you?"

He climbed the ladder and lifted the door into the darkness above him. He managed to squeeze through the hole. Lucy passed him the torch, climbing three rungs to reach. She descended and waited, listening to the odd creaks as Kenny carefully picked his way across the beams. Occasionally, she saw a flash of light as he shone it around.

"It's quite roomy up here," came her husband's slightly muffled voice. "Nothing wrong with any wires though. I can't think why Aunt Bea wanted me to come up here. Oh!"

"What's up?" called Lucy anxiously but there was no immediate reply. Then,

"It's empty up here but I've just noticed something tucked under the lowest part of the eaves. It's covered up. I'm going to investigate."

"Oh, careful!"

She heard some scuffling noises and the sound of something being dragged. Kenny's face appeared at the hole.

"It's a small case. I'm going to pass it down to you."

He put the case sideways down the hole and Lucy took hold of the end and slid it down the ladder. Kenny followed, placing the door back in the hole.

It was a smallish, brown case, old fashioned and now rather delicate. Instead of picking it up by the handle, he picked it up as if it was a box, and carried it to the kitchen. Lucy opened it to reveal some old-fashioned women's underclothes, a dress and an apron. Underneath them was a black and white photograph of a couple with a girl and a younger boy, standing stiffly and looking anxious, a bible plus a small, brown book, obviously a diary. Lucy opened it at the last page that had been written upon The writing was tiny and hard to read, so she fetched a magnifying glass and read,

2nd September 1946
Today I have to say goodbye to my family before I go with my dear Gilbert. We will be leaving about eight this evening. Although I want to be with him, because he is so wonderful, my heart is sore because I will be leaving them. I am going to miss mother and dad and my little brother Joe. I hope I will not be lonely without them. I will contact them as soon as I can. I love Gilbert but I love my family too and it was so hard to choose between them.'

"Oh!" Lucy looked at Kenny. "This is Rosemary's case and her diary. We always wondered where it went. It was thought it went with the car."

"Obviously, Sam took it and hid it here. It's hard to believe it's been there all this time, unnoticed."

"Poor Sam; he loved her so much, didn't he? He couldn't bear for her things to be lost. Perhaps he kept them because he couldn't have her. But as you say, it's strange that it's never been found until now."

"The only people who have been up there have been electricians and they wouldn't bother with whatever might be here. Aunt Bea knew it was though."

"So it seems. You can't put one over on Aunt Bea!"

Lucy felt she should call Dan. She was surprised to get straight through to him. He listened carefully.

"Well, Mrs Baxter, that clears up the last little piece of this mystery. I don't think we need it; we have no suspects now and the case is closed. Let Joseph have it."

They took the case to the Nursery House the next day. Sheila and Tom greeted them cheerfully, always pleased to see them. Butch plodded over for a pat, wagging his tail. They went to Joseph who was in his usual chair in the living room and presented the case to him.

"What's this?" he asked.

"Look and see."

Tom played with John to keep him occupied while Joseph looked through his sister's things with tears in his eyes. When he found the diary, he read the last entry with Lucy's help and clutched it to his chest.

"Thank you. This means a lot to know that Rosemary thought of us like that on her last day. So sad that she thought Trent was perfect and she was going on to live her dream with him but she spared a thought for us. I'm grateful to you both."

"Don't thank us, thank Aunt Bea." Lucy said with a smile. She put her hand in Kenny's and smiled at him lovingly. "And just to end on a happy note, we'd like to tell you that you will soon be a great-granddad again."

There followed congratulations and hugs all round while Butch and Clarry barked their approval with wagging tails, receiving their own pats and hugs. The future was looking good.

If you have enjoyed this story (or if you didn't!) please leave a short review on Amazon – and tell your friends! Thank you. J.T.F.

Books by Jeanette Taylor Ford

The Sixpenny Tiger a poignant story of a boy abused by his stepmother
Rosa a psychological thriller
Bell of Warning a ghostly story

The Castell Glas Trilogy: A fantasy about an orphan who finds her family, the magical Welsh castle she inherits and the wicked ghostly entity bent on destroying them all.
The Hiraeth
Bronwen's Revenge
Yr Aberth (The Sacrifice)

The River View Series
Aunt Bea's Legacy (Book One) Mysterious happenings in the house Lucy inherits from her aunt.
By the Gate (Book Two) Farmer Price finds a buried skeleton, sparking off a seventy year old murder hunt.

Mostly About Bears, a small book of short stories and poems (Paperback only)

For Children:
Robin's Ring a fantasy tale (Paperback only)
Coming soon: **Robin's Dragon**

About the Author

Jeanette Taylor Ford is a retired Teaching Assistant. She grew up in Cromer, Norfolk and moved to Hereford with her parents when she was seventeen. Her love of writing began when she was a child of only nine or ten. When young her ambition was to be a journalist but life took her in another direction and her life's work has been with children – firstly as a nursery assistant in a children's home, and later in education. In between she raised her own six children and she now has seven grandchildren and two beautiful great-grandchildren.

Jeanette took up writing again in 2010; she reasoned that she would need something to do with retirement looming, although as a member of the Church of Jesus Christ of Latter Day Saints she is kept busy. She lives with her husband Tony, a retired teacher and headmaster, in Derbyshire, England.

Join my emailing list on jeanetteford51@hotmail.co.uk
Or follow me on https://www.facebook.com/Jeanette-Taylor-Ford-My-Words-My-Way-699235100160365/
Or my blog: jeanetteford51.wordpress.com

Printed in Great Britain
by Amazon